Pontalba Press presents...Novellas
Vol. 1

Pontalba Press

presents... **NOVELLAS**

Volume One

Autumn Books

Pontalba Presents...Novellas - Volume 1. Copyright 1999© by Pontalba Press. Printed and bound in the United States of America. All rights reserved. No part of this book may be reproduced in any form or by any electronic or mechanical means including quote brief passages in a review. Published by Autumn Books, an imprint of Pontalba Press, 4417 Dryades Street, New Orleans, Louisiana, 70115

First Edition

Designed by John Datri
Cover Art: Kerri McCafferty

Novellas / Pontalba Press
1st. edition
p. cm.
ISBN: 1-891643-01-0

1. Fiction   I. Title

000000000000 1999   000.0
                               00000-000

Charles J. Hebert

Publisher's Notes

W‍hen we founded Pontalba press in 1995, we were determined to counter what we saw as a disturbing trend that seemed to favor mass market formula over unique literary perspective. Since publishing our first title in the fall of 1996, we believe our approach has been richly rewarded.

While our titles have sold respectably enough -- especially for a start-up publisher operating out of a relatively small market -- the "rewards" to which we refer is more subtle than a big bottom line. More important to us has been the respect of our peers in the industry and the opportunity to showcase some of the most exciting new writers in the country -- not to mention established authors who may not have received the exposure they deserved.

Pontalba Press' primary mission is to ensure that fresh, intellectually stimulating literary voices are not obliterated by the flash and glitz of the mass market publishing industry. Too often, those whose voice most deserve to be heard are drowned out by advertising budgets that can scream the loudest. We think the clarity and resonance of the works in this volume deserves to be heard above the noise.

Pontalba Press presents...Novellas, *Volume One*

1 Angels and Pancakes 1
   Charles J. Hebert

2 French Quarter Follies 84
   Dr. Paul Rodenhauser

3 The Life of Christ in the 21st Century 178
   Edwin Christian Allman

ANGELS AND PANCAKES
Charles J. Hebert

ANGELS AND PANCAKES

CHAPTER 1

Tommy fixed his gaze upon the sparkling headband his young daughter wore in her hair, trying to lose himself in its brilliance, to gain a moment's respite from the hell that their lives had become. He had fashioned it himself, out of yards of used aluminum foil, pressing it tightly together, smoothing it out against a lead pipe that he used to protect them under the bridge at night, the hands of a machinist, delicately forming it to fit her tiny head. It had broken his heart to give it to her, to see how excited she had been to have something "new" and "pretty" to adorn her head, too young and innocent to know that it was no crown but a penny's worth of garbage. It had come to signifying, in his eyes, just how he had failed her.

Erica had worn the headband ever since, cherishing it, carefully positioning and repositioning it in her matted hair repeatedly throughout the day, as though she were one of the fashionable ladies that passed by the food line heading to shops or their offices.

After they had lost the house and moved to the city, Tommy had initially hidden Erica during the day, terrified that a passing policeman or concerned citizen might have her taken away from him. He had come to learn, instead, of their indifference. Though those who passed them may be more willing to throw him a dime or a quarter with a child by his side, none apparently wished to be involved with their situation for more than a passing moment.

"I hope they have pancakes today," five-and-a-half year old Erica told her father, calling his attention away from the headband.

"They don't have pancakes, sweetie."

"They could, you never know," Erica responded, her big brown eyes widening as she looked up at her father. She pressed up against Tommy, trying to escape the cold wind. Her dirty dress, worn now for three weeks straight, whipped around her calves, themselves covered with grime. The little red coat that she wore over the dress was two sizes too small, the sleeves barely reaching her wrists, offering little protection from the biting wind. Drawing herself closer and closer to her father, she brought her right hand up to her chin, holding against it the limp, fluffy, stuffed puppy that had once been white but was now mostly a drab brown.

"No, they only serve toast and milk in the morning," Tommy finally responded, directing his attention now to a hole in the elbow of his dirty suit coat.

"But they could. Maybe since tomorrow's Christmas Eve they'll have pancakes," she continued optimistically.

Tommy took hold of Erica's left hand and they moved up in the line. Their eyes met. "She has her mother's eyes," he thought. His mind wandered back to their home in Ohio, to the day that Erica was born. It had been cold that day, too, and his wife, Judy, had been in labor all night. He had remained by her side the entire time. The foreman at the factory where he worked operating a press that produced tractor gears had told him to take all the time he needed. Times were good and he had thought that Tommy should be with his wife.

"Smells like pancakes," Erica continued, smiling at her Dad.

"I don't think it is, sweetheart. Don't get your hopes up," he warned. The three of them; he, Judy, and Erica, had moved into a little house on Sanders Street. Judy had gotten a job doing part-time secretarial work at the trade school, and they were even able to put a little money away in the bank.

Each Sunday morning in Ohio, Judy would get up early and make pancakes; they were Erica's favorite. After breakfast, the three of them would go out and do something together. The park, the zoo, the mall. It didn't matter, only their being together had mattered, whatever they did was fun. They were all perfect together, everything was right.

"I hope it's pancakes. I'm so hungry."

"I know, Baby Doll. What do you think about us going back to Ohio?"

"Back home?" she asked excitedly.

"Sure. Maybe I could get my job back." Tommy thought aloud, knowing it would be almost impossible.

ANGELS AND PANCAKES

He closed his eyes and saw the car coming for them, speeding toward the curb across from the park where they had been holding hands, waiting for the light to change. There wasn't enough time. He pulled, yanked Erica away, her hand out of her mother's. Judy had turned to him and their eyes had met, the final act of communication between them. He could not erase the terrified look on Judy's face from his memory as she, for that split second, stood there, doomed and all alone, just out of his reach.

He blamed himself. He was supposed to have saved her, he had seen it in her eyes the second before she was swept away, thrown across the street, piled in a heap of lifeless flesh. It was all so unreal that time itself had ceased to function properly, instead skipping from scene to scene, like a movie with frames missing. He could only recall parts of the whole.

Erica terrified, wailing on his shoulder, her tiny arms nearly choking him. An old, drunken man stumbling from the vehicle. Women's screams. Sirens blaring. His own soul demanding release from earth's bondage, yearning for its mate.

Suddenly the line surged forward moving Tommy and Erica with it. The jolt, along with an argument that had begun ahead of them, brought Tommy back to the present.

Then the door ahead slammed shut.

"You heartless wretches," an old, bearded man reeking of cheap wine, yelled from somewhere behind them.

Someone else began beating on the door.

"What's happening, Daddy?" Erica asked.

Tommy held his daughter's hand tightly.

"Why did the door close?" Erica asked with obvious worry in her voice.

"Let's go, sweetie," Tommy answered, pulling her away.

"But I want pancakes," she insisted, beginning to cry.

"They don't have any here," Tommy responded somewhat sternly, then softened. "Come on, we'll go where they have pancakes," he said, lifting her into his arms.

"Hurry, Daddy, my tummy hurts," she whimpered, her head buried in his shoulder.

He stopped.

4

"Look" he told her lovingly, wrapping her arms for her around her soft, stuffed dog. "Hold Scruffy real tight and he'll help you to feel better until we get the pancakes."

She did as he had suggested and gave up a little smile.

"Remember who gave Scruffy to you?" he asked.

She nodded her head, smiled. "Mommy," she said.

"That's right," Tommy replied, tears forming in his eyes. "She gave him to her little sugarplum so that she would never be alone. Remember?"

Erica nodded again. "I miss her, Daddy."

"I do too, Sweetie. Just hold onto Scruffy as tight as you can and think of Mommy and we'll get us some pancakes. Can you be a big girl and do that for me?"

"Okay. And then we'll go home to Ohio?"

"And then we'll go home."

Tommy carried Erica quickly down the street, shielding her as best he could against the cold, biting wind. He had not been a good father to her, he knew that. After Judy's death he had lost the will to live, the grief more than he could bear, and Erica had been made to suffer for it.

After Judy's death Tommy barely got out of bed for an entire week, relying on friends to take care of Erica. Neither he nor Judy had any family, so when their friends had stopped coming by, Tommy had been forced to care for Erica, but it was all that he could do. He languished in depression for weeks, then months.

The plant had begun a series of lay-offs a few weeks after Judy's death and Tommy, who had just stopped going to work, had been one of the first to go. By the time that he had finally pulled himself together, the plant was running on only a skeleton crew and there was no other work to be found. It was then that he had made the decision to take the last of what he had and head for the big city in hopes of finding work.

That had been eight months ago and the prospects for work in the city were not much better than they had been in their little town. He did odd jobs at first, but quickly found that he could not afford to rent an apartment, pay for daycare, and buy food and clothing on the pittance that he made. Finally, three weeks earlier, they had been evicted, their possessions thrown out on the street while they were not home, most of it picked over and stolen before they could save it. They lived under an overpass at first, Tommy staying awake most of the night to guard Erica in her sleep, losing his job a few days later because he kept nodding off. Matters had only deteriorated from there. They were forced to beg for food and money and slept wherever they could find a warm sheltered spot.

Tommy was desperate. He had to change their circumstance, no matter what it took. He was not sure exactly how he was going to do it, but the first thing he was going to do was to get his little girl some pancakes. It was the first step. If nothing else, he could at least get her pancakes.

* * *

The Rolls Royce Silver Shadow, its back windows tinted to prevent anyone outside from seeing in, motored along Searcy Boulevard. Rolling past dunes of dirty snow, piled high along the roadside by the morning snowplows that had earlier completed their missions, the limo headed for the downtown high rises.

Ross Potts, *the* Ross Potts, of Potts Manufacturing, an aging man with a receding hair line and the demeanor of a wounded mountain lion, sat in the back seat of the Rolls, attended by his man-servant, Jeffrey. Ever so carefully, Jeffrey poured his employer's second cup of coffee then cleared the breakfast dishes from the small table attached to the floor of the automobile.

"Not so much sugar this time, Jeffrey," Potts ordered in a low, yet demanding tone.

"Yes, Mr. Potts."

"And hurry along with the money section of the Journal."

"Yes, Mr. Potts."

Potts sipped his coffee and received a section of the morning paper from his servant.

The scene had become a morning ritual. Valuing every moment of the day, daring to waste not a single one, Potts had long ago taken to having breakfast in the car en route to his office. He also made a point of reading the financial sections of three separate newspapers before arriving at work so that he would be fully informed before setting foot outside. The burden fell upon Jeffrey to ensure that all ran smoothly and on schedule.

The advent of the cellular telephone had added further complications to Jeffrey's morning duties, as Potts tended to conduct more and more business over the car telephone, leaving much less time for eating and reading. Jeffrey thus found himself with less and less time each day to complete his assigned tasks, the penalty for such failure being the certain loss of his employment. Jeffrey, having handed Potts the financial section of the *Wall Street Journal* stood ready with that of the *New York Times*. Just then, without warning, the chauffeur rounded the corner of Twelfth and Astor at a particularly sharp angle, sending the coffee pot tumbling. In one single, graceful movement, the feet of the man-servant stopped the stainless container, half-full of scalding liquid, just as it seemed certain to roll upon Potts' foot. Anguish clearly exhibited upon his face, Jeffrey, without bothering to look down, quickly grabbed the pot by the handle and placed it in a rack next to his seat, securing it with a rubber cord. Timidly he glanced over at Potts, who had not even bothered to look up from his newspaper. Jeffrey breathed a small sigh of relief. Turning again on Lacy Street, the chauffeur entered the downtown area. Jeffrey watched through the window as they rode past dilapidated warehouses and abandoned buildings, evidence of the hard times that had befallen the city in recent times. The car then made a turn onto Henry Avenue, and Jeffrey turned his attention back to Potts. He received the *Journal* from him and handed him the next section of paper in time to avoid noticing the hoard of homeless beating on the door of the New Reform Mission for their morning meal.

* * *

All stood at attention as Ross Potts entered Potts Towers and headed to the one elevator that serviced only the top floor. He and Jeffrey boarded the elevator and they rode the sixty-four stories in total silence. As usual, Potts stood directly behind the doors, ready to spring out as soon as they opened, Jeffrey lined up in formation directly behind him.

When the elevator reached the top floor, a loud bell sounded and the doors began to slide apart. As though an electrical shock wave had accompanied the tolling of the bell, everyone on the floor snapped into action just as Potts, with Jeffrey in tow, bounded out of the elevator and toward his office. Sour-faced, he hurried past dozens of his employees, each bidding him a good morning. He responding to no one.

The small procession passed the desk of Potts' secretary, Rebecca Jenks, who shouted yet another "Good Morning, Mr. Potts," which was likewise ignored. Accustomed to the ritual, she immediately arose and fell in line behind Jeffrey and followed the men into Pott's office.

Ross Potts' office was as large as any four in the building combined. It consumed an entire quarter of the top floor, two corners of the building, and was completely furnished in authentic Victorian pieces purchased at various estate sales in England. Upon each of three walls hung a single Van Gogh original, complete with gilded antique frame and gallery lighting, the fourth wall being constructed entirely of glass, affording a magnificent view of the city. The office also contained a bar serviced with glasses and decanters made of the finest crystal, and a solid cherry wood desk with gold-plated handles on the drawers, behind which was run the Potts empire.

"Good morning, Mr. Potts," Rebecca repeated, entering and closing the office door as her boss seated himself behind the gargantuan desk. Jeffrey, still standing, had positioned himself behind and to the right of Potts' chair.

"Where are my sons?" Ross Potts asked, with a snarl.

"The President," Rebecca began, referring to his eldest son, Ross, Jr., "is touring the plant this morning. The Executive Vice President," she continued, referring to Potts' younger son, Hampton, "telephoned to say that he had gotten tied up in traffic."

"Again?" Potts screamed.

"He said there was an accident in the tunnel and . . . "

"Spare me, Miss Jenks," Potts rudely interrupted. "We both know he over-slept again and Junior's not at the plant, he's out somewhere boppin' Betty Lou," Potts remarked crudely, referring to someone other than Ross Junior's wife.

"I was just relaying their messages . . ."

"I want them in my office the minute the two of them get in here."

"Yes, sir," Rebecca responded, thinking how nice it would be to quit her job.

"Now what about the pre-year-end reports?"

"I have them right here, sir," Rebecca replied, referring to a stack of paper that she held in her hand.

"Well hand them over," Potts growled, holding his hand out impatiently.

Rebecca rushed over and handed him the documents. She looked for a moment at Jeffrey who stood as still as a mannequin, knowing better than to bat even an eye to acknowledge her glance.

Potts received the stack of paper and flipped through the pages until he reached the projected year-end figures.

"What the hell is this!" he screamed, his brow suddenly turning bright crimson.

"What?" She asked nervously.

"One million, thirty-four units!" he responded loudly. He was enraged to the point of tears.

Rebecca Jenks did not reply.

"This cannot be correct. Someone has made a grave error, Ms. Jenks!" he yelled, shaking the pages in his hands.

"I don't know what you are talking about, sir," Rebecca replied nervously.

"This one million, thirty four!" he roared. "It's a mistake! an aberration! It has to be!" he insisted.

Rebecca now shaking, had no reply.

"If you look back to my January six memo you will plainly see that production was supposed to rise by nineteen percent this year! Nineteen percent, Miss Jenks!" he screamed. "At nineteen percent, we were supposed to reach one million, ninety-eight units this year. With these figures there is no way we will reach those numbers!"

"Yes, sir," Rebecca responded meekly, taking a small step backward.

"How could this happen?" Potts demanded, enraged.

"I don't know, sir, I'm just your secretary."

"I am well aware of who you are, Miss Jenks!"

"Yes, sir," Rebecca replied, nearing tears.

Potts took a deep breath and lowered his tone, "You know what this means, don't you?"

Rebecca did not answer. She could feel her lips quivering, she attempted to stop them, but their movement was beyond her control.

"No winter break, the plant stays open through the end of the year!"

"You mean Christmas?" Rebecca asked, envisioning her mother spending Christmas all alone at home in Connecticut.

"I mean Christmas and weekends and Hanukkah, too, if that isn't over yet!" Potts replied, finally beginning to smile.

"The office staff too?" she asked.

"The whole damned company!" Potts continued loudly, his smile growing with each word. "Officers, secretaries, the door man, janitors, even the guy who stamps the 'P' in the sand in the ashtrays. Everybody! What's the matter with you people?" Potts continued, finding joy in the beating of a fist on his desk. "I gave fair warning. Back in January. You look it up Miss Jenks, January sixth. I want you to make copies and post it in the hallways. I distinctly remember. I said production up nineteen percent and, by God, it will be up nineteen percent!"

Rebecca stood before the raving lunatic, allowing a tear to roll down her cheek.

"Go on now," he said, waving her away. "Make a memo!" he continued as she turned quickly and headed for the door. "No time off until we've reached the nineteen percent and anyone who doesn't like it can be unemployed for the new year!" he said excitedly. "And that goes for you too," he said, turning to Jeffrey.

Jeffrey remained motionless.

Rebecca opened the door.

"And don't forget to get my sons in here!" he called behind her. Potts grabbed the pre-year end report from his desk and flung it toward the door, laughing hysterically as pages drifted around the room.

Closing the door behind her and just ahead of the barrage of paper, Rebecca turned down the hallway and hurried to the lady's room, wiping away tears as she went.

CHAPTER 2

Erica sat bundled up, hugging Scruffy, in the little niche between two buildings where her father had placed her out of the wind. He was standing only a few yards down the street, keeping a watchful eye on her as he attempted to sell a new wrist watch to passers-by. His asking price was half of that on the tag. He figured it would be a quick sale.

Tommy heard a disturbance somewhere behind him and turned to look. He quickly spied a police officer, clad in a blue uniform, hurrying through the crowd toward him.

Panic struck as visions of being arrested and their consequences raced through Tommy's mind. He could not get caught. He could not go to jail. What would happen to Erica?

The street was congested. He could round the block. Lose the police officer, then come back for Erica.

"Erica!" he called as he began to take off.

She looked up, halting the conversation she had been having with Scruffy.

"Don't move! I'll be right back!" he said, running off in the direction opposite of the policeman.

Erica did not respond but watched Tommy run off. Shortly thereafter she saw the policeman hurry past as well. She knew what was happening—she had seen her father take the watch. Obeying him, she did not move.

Tommy weaved through the crowd, his days as a running back on his high school football team rushing back to him. He ran quickly, looking back occasionally to make sure that he was gaining ground on his pursuer. He made it to the corner, rounded it in a hurry and ran directly into the arms of the two policemen whom the first had radioed for help. One of them fell to the ground from the impact, the other held on to him.

"No!" Tommy yelled, struggling against the grip of the officer left standing.

"Hold still, you're under arrest," the bulky officer groaned back at him. He tried to tighten his grasp but Tommy pulled himself free, the big man unable to resist his will to get back to Erica. Turning away to run in the opposite direction, Tommy then found himself face-to-face with the first officer finally rounding the corner. Without a word the man in blue swung his billy club and hit Tommy squarely in the forehead, raising a knot and sending him, unconscious, to the pavement.

* * *

Ross Jr. and Hampton Potts walked into their father's office like two children walking in to see the principal. Hampton, the younger of the two, was thin and balding, taking after his father. Ross, Jr., on the other hand, had inherited his mother's thick, wavy hair and blue eyes, and was much wider around his midsection than his father or brother.

The two men, both in their late forties, stepped over the various pages of the pre-year-end report and made their way to their assigned seats.

"Good morning, Father," Hampton spoke first.

"What's good about it?" the old man snarled, his head buried in a stack of paper on his desk.

"Well the plant's in fine shape," Ross, Jr. chimed in.

"You mean the 'planting', don't you?" his father responded, finally looking up.

"I don't know what you are talking about," Ross, Jr. defended.

"I had Miss Jenks call the plant, no one has seen you there in weeks. Then I questioned your driver and he told me about your wrestling match in the back seat on the way in."

"He told you . . ."

"Don't worry about firing him, I already took care of it. A man's got to be able to trust his driver," Potts threw a menacing glance at Jeffrey.

"Father . . ." Hampton began.

"And you aren't any better, dragging in here at half past nine.

Half of the day is gone before you even get to work!"

"There was an accident on the beltway."

"The only accident was your getting this job in the first place. If you cannot get here for six, don't bother getting here at all," Potts growled. "My God," he continued, "what is going to happen to this company when I am gone? I can't sleep nights worrying about it. I have put my entire life into building this company into what it is today—and for what? To leave it to you two lazy, ingrates?"

Neither attempted a reply. They had heard it all a dozen times before. Experience had taught them to sit and listen as the old man raged on, giving him the occasional nod. Soon enough he would tire of it and the entire matter would be forgotten. Before they knew it they would be back in their respective offices, making their respective lunch plans.

"I have a mind to leave the whole company to Jeffrey here!" Potts screamed, pointing toward his frozen man-servant.

Again, Jeffrey had no reaction. He, too, knew the routine.

"At least he's up in the morning before I am, and he may be dumber than an Irish Setter, but he's as faithful."

Potts turned back toward his sons and Jeffrey quickly stuck his tongue out, briefly panting like a faithful dog at the heels of his master. It was a dangerous maneuver, but one practiced and executed with precision timing.

Hampton eyed Jeffrey's bit of disrespect and struggled to contain his laughter.

"Neither of you deserve anything that you have been given and if you cannot . . ." Potts suddenly stopped, looked at Hampton in disbelief.

"What are you grinning about?" he demanded.

"Jeffrey is panting like a dog!" Hampton squealed in terror.

Jeffrey's ears immediately began to burn, his head grew light and the room began to spin.

Potts turned to Jeffrey, stared him in the eye.

Jeffrey remained frozen. He dared not move.

"Get out of here!" Potts screamed, turning back to his sons after the brief silence.

Ross, Jr. and Hampton did not move, thinking he had been speaking to Jeffrey.

"Are you deaf?" Potts yelled, looking at his sons, "I said get the hell out of my sight, the both of you. You make me want to vomit!"

The two younger Potts both sprang to their feet and scrambled for the door. He watched in disgust as they grasped for the door knob and flung themselves through the doorway in fear. Once they were gone, he turned to Jeffrey.

Standing, Potts positioned himself directly in front of Jeffrey. "At least you have a little backbone," he said.

Jeffrey began to show the slightest makings of a grin.

"But I will not tolerate insubordination!" Potts yelled, his spittle landing on Jeffrey's stone-like face. With that he punched Jeffrey as hard as he could in the stomach. The younger, muscular Jeffrey again showed no reaction. Potts continued glaring at him for a moment, then, rubbing his hand, sat back in his chair.

* * *

Hampton followed Ross, Jr. into his office, a much smaller and much less elegantly furnished version of the old man's.

"He's going insane," Ross, Jr. declared as soon as the door was closed.

"What do you mean going? He been acting this way for forty-five years."

"Well it's worse, now."

"No sense in talking about it, we're in it for the duration," Hampton said.

"Not necessarily," Ross, Jr. replied.

"What are you talking about?" Hampton asked.

"I have a little plan that might just get dear old dad out of our hair."

"You've located a hit-man!" Hampton joked.

"You're such a juvenile," Ross, Jr. responded.

Hampton clenched his jaw. His older brother had been referring to him in the same fashion since adolescence. The thirty odd years since and his degrees from Wharton and Oxford had done nothing to change the situation, Ross, Jr. would always consider himself more mature and more refined than his younger brother.

"I think we may be able to have him committed!" Ross, Jr. said excitedly, moving closer to his brother.

"Committed?"

"Just until we can have him declared incompetent," Ross, Jr. answered.

"Now who's insane?" Hampton responded. "Do you have any idea what he would do to us if we tried such a thing?"

"Nothing if we don't fail."

"We fail, we die."

"We just won't fail, then," Ross, Jr. answered.

"Who are you going to get to say he's insane?"

"Remember the elections last month?" Ross, Jr. continued, barely able to contain his excitement.

"What are you talking about?" Hampton asked, growing impatient.

"When I contributed so heavily to Don Jackson's campaign?"

"Yea, the coroner," Hampton replied. "Most people try to get judges and mayors in their pockets, but my brother goes for the one guy who can do nothing for you until you're dead."

"Do you know why I did that?"

"Because you're not as bright as you thought you were?" Hampton joked.

"Grow up!" Ross, Jr. demanded. "Do you have any idea what a coroner's commitment is?"

"To faithfully dismember bodies in the pursuit of justice?" Hampton continued, smiling.

"The coroner has the authority to commit persons with his signature alone."

"Commit them to what?"

"Commit. As in commit them to custody for psychological evaluation. Lock them up until a doctor can decide whether or not they are competent to handle their own affairs, or whether they are dangerous to themselves or others."

"He does?" Hampton remarked, growing interested.

"Yes, it's called a coroner's commitment and it lasts until the poor soul can prove his sanity!"

"Really?" Hampton replied, considering the possibilities.

"Don Jackson owes me a huge favor, I am responsible for

several large contributions made to his campaign."

"Oh, but you have such the devious mind," Hampton complimented his brother.

"Don't I, though," Ross, Jr. replied with a toothy grin, revelling in the acknowledgement.

The two stood silently for a moment, growing excited at the possibility of moving the old man aside and taking control of the business and the bank accounts.

"But won't we need a psychiatrist to keep him in?" Hampton asked.

"The way I see it, the coroner's commitment will get him out of our hair for at least a week or two. In that time we can have the Board vote him out and us in. After that, I figure it's at least a fifty-fifty shot that any psychiatrist would find him completely and utterly insane, and if not, it will be too late anyway. He'll be out and we'll be in."

"It's very dangerous," Hampton replied with a degree of concern.

"The rewards justify it," Ross, Jr. added. "Of course, it's much better if he gets the full commitment. That way we get control of the bank accounts, but at the very least, Potts Manufacturing will be ours."

"Do we know any psychiatrists that could do with a little extra cash?"

"We can work on that," Ross, Jr. responded.

"When do we do it?" Hampton asked.

"We'll need to wait until he does something a little out of line . . ."

"That shouldn't take long," Hampton interrupted.

"So that we'll have a reason for Don to justify the commitment."

"How about a toast?" Hampton suggested, slapping his brother on the back.

"Brilliant idea," Ross, Jr. agreed.

They walked over to the bar and Ross, Jr. poured two glasses of Scotch. He handed one to his younger brother and they held them up together.

"To the next generation," Hampton said.

"Here, here" Ross, Jr. joined in.

The two touched their tumblers together the gulped down the contents. Each already formulating plans for moving the other out of the way once the old man was gone.

$$* \quad * \quad *$$

Erica waited several hours for her father to return. Darkness had begun to fall and she reasoned that the police must have caught up with him and that he would not be coming back for her. She would have to go to him.

Standing, with Scruffy firmly in hand and her hunger giving way to the more primal instinct of fear, she slowly began making her way down the street toward the bright lights that could be seen flashing in the distance.

ANGELS AND PANCAKES

CHAPTER 3

Erica walked in wonderment through the maze of flashing lights. Cigarette and wine billboards, signs for watches and jewelry, pornographic movie theatre marquees, all bathed in thousands of tiny flashing lights. Dazzling colors and motions, like nothing she had ever seen before. Exciting and distracting for her little mind.

Erica wandered around, looking at the lights, reading the signs and marquees. She had pushed her hunger aside until she walked past a small diner and smelled hamburgers frying on the griddle. Suddenly, a sharp pain began to tug at her stomach and she hurried Scruffy to her belly, pushing him against it, hoping he would make the pain go away as her father had said.

"Look at that dirty little girl, Mommy," Erica heard someone say. She turned to see a girl about her own age in a new, knee-length, red, wool coat with matching hat and mittens and shiny black shoes, pointing toward her.

"Stacey," her mother scolded, "it's not polite to point."

"Look, her coat is too small and she has tin foil in her hair," the little girl continued, laughing, her mother tugging her along, out of earshot from Erica.

Erica stopped cold, took one hand from Scruffy at her stomach and reached up to the metal headband in her hair. She pulled it out and slowly brought it within eyesight. Then, for the first time saw that it was, indeed, made of aluminum foil. The little girl's laughing resounded in her ears and suddenly she felt very alone and scared. Stopped in the middle of the normally heavy pedestrian traffic, made all the worse by the droves of shoppers looking for that last minute gift, it was not long before she was bumped by someone from behind, sending her flying to the sidewalk.

"Whoa! I'm so sorry," the voice said as a pair of strong arms helped her back to her feet. She could see that one of her knees was bleeding through the fresh hole in her old dress.

Erica scrambled and picked up Scruffy and her headband, then turned to see who had knocked her down.

"You okay?" the voice asked. It was an accent that she had never heard before.

She nodded affirmatively, looking up at the man who had knocked her down. He was young, about her father's age. His chin was covered with a scraggly beard and his eyes appeared as tiny black discs, set back in his huge head. Erica immediately noticed his thick fur coat, she had never seen a man in a fur before, and the handful of gold chains hanging around his neck.

"You lost?" he asked.

Erica shook her head no, then placed the headband back in her hair.

"Where's your Mamma and Daddy?" he asked.

"My Mamma's in heaven and my Daddy went to the police station."

"Whoa!" the man exclaimed, "I know how that goes."

Erica smiled. He was funny.

"So who's takin' care of you?" the man asked.

"Just Scruffy," she responded, holding up her stuffed dog.

"Well, hey, Scruffy. What kinda dog is he?"

Erica smiled and shrugged her shoulders.

"Now that's a pretty smile," the man said, causing her smile to grow. "And that's a pretty headband too."

"It's tin foil," she responded.

"Looks like pure silver to me," he smiled, revealing a gold tooth with a little bone carved into it.

"Really?"

"Shore does. Somebody did a real fine job with that fine piece of jewelry, and I know jewelry," he continued, talking fast and exhibiting his gold chains as proof of what he said.

Erica felt better, smiled.

"Heck, if you don't like it, I'll go buy you a brand new one and trade you for that one cause I can tell you, my lady friend would just love a fine piece of jewelry like that. You wanna new one?"

"No thank you," Erica replied, "I like this one."

ANGELS AND PANCAKES

"That's 'cause you got good taste, I can see that. Listen, have you had somethin' to eat today?"

Her smile diminished and she shook her head no.

"You hungry?"

Slowly, shyly, she nodded her head,"yes."

"I was just on my way to get me some supper. What do you feel like eating?"

"Do you know where there are some pancakes?" she asked.

"Pancakes?" he responded. "You mean like hot cakes? Sure. I know the best hot cake house in the city. You want hot cakes?"

She shook her head again, this time with enthusiasm.

"You come wit me. I'll get you the best darned hot cakes you ever tasted. What's your name?"

"Erica," she said, beginning to walk with the man.

"Whoa!" he exclaimed.

Erica smiled again.

"That's my favorite name. I like that lady on the soap opera, what's her name? Erica somethin', I forget. My Momma watches it."

"Erica Caine," Erica answered. "That's my name too. Erica Caine Bloundin."

"Wow! Erica. That's cool. I'm gonna have to tell my Momma I met you. You're named after a star. She ain't half as pretty as you though. My name's Mackbone."

"Mack-bone?" she asked, as though it were two words.

"No, Mackbone, together, not Mack-Bone."

"Mack-bone, what?" she asked.

"Mackbone, Mackbone," he replied. "It's just Mackbone."

"I never heard that name before," she said innocently.

"Well there ain't no one on no soap opera named Mackbone, I can guarantee you that for sure," he responded, guiding her down the street, through the crowd.

Three blocks away Mackbone turned into a little diner named the National House of Hotcakes. Although he had never before been inside, he had passed it hundreds of times. He and Erica walked up to the counter and he raised her up and put her on a stool. Then he sat down next to her. A waitress immediately appeared for their order.

"We don't need no menus," Mackbone said as she began to put them on the counter.

"Okay, shoot," the waitress responded, grabbing her pen and order pad.

"The little girl'll have the biggest stack of pancakes you sell and a tall glass of milk, to help her grow strong and beautiful," he said, touching her hair.

"And what about you?" the waitress asked.

"Water," he answered.

"Just water?"

"No, a glass too, with ice in it. And you can put the water on top of that."

"Ha," the waitress pretended to laugh, then walked away with the order.

"So your Daddy just left you on the street?" Mackbone asked, turning to Erica.

"I don't think so," she replied, looking up at him. "The police must have taken him and they didn't let him come get me."

"Yea, right kid," Mackbone replied sarcastically.

"Could you bring me to the police station to find him?"

Mackbone looked at her in disbelief. "I ain't goin' to no police station," he said.

"Why not?"

"They like me too much there. If they seen me walk in there wit you, they'd want me to stay for sure."

"Can you tell me how to get there?"

"Which one? That's one thing they got thousands of in this town and that's police stations. You'd never find him. No, you just better hang out wit ole' Mackbone for a while, he'll take care of you. Get you plenty to eat."

"I'm starving," she replied.

"Hey!" Mackbone yelled to the cook behind the counter. "What's the story with those flapjacks? How long do it take to fry up a little dough around this joint? Can't you see the little girl's hungry already?"

The cook looked up with a snarl, then returned to his grill.

"What you lookin' at?" Mackbone asked.

In less than two minutes the waitress placed a stack of five steaming pancakes before the little girl who had not eaten all day. Erica's eyes grew wide as Mackbone covered the pancakes in syrup and handed her a fork.

"Don't eat too fast now," he said, lighting a cigarette. "They'll give you a tummy ache."

"How you doin' tonight beautiful?" he winked at the waitress just before she turned and walked away.

Erica took a giant fork full, opened her mouth as wide as possible and pushed the bite in using both hands. With a huge smile on her face, and syrup dripping down her chin, she began chewing, savoring each and every bite.

* * *

Ross Potts was headed for home at his usual eight o'clock in the evening. Potts neither read nor ate on the ride home, considering it wasteful to burn the lights in the back of the car. Instead, he opted to use the time for a nap. Unneeded in the back seat, in the evenings Jeffrey rode up front with the chauffeur. They dared not speak during the ride, however, never knowing whether or not Potts was listening in on the intercom.

Traffic was particularly heavy on the evening before Christmas Eve. Today had been the final day of work before the holidays for most, necessitating a late stay to either finish up work or to have a few drinks with co-workers. Adding in those who were out doing last minute shopping or heading out of town for the holidays, the normally deserted streets were hectic with traffic at this late hour.

The chauffeur stopped at a traffic signal in the middle of the downtown area, he and Jeffrey silently watching the dozens of cars rolled past. The driver paused an extra moment once the light had turned green to assure that the cross traffic had all stopped before finally proceeding across the intersection. The driver of a car in the opposite lane of traffic, however, grew impatient waiting for the Rolls to clear the intersection before making a left hand turn, and sped through his turn just as Potts' driver took off.

The force of the collision threw Ross Potts from his seat to the floor of the car, causing him to strike his head on a metal rack along the side wall as he landed. He rolled over in pain, holding his bleeding eye, screaming for Jeffrey, unaware that both Jeffrey and the driver lay unconscious in the front seat.

* * *

By the time Mackbone had finished his cigarette, Erica had eaten a full half of the stack of pancakes and had finished her glass of milk. She was stuffed and her eyes grew heavy as she pushed the plate away and laid her head on the counter.

"You finished?" Mackbone asked.

She shook her head affirmatively along the counter.

"You had enough?"

She responded the same way that she had to the first question.

"Well let's go, I got a good warm place for you to sleep tonight."

Mackbone threw some cash on the counter and stood up. He took Erica in his arms, she lay her head on the shoulder of his fur coat.

"It tickles my nose," she said, smiling.

"Just put your head there and go to sleep. I'll take care of you."

"What about my Daddy?" she asked.

"We'll have to find him tomorrow, after we have some more pancakes. It's too dark and cold to do it now," he answered.

Mackbone carried the little girl four blocks to his apartment. He walked up the three flights of stairs with her and unlocked his door. Walking in, he found two of his female employees sitting on his couch, drinking coffee, and talking to one another.

"What are you doing in here?" he complained immediately.

"We're takin' a break," one answered.

"A break? What you mean a break?" he said, closing the door behind him.

"Me and Monique was cold so we come in to warm up a bit," the second woman answered.

"This is prime time, baby. Yous need to be out there on the street movin' your asses. This ain't no country club."

ANGELS AND PANCAKES

"What you got there, Mackie?" Monique asked, ignoring his complaints.

"Don't worry about it," he answered, heading for his bedroom.

"What you doin' wit that little girl?" she asked, getting up from the couch. She pulled her mini skirt down as far as it would stretch over her fishnet stockings and followed Mackbone toward the bedroom.

"Don't worry about it," he repeated, louder.

"What you mean don't worry about it?" she replied, raising her voice. "I want to know what you doin' wit that little girl. Where did you get her from?"

"Shut up!" he yelled. "Can't you see she's tryin' to sleep."

Erica opened her eyes briefly and looked at Monique who was now standing right in her face.

"Ahhhh, she's so cute," Monique said, smiling. "How you doin', sugarplum?"

Erica lifted her head with a jerk, looked into Monique's eyes and smiled, then put her head back down into Mackbone's fur, permeated from the air in the small restaurant, impregnated with the comforting scent of pancakes.

"Veronica, come see her," Monique said.

"No," Mackbone responded. "Veronica, get your butt down to the street. Both of yous do that."

He carried Erica into his bedroom and put her in bed under his covers. Then he came out and shut the door. Veronica had disappeared but Monique was standing next to his bedroom door.

"I thought I told you to get outta here," he said, angrily.

"Not until you tell me what your doin' with that kid."

"I found her, okay?"

"What do you mean you found her? You find a puppy or a kitten, you don't just find a kid."

"I found her, I swear. She was wanderin' the Square unattached and I found her already."

"Where's her parents?"

"What do you mean where's her parents, I don't know where her parents are. How am I supposed to know that?"

"Why you didn't bring her to the cops?"

"The cops?" he yelled, incredulously. "The cops, Monique?

What are you talkin' about? I bring that kid to the cops and they ain't never lettin' me see the sun shine again."

"What you mean? It'd be a good deed."

"They ain't seein' it that way. They seein' it as I got somethin' to do wit her bein' on the streets."

"What do you got to do wit that?"

"See what I mean?" he asked, his point proven. "I just found her. See that, even you don't believe me."

"Okay then, answer me this. What you plannin' to do wit her?"

"Don't worry about it."

"I want to know, Mackie. What you gonna do wit her 'cause if it has anything to do wit the streets I'm callin' the cops myself right now."

"What you talkin' about?" Mackbone screamed, rushing to Monique and grabbing her long curly locks with his right hand. "You ain't callin' no cops."

"So help me, you try and work that little angel and you'll have to kill me or I'll call the cops."

"What do you think I am? I ain't no chicken hawk," Mackbone replied, backing off a bit. "I ain't gonna start runnin' no kiddie shit now."

"You better not," Monique answered as he let her go and stepped back.

"I don't play that, you know it."

"Then why do you have her?"

"She's valuable, okay?"

"What do you mean she's valuable."

"She's worth ten gran to the Mob boys, alright?"

"You're gonna sell her?" Monique asked, horrified.

"Ten grand, Monique. That's serious money. It just walked right up to me. Right out there on the street. What was I supposed to do? Leave it there for somebody else to pick up? I don't think so."

"You're supposed to try and get her off the street."

"What do I look like here, Mother Theresa? I ain't got no robe on. I'm a pimp and there's ten grand sleepin' in the next room."

"You don't want to do that, Mackie."

"What? You think I don't want ten gran?"

"You wouldn't be able to live wit yourself."

"I done lots worse."

"Bullshit. You're gonna sell that little girl like a piece of meat on Christmas Eve . . ."

"Oh, for Christ's sake, can we leave Christmas out of it?" he pleaded.

"Let me bring her to Ms. Martha," Monique suggested.

"Are you crazy?"

"You know what they will do to her!" she insisted.

"I know how much they will pay," he answered.

"She will die out there. She's just a little girl, Mackie."

"Just get out of my face," he said, pointing a finger at her.

"Let me take her Mackie."

"Get back down to the street," he ordered, retreating back into his bedroom.

"I ain't gettin' nowhere till that little girl is safe," she replied, trying to follow him.

He slammed the door shut and locked it before she could get inside.

"Open the door, Mackie!" she yelled, pounding on the door.

"Get outta here," he answered, walking toward the bed.

"What are you doin' in there?" Monique insisted, still pounding. "Let me in!"

Mackbone stood at the side of the bed and watched Erica sleeping. He reached down and pulled the covers off of her, ran his eyes down her body. He sat on the bed beside her and grabbed her left hand. Gently he squeezed it, sticky with syrup.

"Open the damn door!" Monique continued, striking the door even harder.

With Mackbone's coat nearby, Erica again caught the scent of pancakes, but did not stir from her sleep. A dream, her mother's face, she was smiling, saying sweet things to her as she had when she was alive.

"My sweet little sugarplum. Mommy loves you."

"I love you, Mommy."

"Don't worry, I'm here."

"I know, Mommy."

Mackbone continued squeezing the little hand until Erica opened her eyes.

"Mommy? Mommy?" she asked, looking into Mackbone's face.

"Jest me," Mackbone answered.

"You asshole!" Monique screamed.

Erica sat up, looked toward the door, Mackbone still holding her hand.

"Don't be scared," he assured her, "she's just mad wit me. Come see Mackbone," he said, reaching out with his other hand and lifting her up.

Erica immediately went to him, putting her head on his shoulder.

"How you feelin'?" he asked.

"Good," she said.

"That's good," he replied softly, overcome by emotion foreign to him.

The pounding on the door grew louder, Monique now half-crazed, was using a chair to beat against it.

"Man, she's one crazy bi . . ." he stopped himself. Then he pulled Erica away so that he could look at her, and continued. "Listen," he began, "Monique there is gonna take you to a real nice lady that's gonna take good care of you."

"I don't want to go," Erica said, scared.

The bedroom door began to give way.

"Okay! Okay!," Mackbone yelled, "I'm openin' the door!"

The pounding stopped.

"Monique is gonna take good care of you, she's a nice lady. And if anybody can find your Daddy for you the lady she's takin' you to can."

"Can't you bring me?"

"No, I can't now," Mackbone answered. "I'm too busy," he said, knowing that if he brought her he might change his mind before she was safely away.

"Thank you, Mackbone," Erica answered.

"For what? Some hotcakes? Sheeee," he waved a hand at her. "Don't mention it," he said walking to the door. He unlocked and opened it, carried Erica out.

ANGELS AND PANCAKES

Monique looked suspiciously at Mackbone. Her hair was in her face and she was breathing heavily.

"Look, it ain't right . . . " Monique began yelling.

"Enough already!" Mackbone said, "Take her to Martha."

Monique was shocked. Then she smiled, wiped her face. "Really?"

"Fast. Before I change my mind," he said, holding Erica out to Monique.

Monique hurried over and took Erica.

"Some pimp I am," Mackbone said under his breath as he handed her over.

"Tell Mr. Mackbone goodbye, sweetie," Monique said, already turning for the door.

"Bye Mack-bone," Monique said.

"It kills me the way she says my name," Mackbone said softly. Monique smiled, mouthed the words "Thank you."

Quickly regaining his persona, Mackbone gave Erica a stern warning, "You stay with Ms. Martha until your Daddy comes, you hear? I don't want you back out on that street, there's lots of bad people out there that's gonna hurt you! You got that? I see you on that street and I'm gonna tan your little hide."

"Ah, Mack-bone," Erica said with a smile as Monique headed for the door.

"And you get back to work after you drop her off, Monique," Mackbone said, trying to sound harsh.

"You'd make a good father yourself," Monique told him as she opened the door.

"What are you talkin' about? I am a father, I got kids. They stay with their mothas," he insisted.

"Ah, Mack-bone," Monique imitated Erica as she walked out and closed the door behind her.

* * *

Monique hurried down the stairs and onto the street, holding Erica close. Martha Albert's Shelter for the Homeless was only four blocks from the front door of Mackbone's apartment and she tried to shield the little girl from the cold as she made her way down the crowded avenue.

Ms. Martha, as everyone called her, was a life-long resident of the neighborhood, living in the same house where she had been born sixty-five years earlier. It had been a much nicer neighborhood then, plenty of shops and apartments with good people living in them. But that had all given way to people and industries catering to the vices of mankind. Ms. Martha was the lone holdover from the old neighborhood. The last true resident, she had opened up the apartment building she owned to the desperate who, like moths to the deadly light, were drawn to the area where a living of last resort could nonetheless be made.

Arriving out of breath, Monique rang the bell to Ms. Martha's apartment building. A voice came over a little speaker imbedded in the wall next to the door.

"Yeeees?" Ms. Martha asked.

"Hi, Ms. Martha, it's Monique."

"I'm sorry child, but I really can't fit anyone else in tonight. The fire marshall's threatened me twice this month. He'll close me down."

"It's not me, Ms. Martha, it's a little girl."

There was no response.

"If you don't take her she'll be out on the street tonight."

Still there was no reply. Monique looked worriedly at Erica, Erica smiled back at her.

"Ms. Martha, please," Monique pleaded into the little box.

"Wait jest a minute," the old woman finally said.

Monique smiled and gave Erica a little squeeze. "You sure are a big girl," she said.

"I know," Erica replied, beaming.

"You gonna like Ms. Martha."

"She's gonna find my Daddy for me," Erica said, laying her sleepy head on Monique's shoulder.

Suddenly the door swung open. Inside a petite Black woman with cotton-white hair and huge, thick glasses, and dressed all in white, stood with the door knob in hand.

"Hi, Ms. Martha," Monique said, smiling gratefully.

Ms. Martha returned the smile and walked out into the cold to inspect Erica.

"My, my, what have we got here?" she said kindly, looking at the child.

"Her name is Erica," Monique said.

"Oh what a pretty name," Ms. Martha answered, her smile growing. "And what a pretty little headband in your hair."

Erica lifted her head and smiled back.

"Do you want to come inside with me and get something to eat?" Martha asked.

"My friend, Mr. Mack-bone already gave me pancakes," Erica replied.

"Did he?"

"Yep."

"Oh, Sweet Jesus," Ms. Martha said, turning to Monique, "this child has been with Mackbone?"

"He saved her, Ms. Martha. Anybody else had got hold of her and she'd be in a bad way by now."

"Suppose so," Ms. Martha replied. "Do you want to come in?" she asked again, turning back to Erica.

"Okay," Erica replied.

"Where's her parents?" Martha asked as Monique handed Erica and Scruffy over to her.

"Her Mamma is dead and her Daddy got picked up by the cops today."

"Do you know where they're keeping him?"

"No, ma'm," Monique answered.

"Never you mind, I'll find out. I'll need to call them about her anyway."

"I was kinda hopin' you could wait until after Christmas to do that," Monique replied quickly, urgently.

"Oh no, I have to let them know. I could get in trouble, lose my license. They have to come get her. I can't keep no children without their parents bein' here."

"I just didn't want her to spend the Christmas like that."

"I've got no choice," Ms. Martha explained in an apologetic tone. "They could shut me down. I'm already about to have to close the doors on my own. There's just too many to help these days and not enough to go around. If I'm not careful I'll be out there soon myself."

"I sure hope that doesn't happen, Ms. Martha. You're the only hope this old neighborhood has left."

"I'm afraid that's not much to hope on," Martha responded. Monique nodded sadly.

"Come along, little one," the old woman said, patting Erica softly on the back.

"Thank you Ms. Martha," Monique said, turning to leave.

Martha merely smiled and walked inside with Erica.

"Who's your little friend?" she asked, as she set Erica on her feet and led her down the hallway to her own bedroom.

"His name is Scruffy. He's my best friend," Erica replied.

"I bet he is," Martha replied, opening her bedroom door. Suddenly something heavy fell against the front door.

"Now what?" Martha asked, quickly guiding Erica inside her bedroom. "You sit in here and I'll be right back," she said, walking slowly back down the hallway toward the front door.

* * *

Ross Potts, his suit coat soaked with blood, and with fresh blood streaming down his face, had managed to walk a total of eight blocks from the scene of the accident before finally collapsing. Disoriented, the entire way he had continued calling for Jeffrey, threatening to fire him if he did not immediately appear.

"Jeffrey, damn you!" he yelled, just as the door he was leaning against gave way causing him to fall to the floor inside.

"Ahhhh!" Ms. Martha screamed, surprised by the bloody figure that had fallen before her. "Sweet Lord, Jesus!" she yelled, staring at Ross Potts' blood-soaked body.

"What is it?" a ragged old man, one of the night's boarder's, asked from behind. With a broomstick in hand he came to Ms. Martha's aid. Soon a small crowd had gathered inside of the apartment building, all prepared to defend Martha Albert.

"Give me some help here," Martha said after finally catching her breath, "bring him to my room. I've got to call an ambulance."

ANGELS AND PANCAKES

Martha hurried down the hall to her room and to the telephone inside. She dialed 911 and summoned an ambulance as the homeless brought the proud Ross Potts into her apartment and laid him on her bed.

"Who are these people?" Potts asked, looking at those around him. "Where is Jeffrey?" he insisted.

Everyone backed away, no one answered Potts.

"Jeffrey!" he summoned from the bed.

"Settle down," Ms. Martha ordered, hanging up the telephone. "You set right there. I'm going to clean you up a little bit," she continued headed to the kitchen for water and a towel.

"I want Jeffrey!" Potts demanded.

No one moved. All eyes were on Potts.

"Don't you know who I am?" he asked. "I'm Ross Potts!"

"I'm Joe Bob Duffy," a tall, slender man with a Texas twang and two days of hair growth on his face said, stepping forward and reaching out to shake Potts' hand. "Pleased to meet ya."

"Jeffrey!" Potts screamed again, ignoring the man's outstretched hand.

"Okay, now ya'll clear out of here," Martha directed, coming back into the room and squeezing through the crowd. "Go wait for that ambulance and bring them in here."

Slowly they all began to back away, leaving the apartment one by one, until only Martha, Erica and Potts remained.

Martha cleaned up the gash in Potts' head. "That's gonna need more than one stitch, that's for sure," she said, handing Potts a piece of gauze to hold against his wound. He looked up at her with his usual sour stare and did not bother to thank her when she was done.

Erica had sat quietly throughout the entire procedure, watching Martha and Potts, not making a sound.

"Now where is that ambulance?" Martha said aloud to herself, as she backed away and rubbed her hands on her white dress. She was more than ready to rid herself of the responsibility of Potts.

"I'm going to go see about it, you stay right there and hold that bandage tight," Martha instructed Potts as she turned to leave the room.

"Sit there and come get me if he tries to get up," she told Erica.

Martha left the apartment and walked to the front door to look for the ambulance. No sooner had the door closed than Erica hopped off of her chair and walked over to the bed for a closer look.

"She told you to stay on that chair," Potts snarled.

"You have a big bo-bo," Erica said.

"Get away from me you dirty little rug-rat. Don't you people bathe? Look at you. Doesn't you mother wash your clothes?" Potts said harshly.

"My Mommy is dead," Erica responded innocently.

"Oh," Potts said, only a little less harshly. Her response had caught him off guard. "Well, your father then. Or is he dead too?" Potts said, recovering.

"The police took him away," she said.

"That figures," Potts mumbled to himself.

"Does your bo-bo hurt?"

"Of course it hurts," Potts replied, growing very tired of the conversation, "are you daft or something?"

"I know how to make it feel better."

"What are you a doctor now?"

"No. But when I hurt Scruffy always makes me feel better."

"Who?"

"Scruffy," she responded, holding up the stuffed animal. "He works every time. You wanna try?"

"No thanks."

"You can hold him, he'll make you feel better, really," Erica insisted, holding the dirty little stuffed animal out toward Potts.

"Get that away from me!" the old man snarled.

"If you hold him really tight it will make your bo-bo stop hurting. I promise."

"That's quite alright," Potts answered.

"It works. Really. When my tummy doesn't have anything to eat for a long time I just hug Scruffy real tight and then it doesn't hurt so much."

"What do you mean when you don't have something to eat? Don't they feed you in here?"

"I don't know. We don't live here."

"Where do you live?"

"A place that has this big iron gate that hot air comes through and keeps us warm all night long," Erica answered with a smile.

"Is that where your house is?" Potts asked, becoming curious.

"We don't have our house any more. Daddy couldn't go back to the plant and we moved here and left our house in Ohio."

"Where do you cook your food?" Potts asked, pushing the gauze tighter against his brow.

"No wheres."

"Then where do you eat?" he asked, incredulously.

"At the Mission, mostly, when they have enough and we get there in time."

"Where do you sleep?"

"On top of the big iron thing that's real warm," she responded cheerfully. "It feels really good when its cold outside."

"That's preposterous," Potts answered.

"What's that mean?"

"That means it's not true. This is America. We pay taxes so you people have a place to sleep and something to eat. What about the soup kitchens?"

"They ran out of pancakes."

"What?" Potts asked.

"They ran out of pancakes. That's why the police got my Daddy. He took a watch to get me pancakes."

Potts did not answer. He stared at Erica, refusing to believe that what she was saying was true. She was, after all, a child and children are prone to exaggeration.

"Try it, it really works," Erica prodded, raising Scruffy once more toward Potts.

"No."

"Just try it."

"I don't want to."

"But it works."

"Stop it! You're making my head hurt worse!" Potts yelled, then noticed the effect on Erica. Her smile disappeared and she folded up, just as his children had all their lives when faced with controversy, when faced with their father.

She turned away.

"If I hold him, will you stop your yapping?" Potts asked in a strangely gentle tone.

"He'll make you feel better. I promise," Erica yelped, turning back around.

Potts took the dog and placed it on his belly below the point where his blood had soaked his shirt.

"Not like that," she said, climbing onto the bed. "You have to hug him tight."

Erica sat on Potts' lap and demonstrated the proper way to hug Scruffy. Then she handed him back to Potts.

Ross Potts glanced toward the doorway to make certain no one was watching, then he gave the little dog a short squeeze.

Erica smiled.

Potts paused a moment, as though deep in thought. "Didn't work," he announced.

"Maybe you need to do it longer," Erica urged.

"I don't think…" Potts began, but they heard a big commotion in the hallway. Erica, sensing someone was coming, jumped off of Potts' lap and ran back to her chair, leaving Scruffy behind, just as the door flew open.

The ambulance crew rushed in, pushing a wheeled stretcher, Ms. Martha following closely behind. Minutes later, Potts was being rolled out of the apartment building, Scruffy riding atop his chest and Ms. Martha still in close pursuit.

Suddenly alone again, Erica stretched out on the bed and thought about her Dad. She worried that Ms. Martha would not be able to find him, then raised a hand to her head to feel the headband, the last reminder that she had of him, but it was gone. She panicked, suddenly feeling alone, as though she may lose contact with her father forever and she knew she had to find the headband, that she could not feel right again until it was atop her head. Erica jumped up to search, but froze by the side of the bed at seeing who was now sitting where Ross Potts had been.

"Hey Sugarplum."

The little girl stood in silent amazement, wanting desperately to believe what she was seeing. Then tears welled up in Erica's eyes, followed closely by a smile that engulfed her entire face.

"Mommy!" she screamed, running over and into the bosom

of the woman sitting across the room.

Judy Bloundin held her young daughter tight in her arms.

"Mommy, Mommy," Erica repeated. "You're here, you really are."

"I'm here, Sweetie."

"You're really, really here," the young girl cried, her deepest of prayers finally answered.

"I never really left you, my love."

"Oh, Mommy."

"Listen, Sugarplum," Judy finally said with some urgency, pulling Erica back to see her face. "That was a great thing you just did. You make me so proud of you."

Erica continued smiling, tears running down her fat little cheeks.

"You're such a good girl. I know you are scared but I promise you, everything is going to be alright. Please don't worry. There's a lot of people looking out for you and everything is going to work out."

"I can't find Daddy," Erica responded worriedly.

"You're Daddy's just lost his way, Sweetie, but we're gonna help him find his way back. He's a good man and he's gonna take real good care of you. It's not his fault, really. Sometimes grownups just can't help the things that happen to them."

"Like when you left."

Judy nodded affirmatively. "You're such a smart girl. I love you so much."

"I love you too, Mommy," Erica responded.

Judy did not go on, content to look upon the beauty of her innocent young daughter in the short amount of time that she had left.

"You're not coming back, are you?" Erica asked, somehow understanding much more than her mother had expected.

"If I could I would, sweetheart, but you have to know that I am always looking out for you. I promise you that. I am always with you. I got to come back for just a minute because of you, darling, because you have such a good heart. But I can't stay here."

"Okay, Mommy," Erica responded, smiling, though still crying.

"You just keep being good, okay?" Judy asked as she placed the headband back in her daughter's hair and wiped her tears away with her thumbs.

"Okay."

"You promise?"

"I promise, Mommy," Erica answered as they kissed and made one final embrace.

"You hungry yet, Sugarplum?" The familiar voice asked from somewhere behind Erica.

The little girl turned, with tears in her eyes, away from the empty bed, and toward Ms. Martha standing at the door.

"Oh, child, what's the matter?" Ms. Martha asked, seeing the little girl's tears. She hurried over and took Erica in her arms to comfort her.

"Nothing," Erica replied, hugging the old woman tightly, smiling through her tears.

* * *

CHAPTER 4

As the ambulance pulled away from the curb, the attendant administered a pain killer and placed an oxygen mask on Ross Potts' face. He closed his eyes and tried to relax, found himself falling asleep. Sometime later he realized the ambulance personnel were talking about him.

"He's a real piece of work, that one," the one in front, driving, said.

"What you mean?"

"You know who that is, don't you?"

"This old lizard?" the one in the back asked.

"It's Ross Potts."

"No way."

"Sure. Don't you recognize him from the paper?"

"Dang it, you're right!. I'll be a . . . "

"You know, if you turn off that oxygen you'd be a hero to half this city," the driver suggested. Potts, on the edge of consciousness understood the threat, but was helpless to protest or resist.

"This sorry excuse for human being. Look at him. He don't look so rich and mighty now lying there half-dead with blood all over his starched shirt."

"I personally know eight people he's put out of work, just buying up companies and shutting them down and selling off the pieces like he's playing some kind of game," the driver continued. "My uncle lost his job, had to go on welfare."

"If he arrests, I'm takin my time."

"I won't tell."

Potts struggled to move, to let them know he could hear them, but could only managed to close his fingers. He squeezed and squeezed, something soft and fluffy in his grasp, then all was dark.

* * *

Perfect silence. Absolute darkness. Neither sound nor sight. Ross Potts found himself walking down a long, dark hallway, to a door that opened before him. Inside he could see a young man, a hungry man, returning from a long day's toil to his waiting wife. Upon their table, the same staple he had eaten for breakfast and dinner at countless meals, fried dough, pancakes. The two embrace and she cries from the hunger within her and he is moved.

"I swear to you," he whispers to his dear love, "I'm going to change all of this. You'll be the richest woman in town, and they'll all know it, and we will never be hungry and never have to eat like this again."

"I know," she responds. "I know you will, Ross. I know you will."

* * *

The thud of the stretcher wheels dropping to the curb roused Potts from his slumber. Too drowsy to open his eyes, he strained to maintain consciousness, to at least hear what was going on around him. They whisked him inside.

"Oh my God!" he heard Ross, Jr. exclaim from somewhere nearby.

Potts could feel the warm air on his face and his hands, but still could not move. He held tightly the soft object in his hands but was unable to offer any real resistance when it was taken away. He suddenly felt alone, desperately alone and unloved, and strangely concerned for the little girl who had given up the stuffed animal for him only minutes earlier.

* * *

Tommy Bloundin, desperate with concern for Erica, had demanded the meeting with his attorney. He sat at a small desk separated from Victor Adams, by a chain-link fence.

Adams, three years out of law school yet only six months

beyond the bar examination, had landed a job with the Public Defender's Office, due in no small part to the current administration's indebtedness to his father. The elder Adams had great plans for his son, his sights set on the Governor's Mansion, and was convinced that the road began in defense of society's most helpless and vulnerable. After six months, Victor was ready to proceed to the next step, perhaps a judgeship, or the District Attorney's job, or Mayor, he thought. Nonetheless, in the waning hours before Christmas, he was still an assistant public defender and Tommy was his twelfth interview of the evening. He was hard-pressed to spare much of his attention.

"You have to get me out of here, I don't care what it takes," Tommy stressed immediately following Victor's self-introduction.

"I'm working on that," Victor replied, using one of his favorite pat responses.

"No," Tommy demanded, panicking. "I mean now. Today. I have a seven year old daughter out on the street somewhere. She's all alone and I have to find her."

"Mr. Bloundin, it's December 23, the courts are closed. Only Judge Holliday is sitting over the holidays." Adams chuckled, "Pretty ironic, isn't it? Holliday working over the holidays?"

"Fine, I'll see him," Tommy, unamused, demanded.

"He already has over two hundred arraignments set on his docket. Not only that, but anybody who wants anything legal done before Christmas is going to be crowding his courtroom to see if he can squeeze them in, too. I don't know about you, but I don't relish the idea of spending my Christmas waiting in Holliday's courtroom to see if he can fit me in."

"Maybe you didn't hear me," Tommy said impatiently. "She's only seven."

"That is not a valid reason for expediting your hearing," Adams responded. "In fact, it could ultimately come back to haunt you—blow up in your face. Judge Holliday is a family man. He's not going to like it that you left a seven-year-old out on the street by herself..."

"The police knocked me out and dragged me away before I could tell them."

"And where was she?" Victor asked.

"Sitting against a building next to where I was before I ran ..."

"...Before you left her," Victor interrupted.

"Don't you understand?" Tommy said more softly, beginning to cry. "She's my life. She's just a little girl and she's out there all alone.   Anything could happen to her. I would move mountains to get out of here and get to her, I'll do whatever I have to. Do you have any kids?"

"Yes," Victor replied, finally really beginning to listen. "A boy and a girl."

"What if one of them was alone out there tonight? What would you want to do then?"

"That wouldn't happen," Victor replied sheepishly.

"Because you're a lawyer?" Tommy asked. "Because you have lots of money?"

"Because I would not allow it to," Victor answered. Privately knowing that his situation was vastly different from Tommy's, secured by his father's wealth and name.

"I used to think that. When I had a good job, a house, lots of friends. I never thought I could let it happen. But somehow it did," he explained, a tear rolling down his cheek. "It happened to me and it's happened to my little girl. She's paying for my mistakes and my weaknesses and I have no right to make her do that, that's not the way it's supposed to be. I have to see that judge, don't you see? You have to get me in to see him."

Adams paused for a moment, considered the desperation on Tommy's face.

"Mr. Bloundin, what do you want me to do?"

"Get me in front of Judge Holliday," Tommy repeated, wiping the tear from his cheek, growing angry once more. "Get him to let me out of here."

"Can you afford bail?" Victor asked, returning to reality. Tommy had begun to get to him, but he fought back the impulse.

"If I could, I wouldn't be in here in the first place."

"Forgive me for saying so, Mr. Bloundin, but you are not with reality here. You are living in some kind of Christmas fantasy land. You have no money, you have no home, no job. You steal a watch, try to peddle it on the street and run away from where your daughter is when the police come. Do you think any judge in his right mind is going to let you out without bail? You're too great a flight risk. We'd never see you again."

"'We'? Who's side are you on?"

"I mean the good people of this city."

"Is that who you represent?" Tommy asked.

"They pay me to represent you."

"My little girl is out there," Tommy tried again, realizing what he was up against. "Alone. Tonight! I will do anything to get out of here and find her. No one in here will listen to me. I tell them there's a kid out there and they don't try to find her."

"They don't care," Adams responded.

"Then you have to make them care!" Tommy screamed, rising to his feat and grabbing hold of the fence between them.

Victor paused a moment, stared Tommy in the eye. "I represent sixty of your fellow inmates. It's two days before Christmas. They all want out and they all want me to do them favors on the outside. You are right, I do have a family. A family that I'll get to spend perhaps one day with, tops, for Christmas."

"She's all alone," Tommy pleaded desperately. "What if she were one of your kids?"

"We've already been through this, sir. It's been a very long day," Victor responded, standing.

"Mr. Adams, I know that I'm just a number to you," Tommy said, as Victor pulled himself away from the table. "I am not asking you to do anything for me. I'm begging you to help a sweet, innocent, defenseless little seven-year-old girl who is going to have to find herself something to eat and somewhere to sleep because her father is a stupid, worthless, loser…"

Victor Adams walked away, turned a corner, out of view. He was thinking of his own family, his own children, who wanted to see him for Christmas. It was only right that he spend time with them and not with his work.

". . . who doesn't deserve her," Tommy said to himself as he fell back into his chair. He hung his head, grabbed his hair tightly with both hands and began to weep.

Victor walked up the hallway, hesitated, then stopped. He turned around, walked back in and threw his brief case against the chain-link fence. "Where were you arrested?" he asked.

Tommy stood, smiled and grabbed the fence, "Thank you!" he said.

* * *

Ross Potts was resting comfortably in the largest room of Mt. Temple Hospital. There were three nurses at his disposal, one in the room at all times, the other two a moment's notice away. Ross, Jr. and Hampton arrived together and walked in, standing at their father's bedside.

"The vultures are already circling," Potts remarked, opening one eye to his sons.

"Father, are you alright?" Hampton replied dramatically, taking his hand.

"What a nightmare," Potts responded, snapping his hand away from Hampton's grasp.

"Don't get yourself upset now," Ross, Jr. replied, stepping forward, placing a hand near his father's leg.

"Where is Scruffy?" Potts demanded sharply.

"Who?" Hampton asked.

"Scruffy, the little white dog I came in with."

"He's hallucinating," Ross, Jr. told the nurse. "Get Doctor Fangaro."

"I came in here with a little white dog."

"Father, you have a very nasty wound on your head. I am sure you were just dreaming," Hampton answered.

"Don't tell me what I'm doing," Potts retorted. "I know very well what I'm doing. They gave me something that knocked me out, somebody took my dog and I want it back. Where is my dog?" he demanded.

"Settle down father," Ross, Jr. urged.

"The little girl at the shelter gave me a white dog," Potts said, slightly more calmly. "Now it would make me very happy if . . ."

"What shelter?" Ross, Jr. interrupted.

"The one I was in after the accident."

"There you go," Hampton replied. "You weren't in any shelter, they took you out of the car."

"What do you mean they took me out of the car? Do you

think I'm an idiot?"

"Father, we've spoken to Jeffrey, he said they took you all out of the car," Hampton continued.

"Impossible. I was in a shelter. With a little girl."

"It's quite understandable, Father. You've received a severe blow to your head. The mind can do strange things under such circumstances," Ross, Jr. interjected.

"But I was there."

"It doesn't matter, now anyway," Hampton said. "You're obviously back to normal."

"You mean to tell me it was all a dream? You think I believe that?"

"If you think you were in some kind of shelter then certainly, yes. It was a dream," Hampton answered.

"Father, you didn't have a dog and there was no shelter," Ross, Jr. added softly.

"There was. I know there was," Potts said, confused.

Dr. Fangaro and a nurse entered the room. Fangaro, an internist, had been Potts personal physician for more than thirty years.

"What's the problem, Ross?" the doctor asked, squeezing between Hampton and Ross, Jr.

"Father seems to be hallucinating," Ross, Jr. replied.

"I just had a dream," Potts protested.

"Let's see," the doctor answered, pulling out a small flashlight and looking into the old man's eyes.

"I'm alright," Potts demanded.

"Hmmm," the doctor responded, moving to the other eye, "why don't you let me be the judge of that."

"Do you think there could be permanent damage?" Junior asked as Fangaro continued his examination.

"It appears that you still have a slight concussion," the doctor began. "Nothing serious and it isn't unusual that you may have some pretty realistic dreams that go along with that. I really don't think it's anything to worry about."

Ross Jr. and Hampton's faces fell in unison.

"When can I get out of here?" Potts asked, annoyed.

"Let's wait at least until morning," the doctor replied.

"I feel fine," Potts replied.

"I'll be by again in the morning to check on you. Your X-rays came back negative, so if nothing changes you should be okay to leave in the morning," Dr. Fangaro explained.

"I'm fine to go now," Potts insisted.

"Ross, let me do my job," the doctor pleaded.

"I am going to be in my office first thing in the morning," Potts insisted.

"I'll put you first on my rounds."

Potts did not respond at first, then relented. "Thank you, Eddie."

The words caught Doctor Fangaro off guard. He froze for a moment, stared at Potts.

"You're welcome, Ross," Fangaro finally replied, smiling. He patted Potts on the shoulder, then walked back between Potts' sons to the door.

"Doctor, could I have a word with you?" Hampton asked, following him.

"No, wait," Potts called to Hampton, "I would like a word with you and your brother."

Hampton stopped, allowed the doctor leave and reported immediately back to Potts' bedside.

Ross Potts motioned for the nurse to excuse herself, and she promptly complied.

"Why don't you guys have a seat," he began in a concerned voice.

His tone of voice caught them off guard, confused them. Neither moved. Then Potts frowned and the two of them scrambled to find chairs, pulling them in close and sitting down.

"I need to talk to you boys."

"Certainly father," Hampton replied.

"I want to speak to you like I am not used to speaking to you. As your father and not as your employer. Something miraculous happened to me in that ambulance. I can't quite explain it. There I was, riding back there, the same old Ross Potts, holding that little..." he stopped himself. Ross, Jr. and Hampton looked at one another. "I had a lot to think about in the back of that ambulance," Potts said, then paused. "I don't know, maybe it was all just a dream, but what are dreams if not our own subconscious giving us direction at the only time that we will listen, the only time that we are forced to give our undivided attention?"

"Anyway," he continued, "mostly what I thought about was you two, and I tell you it was as though somebody flipped on a light switch. It was that quick and that clear. Suddenly, I could finally see it all, it was all clear to me for the first time in a long, long time. And that is what I want to share with you, to keep you from living in the same trap that I built for myself. I want you two to listen carefully, because I really think you're going to really benefit from what I have come to realize."

"Wonderful, father," Hampton replied.

"What is it?" Ross Jr. asked anxiously, anticipating the announcement of his father's retirement.

Potts looked into his sons' smiling faces.

"I haven't been much of a father to you boys," he began.

"Sure you have," Ross, Jr. interrupted.

Potts frowned again, Ross, Jr. bit his lip.

"I know that I've supplied you with the basics of life," he continued. "Food, clothing, shelter, an education and employment."

"I would say that Harvard and Oxford are a little above and beyond the basics of life," Hampton joked.

Ross, Jr. chuckled knowingly.

"But I was never there for you as a Dad," Potts went on, ignoring Hampton's comment. "I worked hard. Long and hard, and you two grew up, it seemed, almost overnight. And now I look back—riding in that ambulance, I looked back—thought of a father and his children and what that is supposed to mean, what it should be. And then I thought of you two and what you have made of yourselves under my tutelage."

Ross, Jr. and Hampton, dressed in their thousand dollar suits, sat up, smiling proudly.

"I've raised a couple of worthless, snivelling, ostentatious, greedy, self-centered, cowardly brats."

Their faces dropped.

"I have given you everything and made you nothing. Nothing, because I failed to give you the one thing that you really needed and that was myself. I was too busy giving all of that to my work and there was none left for you and none left for your poor, dear, sweet mother, God rest her soul. I promised her that I'd make her the richest woman in town, I thought that's how you gained respect..."

"And you did. Gracious, Father, she was easily the richest in the state, everyone admires and respects you, even the governor," Ross, Jr. assured him.

"I doubt that now, son. She might have had more money than the rest, but she died a very sad woman. If you had only known her before, before I was consumed by all this, you would know. Sadly, I must admit," he continued, his eyes growing red, "that as successful as I have been with my business, I have been a complete failure where it really counts, and that is as a husband and as your father."

"Father, it isn't true," Hampton protested.

"Oh, but yes it is. I see it. Every day I see it. I see it in the way you treat people. As though they were objects, pieces of machinery that make you rich. And I know where you learned that, you learned that from me. I see it in the way you treat your own families and cheat on your wives, and you learned that from me as well. The truth be known, were it not for my bank account, you two would be nothing more than worthless white trash, with not an ounce of redeeming social value between you."

"Father, I think this accident has affected you..." Ross, Jr. began.

"You're damned right it has," he said loudly. "It has affected me, it's woken me up. It's given me a new lease on life. My God, I have a bank account with seventy million dollars in it and I'm probably the unhappiest man in this entire God-forsaken town. And you two aren't far behind. There are people out there who don't have enough to eat, children wearing rags and sleeping on iron grates to keep warm at night and they have more than you or I will ever have. Somehow, through all of their struggle and sadness they have managed to retain the one thing that has eluded each of us—their sense of human dignity and their ability to care about what happens to a fellow human being."

"Father! We attend several charity balls each year, paying

dearly for overpriced tickets that go to help such people," Ross, Jr. protested.

"Quite painless, isn't it?" Potts continued. "Help the poor dressed in your tuxedo, eating caviar and gulping down champagne. Always giving from your excess, never from where it hurts. Look at us, we consume too much, we hoard too much. We hold it in bank accounts where it will never be spent, counting it while so many have none in their pockets. But still, they manage to have so much more than we do. And you know what? I would bet you that if they did have my money, they'd probably give half of it away to others less fortunate."

"Precisely why they are where they are today," Hampton blurted out.

"You see what I mean?" the old man yelled. "You haven't the least idea of what I am talking about. You are a couple of monsters and I'm the Dr. Frankenstein who created you."

"Father, settle down," Ross, Jr. demanded, standing.

"No, you settle down," Potts retorted, "I am not going to settle down. I am going to get out of here and I am going to start living life the way it is supposed to be lived, caring about something and someone other than myself. Before it's too late. And I am going to start right here, in my own town, and in my own house, by being a much better father. And by spending a lot less time in pursuit of the almighty dollar and a lot more time in pursuit of the Almighty."

Finally, he was getting around to what Ross, Jr. had hoped to hear. He smiled and sat down again. "I see what you are saying, Father," Ross, Jr. declared.

"I want you two to try and accept me as your father, let me know what is bothering you. Let me try and help you work it out."

"I can do that," Hampton said, quite merrily. Realizing the interdiction would not be necessary after all.

"I know it is going to be hard on you at first."

"Not at all, Father," Ross, Jr. disagreed. "We've been raised to take over the reins when you felt the time was right. And it is a great comfort knowing that you will still be there should we ever have a problem. We can still come to you for your expert advice. You can even maintain an office in the building if you'd like."

"What are you talking about?" Potts asked.

"After your retirement," Ross, Jr. explained. "It doesn't have to be a full retirement, you can have my office. Come in whenever you get the urge."

"I'm not retiring," Potts stated incredulously, "you are. At least from Potts Manufacturing."

"What do you mean?" Hampton asked, confused.

"I'm firing you, setting you free to spread your own wings. Pushing you out of the nest to make your own way in life."

"Ha!" Hampton laughed, unable to control himself.

"You've gone mad," Ross, Jr. added, a little more concerned.

"I am not mad, and one day you are going to thank me for this. You are both fired, effective immediately. You have fine degrees, go out and find yourselves good jobs, start at the bottom and work your way up, make me proud of you."

"You can't be serious," Hampton huffed.

"As serious as I have ever been. And not only am I firing the two of you, but I am cutting you out of your inheritance as well. I'll maintain the trust funds for your children's educations, but the rest is going to go for doing some good in this world while I still have time."

"He has gone mad," Hampton said to his brother.

"We will see about this!" Ross, Jr. exclaimed, standing.

"I take responsibility, boys, it is all my fault," Potts continued to explain. "You can make it on your own, have confidence in yourselves. I'm not deserting you, I'll be there if you need some advice, a recommendation, but I won't let you turn in to what I have become. I want you to be happy."

"Happy?" Hampton yelled, standing. "You think it will make us happy to be thrown, with our families, out into the streets?"

"Don't be so dramatic, Hampton. No one is throwing my grandchildren out into the street. I'll give you a severance. You own your homes and cars. You have your bank accounts. You have a hell of a lot more than most have when they strike it out on their own. A lot more than I had when I started out."

"We will not be cheated out of what is rightfully ours," Ross, Jr. insisted, taking his brother's arm and pulling him toward the door.

"That's right, you won't. Make me proud, boys," Potts

repeated as his sons hurried out of the door.

Once his sons had gone, Ross Potts threw his head back on his pillow, wearing a huge grin on his face. He felt great, rejuvenated, better than he could remember having felt in a very, very long time.

* * *

CHAPTER 5

Tommy Bloundin telephoned his attorney's office at precisely 9:00 in the morning.

"P.D.'s office," the receptionist answered.

"Mr. Adams, please," Tommy requested impatiently.

"I'm sorry, but Mr. Adams is not in today," the receptionist replied.

"When do you expect him?" he asked.

"After the Christmas holiday," she said.

"No, ma'am," Tommy replied. "Mr. Victor Adams, he's working the holiday."

"I'm sorry, but Mr. Adams will not be back in until the twenty-seventh."

"No, you're mistaken," Tommy insisted. "This is Tommy Bloundin, I'm one of his clients. I spoke to him yesterday and he was going to take care of something for me today."

"I'm sorry sir," she replied. "All I know is that when Mr. Adams left here last night he said he would be back on the twenty-seventh."

"Is it possible he left a note for me?"

"No note sir."

"How do you know? Did you check?" Tommy asked angrily.

"I'm sorry, sir, but I have other lines ringing, I'll have to disconnect."

"No! Wait! Please!" Tommy pleaded, but the line went dead.

"No!" Tommy yelled, slamming the telephone against the wall.

* * *

"Okay, you're free to go," Dr. Fangaro announced walking into Ross Potts' room.

ANGELS AND PANCAKES

Potts, grinning broadly, hopped out of bed.

"Ross?" the doctor began, partly out of curiosity but also with concern.

"Yea, Doc?" Potts replied, standing to dress.

"I've never seen you like this," Fangaro continued.

"Eddie," Potts replied, pulling up his trousers, "I've never been like this."

"What's come over you?"

"I'm not really sure," Potts answered, then reconsidered. "You really want to know?" Potts asked, tightening his belt.

"Absolutely."

"Do you believe in angels, Doctor?"

"You mean like cherubs, little wings flying around in heaven and all?"

"Or visiting earth," Potts added, stopping to give the doctor his full attention.

"I suppose I do. I read the Bible and it talks a lot about them, just seems they're not as prevalent as they were back then."

"Well, I think I saw one last night," Potts said in earnest.

"Really now?" the doctor replied, humoring him.

"In a dream. You know, like when Gabriel came to Joseph, in a dream."

"So the Angel Gabriel came to you last night in a... "

"No, of course not," Potts interrupted. "Not Gabriel, just a little girl."

"A little girl angel?" the doctor asked with growing concern.

"Yes. A dirty little girl. No wings or anything, just a plain ol' ordinary looking little girl."

"What did she look like?"

"Just what I needed her to look like, Doc. A little homeless waif, with nothing in the world. Coming to me, who seemingly has everything in the world. I tell you Doc, she changed my life."

Doctor Fangaro smiled, Potts resumed his dressing.

"I was a self-centered, crabby old man. Life wasn't fun anymore," Potts continued. "But you know what, Eddie?" he said, buttoning his shirt.

"What, Ross?"

"It's gonna be a hell of a ride from here on out!"

The Doctor smiled as the door behind him swung open. Ross, Jr. and Hampton walked in along with a doctor and a deputy sheriff.

"Oh, the family is here to escort me home," Potts said half in jest.

"Mr. Ross Potts?" the deputy sheriff asked.

"In the flesh," Potts responded.

The deputy began reading from the order in his hand. "Under the authority of the County Coroner's Office, you are hereby placed under custody for psychiatric evaluation. You are to remain under such custody until such time as the evaluation has been completed and the coroner has had the opportunity to review the findings. If you will come with me, I will escort you to the eighteenth floor of this building."

"What?" Potts asked, concerned.

"It's the psychiatric ward, Ross," Dr. Fangaro answered. "May I see those commitment papers please?" he requested of the deputy.

"Boys, you can't be serious," Potts said to his sons.

"Quite the contrary, Father," Ross, Jr. replied.

"It's all for your own good," Hampton added.

"These appear legitimate, Ross. Was the Coroner in here to examine you earlier?" Dr. Fangaro asked.

"No, I haven't seen him," Potts answered.

"I am afraid that the commitment was made upon my recommendation after having spoken with the family last evening," the doctor who had walked in with the deputy answered.

"And who might you be?" Fangaro asked.

"Dr. Edmund Fischer, I have a Phd. in psychiatry."

"You obtained a coroner's commitment without even examining Mr. Potts?" Dr. Fangaro asked incredulously.

"That is why I am here now. As soon as Mr. Potts has been escorted upstairs, I will examine him and make a preliminary determination. Should it be negative, he will be released immediately."

"What ever happened to innocent until proven guilty?" Potts asked.

"You are not on trial, Mr. Potts. Your family is quite concerned about you and thinks that you may be a danger to yourself. I am merely going to make sure either that that is not the case, or that you receive the appropriate treatment should their fears prove correct."

"This man is not dangerous," Fangaro said.

"I beg your pardon, Doctor, but this is not your field of expertise. I will have to make that determination."

"This is outrageous," Dr. Fangaro continued. "Ross, who is your attorney?"

"Alton Green," Potts responded.

"I'll get him down here. It's the holiday but I'll find him," Dr. Fangaro assured Potts as the deputy led him away.

"Thank you, Eddie," Potts replied, winking an eye at the doctor.

"Dr. Fischer," Fangaro called out as the psychiatrist was leaving the room.

"Yes?" Fischer responded.

"I want you to know that I am going to bring this up with the Chief of Staff."

Fischer did not respond. He turned and followed the others out of the room and down the hall toward the elevators.

* * *

An hour after Doctor Fischer's preliminary examination had ended, Alton Green, with the help of Doctor Eddie Fangaro, was allowed onto the eighteenth floor of Mt. Temple Hospital. A nurse unlocked an iron gate and Green walked in.

"He's in 1824," she said, closing and locking the gate behind him.

Green, a heavy-set man in his mid-fifties, with a tuft of bright red hair combed across the top of his head in a futile effort to hide his baldness, ambled down the hallway in search of room 1824.

Many of the ward's residents were also in the hallway, most walking, zombie-like, from doorway to doorway, stopping momentarily at one before proceeding on to the next.

"Doctor!" a young man yelled from down the hallway. Although he was looking directly at Green, the attorney ignored him, believing no one could mistake him for a doctor.

"Doctor! Doctor!" the young man continued yelling as he ran, with a limp, down the hallway toward Green.

Alton Green looked around for a nurse or an orderly, but none were in sight.

"Doctor!" the young man yelled, screeching to a halt directly in front of Green.

"I'm sorry, son, but I'm not a doctor."

"Doctor," the young man continued, relentlessly, "I feel much better now. Can I have some candy now?"

"I am not a doctor," Green insisted, stepping aside to move up the hallway.

"I'm feeling better, Doctor," the young man continued, stepping in front of Green.

Green responded with an angry stare, hoping to intimidate the young man into silence.

"Can I have candy, Doctor? I feel much better today," the young man repeated, unaffected.

Abandoning his initial tact, Green replaced his angry look with a smile and spoke softly to the young man.

"You do seem to have improved," he said. "I don't see what harm a few pieces of candy would do. Go ahead."

"Thank you, Doctor!" the young man yelled, immediately turning and running back down the hallway. "Candy! I get candy!" he yelled as he went.

Green hurried to room 1824.

"Alton!" Ross Potts called out upon seeing him in his doorway.

"Hello, Ross," Green said, hurrying in and grabbing the door to close behind him.

"You have to leave it open," Potts said.

"I'm trying to get away from… " he began to explain, but Potts interrupted him.

"It's a rule."

"Okay," Green relented, nervously walking in the rest of the way and shaking Potts' hand.

"It sure is good to see you, Alton. Makes me feel like the farmer whose hired gun just rode into town to take care of the ranchers."

"What's going on, Ross?"

"Those two boys of mine are making a power play."

"That's what it sounded like when Eddie called me. Look, you've got nothing to worry about. I already have two psychiatrists lined up, tops in the field, both on the West Coast. They'll be here the day after Christmas."

"Alton, I want out today," Potts said.

"Ross, be reasonable. It's Christmas, for Christ's sake. We are going to need expert testimony to rebut their witnesses. No telling who they're going to bring in and how much they're going to pay them."

"To lie?" Potts asked.

"To give them a favorable result," Green replied diplomatically.

"Is that what these two from the West Coast have agreed to do? Give us a favorable result?"

"I'm certain they will be able to clearly see just how sane you are and to honestly present that to the Court."

"And if not, they'll say so anyway, right?"

"You do want out of here, don't you?"

"Today," Potts insisted.

"They can't be here today, and I can't prove my case today. Besides, you'd never find a judge to hear the matter on such notice. The courts are closed. It's the day before Christmas."

"Alton," Potts answered calmly, "every year you come to me with your hand out, asking me to make contributions, sizeable ones, to your friends vying for the bench. And every year I dole it out, just as you suggest. Now I have my hand out. I want a hearing, and I want it today. I don't care what kind of judge he is, a traffic Judge for all I care, as long as he out-ranks a coroner and can have me out of here today!"

"We have no witnesses!"

"That is not your concern. You get me the hearing. If it fails, it will be my fault. I won't hold you accountable."

"Ross," Green complained.

"Alton, that's all I'm asking of you. And if you fail me," Potts continued, in a much more serious tone of voice, "you will never represent me again."

Green picked up his briefcase and looked at Potts.

"Okay, Ross," he relented, "I'll find you your judge. And I want you to know I'm going to have to go to the Supreme Court to do it. It's going to take my calling in some very big chips. I'll get you your hearing, but this is going to wipe the slate clean."

"Agreed," Potts said.

"Doctor! Doctor! Doctor! Doctor!" the young man in the hallway yelled as he ran past Potts' door.

"Somebody get an orderly!" a nurse yelled.

"Doctor! Doctor!"

"Who's the asshole that told Jimmy he could have candy?" the nurse yelled out as two orderlies ran past Potts' room on their way down the hall.

A look of concern came over Green's face. "I'll see you this afternoon," he told Potts as he cautiously looked down the hallway, then rushed out, toward the gate.

"Doctor! Here I am," Jimmy yelled from down the hallway, breaking free of the orderlies and chasing after Alton Green.

Potts shook his head then sat at the little desk in his room. He put his hands over his ears to block out the noise, then he did something that he had not done for years. Ross Potts began to pray.

* * *

"Excuse me. Excuse me," Potts finally heard someone repeating the words. He looked up and saw one of the nurses from the night before standing in the doorway. He moved his hands away from his ears.

"Mr. Potts?" she said in a low tone.

"Yes," he replied. "You're the nurse who was with me last night, aren't you?" he asked kindly.

"Yes, sir. I sure am," she answered. "May I come in?"

"Certainly," Potts replied, motioning for the young Black woman, dressed in a white uniform and holding a purple gym bag, to enter.

"What can I do for you?" he asked.

"Well, I'm not really supposed to be here," she began. "I'm off duty and only the nurses that work on this floor are supposed to be up here. But a friend of mine minds the gate and she let me in."

"I see," Potts answered.

She stared at him for a moment.

"Is your head alright?" she asked.

"Oh, yes, just fine," he answered. "Is that why you're here?"

"No, not really," she hesitated. "I came to bring you this," she said, holding up the gym bag.

"I'm sorry, but that's not for me," he responded

"Yes it is," she insisted.

"It's not mine, I've never seen it before."

"I was in the ward when they brought you in last night. The bag is mine, I keep my change of clothes in it," she explained. "You were pretty much out of it, even after your boys came in. They aren't too nice, are they?"

"No, I'm afraid they aren't," Potts answered.

"Hard to believe they're your kids. Most nice people like you seem to have nice children," she continued.

Potts smiled.

"Anyway, I heard what they was sayin' and all, 'bout you bein' crazy. I didn't believe a word of it. I said to myself, 'Darlene, they're just trying to get that old man's money'."

"You are quite perceptive."

She smiled. "And then when they told you that you didn't come in here with no dog…"

Potts' heart skipped a beat, his eyes immediately filled with water.

". . . I just couldn't stand it. They told me to throw it away."

"You mean she wasn't a dream?" Potts asked, envisioning Erica, the tears falling from his swollen eyes.

"Who?" Darlene asked, confused.

Potts swallowed hard, composed himself.

"You mean I did have a dog with me?" Potts continued.

"Yes, sir, you sure did. And I kept it too. I have it, right here in this bag."

Potts concentrated intently on the bag as Darlene began to unzip it.

"I wasn't about to throw it away. I don't care who the man

said he was. He said he'd have my job, but I don't care because what they're doing just ain't right," she continued pulling the little stuffed dog out of the bag. "Jesus wouldn't want me to take the easy road and just turn my back on you in need, not the day before his birthd…"

At the sight of Scruffy, Potts fell back in his chair and began to weep openly. Darlene shut up, walked over and handed him the dog.

Potts grabbed Scruffy, gazing blurrily through teardrops upon his stained white coat, then held him close to his cheek. "Thank you! Thank you!" he said between gasps of air.

"I'll surely go and testify for you too if you want me to," Darlene continued. "They was tryin' to drive you crazy, I know they was."

"You will never know how much you have done for me," Potts said, forcing himself to calm down. "That poor, dear, sweet child. She's still out there."

"You really love that little doggie, don't you?" Darlene asked innocently.

"More than you can imagine," Potts answered, wiping his eyes. "Well I am glad that I didn't throw it away."

"This is quite embarrassing," Potts admitted, reaching for a tissue to dry his eyes. "I've never done this before."

"I'm just the same way," Darlene rambled on. "Sometimes I just have to open the flood gates and let all those pent-up feelings come flowing on out."

"Well I haven't done that for fifty or sixty years now," Potts confessed.

"Oh my, darlin', well you sure deserve to now after all that time."

"I hate to ask," Potts said, turning back to Darlene, "but could you do me one more favor?"

"I'd be proud to," she answered.

"I'd be more than happy to pay you," he said.

"Don't be silly, it's Christmas," she insisted. "That's the best part about Christmas, doin' unto others, especially those less fortunate."

Potts smiled, never before having considered himself of one of the "less fortunate."

"You think any amount of money would make me feel better than seein' you so happy to see your little doggie again?" Darlene continued. "I know just how you feel. I lost my favorite little doll when I was a child. I cried and cried for days. I don't want no money from you, Mister, you've already given me enough just sharin' that special time with me."

"Well you see," Potts began, "it's not my little dog."

"It's not?" Darlene said, surprised.

"No, it belongs to a little girl. She let me use it because she thought it would make my head feel better."

"Ahhh, ain't that sweet? Is she your grandbaby?"

"No. No she's a little girl that doesn't have a home and her father's in jail. She's going to be all alone for Christmas."

Darlene began to cry. "That poor child," she said. "She could come to my house, she'll fit right in with my babies. Where is she? I'll go get her."

"That's very kind," Potts said. "But that's just the problem, I don't know where she is. Will you help me find her?"

"Mister, you don't even have to ask that question. You done broke my heart," Darlene answered. "Where did you see her? What did she look like?"

"No, no, not like that. You see, I am a very wealthy man…" Potts paused. "I have the resources to find her, but I need you to get word to the outside for me."

"You mean like sneak a note out or something?" Darlene said, still crying, but excited.

"Exactly!" Potts responded.

"Ohhhh. Jest like in a movie!" she said.

"So you'll do it?"

"You just write it. I'll get it out."

"I'll write it all down. All you have to do is give it to my secretary, Ms. Rebecca Jenks…"

* * *

After having spoken briefly with Rebecca Jenks over the telephone, Darlene headed to the bench in Circle Park that she had designated as the "drop-off" point. Darlene had told Rebecca Jenks how to recognize her, an idea she had gotten from a movie once and that she had always wanted to try out.

"Darlene?" Rebecca asked, having no doubt that the young woman seated in the nurse's uniform, wearing one white shoe and one red shoe was the person she was supposed to meet.

"Don't use my name. Who's asking?" Darlene inquired without looking at Rebecca.

"I'm Rebecca Jenks, Mr. Potts' secretary."

"Do you have some I.D.?" Darlene asked, still not looking at Rebecca.

"I have a driver's license," Rebecca said, digging in her wallet and pulling it out.

Rebecca handed the license to Darlene, who inspected it, then looked at Rebecca and handed it back.

"Okay," Darlene began. "See that garbage can over there?"

"Where?" Rebecca asked.

"Right there in front," Darlene said, referring to a green garbage can directly across the path about ten feet away.

"Okay, I see it," Rebecca said.

"You see that big rock next to it?" Darlene asked.

"That one?" Rebecca asked, pointing.

"Yes," Darlene responded, looking around nervously to see whether anyone had noticed Rebecca pointing.

"Yea, I see it."

"It's under there," Darlene said.

"What is?"

"It," she insisted. "Your boss' note."

"It's under that rock?"

"Right."

Rebecca walked over to the garbage can, leaned over, moved the rock, and picked up the folded piece of paper underneath. She unwrapped it and immediately began reading:

"Dear Ms. Jenks, No time to explain. Contact Ace Private Investigations, a Mr. Jimmy Mitchell. Tell him that I want to find a little girl who gave me a stuffed dog last night in a shelter for the homeless. It is run by a kindly old woman in the downtown area and it is where the ambulance picked me up after my accident. Find out where I was and who the little girl was and where she is now. If she needs anything get it for her out of petty cash. Report back through Alton Green. Also, make arrangements to give the angel of mercy who delivered this note to you $1,000.00 out of my personal account..."

Rebecca looked up in disbelief. She looked over toward the bench, but Darlene had disappeared. Her eyes darted around the park, but Darlene was nowhere in sight. She continued reading:

"Also, write a new memo: All employees are officially off effective immediately, through the fifth of next month, with full compensation. I beg you not to rest until you have found this little girl, she is in great need. I promise to make it all worth your effort. And Ms. Jenks, I truly regret, from the bottom of my heart, the way I have treated you in the past. If you stay with me and aid me in this, my time of need, I promise that you will not regret it.

Respectfully,

Ross Potts"

"Oh my God," Rebecca said aloud, "he really has lost his mind."

* * *

CHAPTER 6

Judge Harry Holliday took the bench of Section B of the Municipal Court at precisely one o'clock in the afternoon. It was the day before Christmas, and his was the only court holding session in the entire county. Consequently, the courtroom was packed with attorneys and spectators, all hoping to be heard before the Christmas break. Ross Potts, clutching Scruffy under his left arm, sat in the front row of the courtroom, flanked on either side by Alton Green and a deputy sheriff. Hampton and Ross, Jr. were seated across the aisle, directly behind the Assistant District Attorney, with whom they were chatting gleefully.

As a Municipal Court Judge, Holliday's main duty was to conduct arraignments and set bail for those imprisoned for the relatively minor offenses prohibited by city ordinances. He was the last hope for nearly a hundred prisoners on his docket to be released from custody in time to be home for Christmas with their families.

The Judge rapped his gavel on the block of wood sitting atop the bench, the loud crack resonating throughout the room, demanding silence.

"Good evening," he stated sternly.

The attorneys present each responded aloud with "Good evening Judge," or "Good evening, Your Honor," or something similar.

"I would like to open this session with a little statement, if the gallery and the members of the bar would be so kind as to allow me," Judge Holliday began, knowing there would be no objection.

"I have a confession to make," he continued after a brief pause. "I have been involved in a tepid love affair for the last twenty-seven years." He paused again for effect, now having the undivided attention of all present.

"My wife is fully aware of the situation and has, albeit some-times begrudgingly, allowed me to carry on. She's had no choice, actually, for without my extra-marital love life, we would soon find ourselves in indigent circumstances." He savored the shocked looks on the faces of his staff and the lawyers with whom he worked daily for another moment, before coming clean.

"My mistress for all these years, you see, has been the law." He noted the disappointment and delight of the various faces in the courtroom as he continued. "The law of the greatest nation on earth, and what a jealous mistress she is. I have always believed in the law, and in the principles upon which this land is based. Liberty and justice for all. The law is blind. It plays no favorites." Again he paused. "Or so I thought until today."

Judge Holliday focused his gaze upon Alton Green.

"I have always kept my courtroom open on the day before Christmas. My mistress has demanded it of me. Much has been entrusted to me by the people of this city in electing me to the bench. My sense of duty demands that I be here on this day, when all of my colleagues are home getting ready to put the turkey in the oven, or dress up like Santa Claus, or to watch a football game—I don't know what they do. But I know what I do," he said, suddenly raising his voice, "I sit at my appointed post and humbly wield my authority to allow some of your children out there to spend the holidays *with* their parents rather than having to visit them in jail. How could I enjoy myself on Christmas Day, knowing that some child is unable to enjoy the holiest of days because I wouldn't get up off of my duff and hear the hundred or so matters that have a right to be heard the day before?"

"Don't misunderstand me. I am a deeply religious man, and I do not work on Christmas day, refusing to deny my children and those of my staff the very thing that I aim to accomplish today. Christmas is a time for families, and mine is no exception.

"I normally have thirty or forty cases on my docket, but today I have considerably more..."

He looked to his docket clerk, "How many do we have exact-ly today, Jerry?"

"One hundred twelve," Jerry immediately replied.

"You're wrong," he publicly admonished the young clerk. "But it's not your fault. I'll get to that in a minute." Then he turned back to the courtroom. "I have considerably more cases on my docket today because I am taking up the slack of my brethren who apparently do not answer to the same jealous mistress that I must."

He paused again. The courtroom was silent.

"But I digress. I am not here to get your collective pats on my back. I have already explained to you why I am here."

He paused again.

"And justice for all! it says," he yelled, startling the room. "My clerk informed me that I had one hundred and twelve matters on my docket today, but that is not correct. I had one hundred and twelve matters on my docket this morning when I woke up, but then, about an hour ago, my boss, the Chief Justice of our State's Supreme Court, telephoned me and asked that I add one more. And I use that term 'asked' very loosely. Never mind the fact that the matter concerns an issue that I, in my current position, do not even have jurisdiction to hear, because I received special permission. Never mind that it's of such a sensitive nature that I am going to have to clear my packed court room of all but the parties involved and consume a precious hour that could otherwise be used deciding the fate of twenty or thirty or forty others. No, never mind any of that. For today it is truly justice for all. Justice for the poor," he said, waiving his arm over the crowded courtroom, "and justice for the rich," he continued, letting his arm fall in front of Ross Potts.

"But that's what I get for doing a good job. More work. You'd think that..." he stopped himself. "Never mind. Bailiff, clear the courtroom except those involved in the Potts matter," he ordered, throwing himself back into his chair.

"This is what I tried to warn you about, Ross," Alton Green whispered in his client's ear. "You'll find no sympathetic ear on the bench today."

The deputies saw to it that the courtroom was cleared and the doors barred. Potts and Alton Green walked up to the defendant's table and took their seats, Ross, Jr. and Hampton walked up and sat beside the Assistant District Attorney.

"What have you done so wrong in your life to have the misfortune of being before me this day visited upon you, Mr. Gates?" the Judge asked the prosecutor.

"I volunteered, your honor," Gates answered, smiling.

"Brown-noser," Green whispered to Potts.

"Call the first matter," the Judge ordered his clerk.

"Case number 994-125, In the Matter of Ross Potts. It is a coroner's commitment, Your Honor."

"Mr. Gates, are you ready to proceed?" the judge asked.

"Hardly, Your Honor," Gates said rising. "The People would like to enter an objection. This entire matter is procedurally impossible. First of all, this Court does not have the proper jurisdiction to hear testimony regarding a commitment. Secondly, the State has not had time to properly prepare its case..."

"Mr. Gates, your objections are overruled. They will be noted for the record, however; considering my earlier statement and the fact that the body to which you would ultimately appeal my ruling is the identical body that has ordered this court to hear this matter today, I would suggest that you proceed."

"Your Honor, the People call Ross Potts, Jr. to the stand," Gates replied without further hesitation.

Ross, Jr. stood and walked to the witness stand. He was sworn in, and Mr. Gates began immediately.

"Mr. Potts, is it correct that you and your brother asked that the coroner intervene and have your father placed in custody for observation?"

"Yes, sir, that is correct. We were very concerned and felt that he may be a danger to himself."

"And what caused you to develop these beliefs?"

"Well, a lot of things," Ross, Junior replied.

"I understand that," Gates prodded, "but could you explain them to the court?"

"Well, it began a long time ago. It seems that father has been slipping further and further away from reality... from us... since my mother's death. My brother and I have been concerned for quite some time, but yesterday's events really frightened us." Ross, Jr. said.

"Go on," Gates urged.

"We went in to see him yesterday, in his office. You would have to know my father, but we were both shocked to see pages and pages of paper scattered everywhere. This is very unlike him, he is ordinarily very neat and orderly. I suppose you'd even say anal retentive," Ross, Jr. continued, daring not to look in his father's direction. "When we got into his office he began ranting and raving and comparing his man-servant, Jeffrey to a dog. Anyway, he issued a memo commanding the entire company to work through the holidays, even though we had already exceeded our year-end projections."

"Now this is strange behavior, perhaps, but I don't see what might be life threatening about it," Gates moved him along.

"Well, later we found out that he was causing a furor in his car on the ride home and that an accident had ensued. Although he was bleeding and covered in blood, he wandered off—into the ghetto—and finally collapsed, thank God, at the door of a homeless shelter. Then, later at the hospital, he kept talking and rambling on about a little white stuffed dog. I suppose much like the one he's holding now," Ross, Jr. said, pointing, finally facing his father, "and how he was going to give all of his money away and leave us and his grandchildren penniless. All of this, of course, caused great concern on the part of my brother and me. He was wandering the streets, playing with stuffed toys and talking about giving away everything that has always meant so much to him. We were scared, there was no telling what he might do next, so we sought professional help."

"And this professional help that you sought, this would be Doctor Fischer?" Gates asked.

"Yes, sir, Doctor Edmund Fischer, he's a psychiatrist. He suggested we attempt to get the coroner's commitment just as a safety precaution, until we knew for sure whether Father was ever going to be the same again. We are only acting out of love and concern, Father," Ross Potts, Jr. addressed his father directly. "We just want you to come back to us, and to be safe."

Ross Potts sat at the table shaking his head.

"I have no further questions of this witness, Your Honor."

"Mr. Green?" Judge Holliday said.

"No questions, Your Honor," Green replied.

"You may step down," the Judge told Ross, Jr. "Call your next witness."

"I call Hampton Potts."

Hampton rose.

"Your honor," Alton Green stood. "I am certain that Hampton Potts is going to testify to the same facts as his brother has, so in the interest of the Court's time and those waiting outside, we would be willing to stipulate that Mr. Potts would testify as such."

"Is that acceptable, Mr. Gates?" the Judge demanded more than asked.

"Yes your Honor," Gates replied.

"Call your next witness."

"The People call Dr. Edmund Fischer," Gates responded, pushing Hampton back into his seat.

Dr. Fischer took the stand and went through his analysis of Ross Potts which he had conducted earlier that morning. After twenty minutes of explaining the various tests administered, Emile Gates asked Dr. Fischer his opinion regarding Ross Potts' condition.

"Inconclusive," Fischer responded. "I simply have not had adequate time in which to form an opinion. I shall require several more diagnostic tests and other evaluative procedures before I can properly answer that question."

"In your opinion, Doctor, as an expert in the field of psychiatry," Gates asked, "is there anyone else who could provide us with an answer to that question at this particular point in time?"

"Knowing that no other professionals have seen Mr. Potts, there is absolutely no way that anyone could provide this court with a conclusive answer to the question today, or even this week. It will simply require more time."

"No further questions, Your Honor," Gates said.

"Mr. . ."

"No questions, Your Honor," Alton Green said, rising.

"The witness is dismissed. Call your next witness," Judge Holliday said.

"The People rest, Your Honor," Gates said, returning to his seat.

"Very well," Judge Holliday answered. "Mr. Green."

"Your Honor," Alton Green began, rising to his feet, "we have no witnesses, we have not had time to have an evaluation made. However, Your Honor, it is painfully obvious that the People have the burden of proof here and they simply have not proven that Ross Potts should be detained one moment longer under the Coroner's commitment. Indeed, they have not shown that enough evidence existed to obtain the commitment in the first place. What? A man wanders around after a car accident? Holds a stuffed toy? Threatens to disinherit his children? Your Honor, if a man can be committed to the psychiatric ward for having papers on the floor of his office I am afraid they will be coming after me next."

The muscles in the judge's face tightened, his cheeks turning red. "Mr. Green, am I to understand that you had this hearing called today, under these circumstances, and that you are not going to put forth a case?" Judge Holliday asked.

"In my opinion, the State has not put forward a case as is their duty, Your Honor. Therefore we must prevail."

"Only because you have not allowed them the proper amount of time to prepare one. You've rushed them into court so that you can claim they don't have enough evidence? These things take time, that's why the Coroner has the authority to detain such people."

The Judge was flustered. He continued, "If you have no case, then rest. I am prepared to make my ruling and I dare say you are not going to like it, Mr. Green. This is the most preposterous case of trial by ambush that I have ever heard of, and this won't be the last you've heard of it either!"

Green put his head down.

"Your honor, may I speak?" Ross Potts asked, rising, Scruffy still in hand.

"No sir, you may not, you are represented by counsel," the Judge responded.

Ross Potts turned to Green. "You're fired." Then, turning back to the judge he asked, "May I speak now."

"Your honor," Mr. Gates interjected, "this is highly irregular. This is a sanity hearing. Are we really going to have the defendant represent himself?"

"He has that right," Judge Holliday answered. "Objection overruled."

ANGELS AND PANCAKES

"Your honor," Potts began, "I know why I am here. I am here because I have failed my sons as a father. I've raised them to be greedy and selfish, just like their old man," he said, walking toward the bench with dog in hand. "Two days ago, I was exactly like them."

The judge pursed his lips, considered whether to let Potts continue.

"I know what this must look like, walking around with this bandage on my head, carrying around a dirty old rag doll of a dog. But your honor, I am a changed man. In two days my life has been totally and completely turned around and it's all because of this dirty little 'doggy'," he continued, holding Scruffy up for the judge to see.

"His name is Scruffy," Potts continued.

The judge frowned. Ross, Jr. and Hampton smiled at one another as their father demonstrated his insanity before the court.

"Two days ago the only thing that was important to me was my product. You see, I am a manufacturer. It is what has defined me for most of my life. I make things and I'm good at that. I always have been. I make things and people buy them and I make more. Every year I make more than the year before, it's what has kept me going for all these years. It is what I have lived for. A pretty sad story, wouldn't you say?" Ross asked the judge earnestly.

The judge did not answer the question, seeing fit instead to caution Ross Potts. "Mr. Potts, this is a court of law, and in a court of law there are certain rules, and whether you are represented by an attorney or whether you represent yourself you are expected to know those rules and to abide by them. One of these rules is that you don't ask me questions like that. Another is that you don't ramble on about worthless pieces of information that are not going to help this Court to decide the issue at hand, which is whether or not you are capable of handling your own affairs and whether your sons should be appointed to handle those affairs for you."

"Yes, your honor, I understand," Potts responded.

"With all of that in mind, I am going to allow you to continue, for now. But I caution you to be brief and direct."

"Thank you, Your Honor," Potts answered. "As I was saying, yesterday, I was involved in an automobile accident. I got a bump on my hard old head," Potts said, pointing to his bandage.

At that moment there was a knock on the court room door and the bailiff let Rebecca Jenks in. Potts turned to her, then to the Judge.

"Your honor," he said, "could I speak to my secretary for just a moment? It's concerning a witness."

"Briefly," the judge answered, looking over at Alton Green. Green threw his arms up in confusion, knowing nothing about any witness.

Potts hurried over to where Rebecca was standing and whispered in her ear. She responded in his ear and he gave her a huge hug. She was flabbergasted. Then he spoke to her again and handed her the puppy dog and returned to the Judge smiling.

"Your honor, my sons, the monsters that I have raised them to be, are incapable of understanding that I have so suddenly and so abruptly turned my life around. To them, with their limited knowledge of the human side of people, they see my change as insanity. It is not that, I assure you. Judge, there is a little girl of about seven years of age outside who can help me explain how a selfish, loveless, mean old man like I was, could somehow miraculously turn his life around overnight. I fear that if she is not allowed to testify on my behalf, I will be incapable of explaining to this Court the impact that such a little angel could have on the soul of a hard old man."

"Your honor, I am going to object..." Mr. Gates said, standing.

"You go ahead and do that," the Judge interrupted, "but it's Christmas Eve and if there is an angel out in that hallway I'm going to want to hear what she has to say."

The bailiff and Judge's clerk laughed.

"Thank you, Your Honor, objection withdrawn," Gates said, retaking his seat.

The bailiff opened the door and little Erica Bloundin, with silver headband in place and Scruffy firmly in hand, walked through, Martha Albert by her side. A knee poked out of the new hole in Erica's dirty dress with every step she took, but still she smiled brightly as soon as she laid eyes on Ross Potts.

Potts walked over to meet Erica, squatted down as she ran into his arms.

"You brought Scruffy back," she said happily.

"He missed you," he told her, holding back tears. "We both did."

"You're all better," she said.

"Thanks to you."

Pulling her away and holding her firmly by the shoulders, he spoke more seriously to her.

"Would you do one more favor for this old man?" he asked.

"What?"

"Would you go sit up there and talk to me and the nice judge?"

"About what?"

"About you and about me. And about him," he responded, patting Scruffy on the head.

"I guess so."

"It would really help me out."

"Okay," she smiled, leaving Potts and walking up to the witness stand.

"Your honor," Mr. Gates rose again, "are this child's parents present today?"

"Her Mamma is dead and her Daddy is in jail here," Martha answered from the back of the court room.

Ross turned around and smiled at Martha. She smiled back.

"What's he been arrested for?"

"Shoplifting to buy his little girl some pancakes," Martha replied. "His name is Tommy Bloundin."

"Your honor!" Gates protested. "Is this a courtroom or a public meeting hall?"

"It is a courtroom counselor. It is my courtroom, and if you don't like the way I run it then I suggest you find yourself another profession," Holliday scolded.

Gates, humiliated, sunk slowly back into his seat.

"Ernie," the Judge called to his bailiff, "see if you can find this child's father and have him brought up."

"Yes, Judge," Ernie responded, walking out into the hall.

"Hi," the Judge said, turning to Erica.

"Hello," she said shyly, but smiling.

"What is your name?" he asked.

"Erica Cane Bloundin," she replied, "I'm named after one of my Mamma's favorite characters."

"Is that right?" he asked.

"Before she died," Erica added.

"Well I'm really sorry to hear that," the Judge answered. She looked into his eyes, smiled. "But she's still sees me."

"I bet she does." he said, then, "Erica?" he asked.

"Yes, sir?"

"Do you know what a lie is?"

"It's when you don't tell the truth about something."

"Do you know what happens when you tell a lie?"

"You get in big trouble," she said, clutching Scruffy against her neck.

"If Mr. Potts and I ask you some questions, are you going to lie to us?"

"Oh, no sir. That would be wrong. I have to be good 'cause my Mamma is watching me all the time."

The Judge swallowed hard, turned away to softly clear his throat. "That's right," he agreed. "Now, Mr. Potts is going to ask you some questions and you tell the truth, okay?"

"Okay," she said, turning toward Ross Potts.

"Hi, Erica," Potts began.

"Hi," she answered.

"I didn't know that was your name, it sure is pretty."

"Thank you."

"Do you remember who I am?"

"Sure, you're the old man with the big bump on his head."

"That's right," Potts replied with a laugh. "And do you remember when you first met me?"

"Last night," she said.

"Where did you meet me?"

"At Miss Martha's."

"Miss Martha's shelter?"

"Yes, sir."

"What were you doing in her shelter?"

ANGELS AND PANCAKES

"That nice lady, Monique, brought me there after Mr. Mackbone bought me some pancakes."

"You like pancakes?"

"Yes, sir. They're my favorite."

"And where was your Daddy?"

"Some policemen chased him and took him away."

"And they left you all alone and these people Monique and Mackbone brought you to the shelter?"

"That's right. Miss Martha said she was full, but she let me come in anyway."

"And you were there when they brought me in with the bo-bo on my head, right?"

"Yep."

"Do you remember what I told you?"

"Yea you said, 'Get away from me you dirty little rug rat.'" Everyone in the courtroom laughed.

"That's right," Potts replied, tears forming in his eyes. "Shame on me. I'm really sorry for that."

Erica smiled.

"And do you remember what you told me?"

"I asked you if your bo-bo hurt and you said, 'are you stupid or something, of course it hurts.'"

"I wasn't very kind, was I?" Potts asked, obviously embarrassed.

"No but I knew it was just 'cause you had problems. My daddy gets mad when he gots problems."

"And you didn't leave me alone either, did you?"

"Nope," she replied shyly, "I didn't listen."

"What did you do?"

"I gave you Scruffy," she said, exhibiting the dog to the courtroom.

Potts smiled broadly through tears, "Yes you did, didn't you? You gave me Scruffy and you told me that if I held him really tight he would help me to stop hurting like you did when you didn't have anything in your tummy, right?"

Erica shook her head affirmatively, nearing the point of tears. She did not understand why Potts was crying, she was afraid that she had said something wrong.

"Your honor," Potts began, turning to the court and pausing to attempt to clear the huge lump from his throat. "I have seventy million dollars in the bank. That doesn't include the value of my business or of my four houses, twenty-eight cars, and the millions I have tied up in other worldly goods. I have all of this, and two days ago I would not have stopped on the street to give this hungry child a dime. Yet, I get put in this ungodly place," he continued, another tear rolling down his face, "a place fit to live only because the only alternative is the street. I get put in there with a bump on my head and this little dear, this absolute angel who hasn't even enough to eat, gives the only possession that she has to *me*," he said, striking his breast, "to selfish old me, to make me feel better, and suddenly I realized what a waste my entire life has been. In a split second, a single second, with a single act, this little girl showed me that despite all I own, what a dismal failure I have been.

"Your honor, I have wasted seventy-four years. An entire lifetime of being selfish, always putting myself first, before everyone else, including my own children. They wheeled me away, Your Honor, and I kept this little girl's dog, her only possession, again out of selfishness. I did it to get her to leave me alone. But the more I thought about it, the more I realized what a great gift she had given me. She gave of herself, Your Honor. Who teaches a child that? In all my seventy-four years, I can't remember having once done it myself.

"Judge, I stand before you today a new man. I have thrown off the yoke of selfishness and have vowed to live my life out with the one thing that has eluded me for most of my life. I am going to be a happy man. I am going to treat people with dignity, treat my employees like human beings, and I am going to use my money and my power and my influence to do some good before my meager little life has ended. I apologize to my sons if they cannot see this, if they cannot share in my rejoicing in having this second chance, but I declare that it is not insanity that drives me, but sanity, and all of it, every bit of it, attributable to that little girl sitting right there," Potts concluded, pointing toward Erica.

"Your honor," Mr. Gates interrupted, gathering his courage to rise once again.

"The court will recess," the Judge declared, ignoring Gates, slamming his gavel on the table and hurrying to his chambers.

Potts wiped his eyes and helped Erica down from the witness stand. They headed toward Martha, stopped by Alton Green along the way, who wanted to shake Potts' hand.

"I'm lucky you never went to law school," Green said.

Potts only smiled as he and Erica continued on to Martha.

"You kept her?" he asked, smiling.

"I never called the police," she admitted. "It wouldn't have been a happy Christmas knowing she was sittin' all alone down at Juvenile. I decided to bring her to my daughter's with my grandkids for a couple of days."

"I've got some big plans for that shelter of yours," Potts said, looking slyly toward Martha.

"You do?" she asked.

"Actually I'd like to open a chain of them and I'd like you to help run it," he said.

"A chain of homeless shelters," she said, "I guess you're just gonna franchise them out."

"I might just do that," Potts answered, smiling.

The door opened behind the bench.

"All rise," Earnie, the bailiff, commanded, walking in ahead of Judge Holliday.

Potts returned to the table.

"Be seated," the Judge said, blowing his nose.

"In the matter of Ross Potts, I find that the defendant is about the most lucid individual that I have ever had the pleasure of meeting. How anyone could obtain a Coroner's commitment against such a man I have no idea, but I can promise you that I'm going to suggest to my new friend, the Chief Justice, that it is well worth investigating to ensure that such a miscarriage of justice does not again occur in this State. The parties are free to leave." Judge Holliday slammed his gavel down.

Alton Green slapped Potts on the back and Potts turned to him.

"No hard feelings?" Potts asked.

"Are you kidding?" Green replied, "You've just given me the best Christmas war story I'll ever tell."

Potts looked over to his sons, they were already on their way out of the courtroom, Emile Gates following closely behind.

"Mr. Gates," Judge Holliday called from the bench.

Gates froze, turned. "Yes, your honor," he replied, walking back toward the bar.

"I would like to take up the matter of Tommy Bloundin now, if you would be so kind as to sit in for the People."

Erica's eyes grew wide as she heard her father's name called out.

"Your honor, that's not on my docket," Gates protested.

"I would really appreciate it," Judge Holliday said in a tone which Gates dared not refuse.

"Yes, your honor."

"We have to move out of here," Green told Ross Potts.

"I want to stay for this," Potts answered.

"We have to get behind the bar," Green said.

Potts followed Green to the courtroom seats near where Erica was sitting with Ms. Martha. Ernie escorted Tommy Bloundin in from a door behind the judge's bench.

"Daddy!" Erica screamed.

Tommy Bloundin's face lit up, "Oh, God! Erica!" he yelled, having no idea that she had been found or would be in the courtroom. Tears of joy immediately began to streaming down his face.

"Order in the courtroom!" Ernie commanded.

Erica made a run for her father, but Ross Potts grabbed her.

"It's my Daddy," she protested.

"Erica, Sugarplum, listen to me," Potts said softly, yet sternly.

Still pulling, she listened.

"Your daddy is in some trouble. Now, I promise you we are going to get him out of trouble, me and Mr. Green are going to make sure of that, but you have to be quiet, you have to wait."

"But it's my daddy," she protested, crying.

"I promise you, this will be the last time you have to be without him. I am going to see to that, but if you aren't good we aren't going to be able to help him. Now you sit right here, and I'm gonna get your Daddy for you. Do you believe me?"

She looked at him, skeptically at first, then nodded.

"Okay," Potts responded, loosening his grasp on her. "Hold Scruffy," he said, wrapping her arms around the dog. "Mommy's watching, it's going to be okay." He guided her back to Martha's lap.

"Your Honor," Alton Green called out.

"Yes, Mr. Green."

"May I have the honor of sitting in for Mr. Bloundin?"

"You saved me the trouble of asking. As long as Mr. Bloundin has no objection, that is."

Tommy quickly shook his head no. Alton Green returned to the defendant's table.

"Gentlemen," Judge Holliday began, "I would like to conduct this as informally as possible. I believe I know what's going on here but there is a minor who is affected by all of this and this court's interest at this point is primarily with her."

There was no objection.

"I understand," Judge Holliday continued, "that Mr. Bloundin would like to enter a guilty plea to the charge of possession of stolen items and with the permission of counsel and the defendant, I would like for the defendant to take the stand and be questioned directly by the Court."

Green leaned over and spoke to Tommy, then he rose and addressed the Court.

"We have no objection, Your Honor."

Mr. Gates rose, "Of course, the People have no objection, Your Honor," he said, daring not to cross the Judge again.

Tommy stood and walked to the witness stand.

There was another knock on the courtroom door and the bailiff let Rebecca back in, this time followed by an elderly gentleman walking with the aid of a cane. They walked over to Potts and the two men shook hands before he and Rebecca took their seats.

"Mr. Bloundin," Judge Holliday began after the clerk had sworn Tommy in. "I understand that you wished to plea guilty to the charge of possession of stolen property."

"Yes, your honor," Tommy replied.

"You understand that you could receive a sentence of up to six months at hard labor for this crime."

Tommy's heart froze with fear.

CHARLES J. HEBERT

"Mr. Bloundin?" Judge Holliday prodded.

"Your honor," Tommy pleaded, "I can't do six months, I can't do six days. I have a little girl who has nobody else in the world to take care of her."

"It appears to me that you haven't been doing a very good job yourself of taking care of her. It is quite apparent that she may very well be better off in the hands of the State," Judge Holiday interrupted.

"No, Your Honor. Listen to me, please," Tommy begged. "I've done a good job raising her, she's a great kid. I let myself get down, and by the time I was ready to pick myself back up the world had moved on without me, I didn't fit any more. My wife was hit and killed by drunk driver, she died right in front of us," he continued, beginning to cry. "Suddenly, she just wasn't there anymore and everything had changed. I was devastated, it were as though I had died. I couldn't eat, I couldn't sleep, I couldn't work. I thought my life had come to an end. But then I realized... I thought of Erica and I realized that I had not died. I pulled myself together, I became a real person again. I had been laid off during that time and there was no work in town. I went through our savings and took welfare, but we just kept sliding further and further into the hole. I thought that if I came here I could find a job, start all over, but I was wrong. Things were even worse here, no one wants to hire you when you have only own one set of clothes and you don't have an address to put on an application. I was all set to head back to Ohio, get back on the welfare and flip hamburgers until I got on my feet, but she was hungry. She wanted pancakes. That's all she wanted were some lousy pancakes. Most kids want clothes and dolls and bicycles, all she wanted were some lousy pancakes and I couldn't give them to her," he stopped to wipe away the tears that were rolling freely down his cheeks.

"Take your time," Judge Holliday said. "Would you like some water?"

Tommy shook his head no, continued. "I did something I shouldn't have done, I know that. I took something that wasn't mine and I was going to sell it to the first person I met and then march my little girl over to the nearest diner and buy her the biggest stack of pancakes she ever saw. And after she had eaten them I was going to get so far away from here…"

"Where did you take the watch from?" the Judge interrupted.

"I don't even know," Tommy answered.

"Nathan's Swiss Emporium," the man with the can sitting next to Potts, answered in a heavy Irish accent.

"Who are you, sir?" the Judge asked.

"Martin Nathan, Judge," the old man responded, rising.

"You have something to do with Nathan's Swiss Emporium?"

"Yes I do. I own it, Judge," the man answered.

"What are you doing here?" Judge Holliday asked.

"Well, this nice young lady," Nathan said, pointing to Rebecca, "came to my store this afternoon and offered to pay for the watch and explained to me what was going on, so I came on down here. I was closing up early for the holidays anyway."

"So the watch has been paid for?" the Judge asked.

"Not exactly," Nathan answered.

"Well, either it has or it hasn't," the Holliday answered testily.

"Well, you see," Nathan continued, speaking slowly and deliberately, "when I found out what the man had stolen the watch for I wouldn't accept the young lady's money."

"You wouldn't let her make restitution?" Judge Holiday asked.

"I felt so bad about having reported it to the police that I felt I should come down here myself and make sure that it all turned out alright. You see, I've been a very fortunate man, Judge. The Good Lord has always put plenty on my table. But had one of mine gone without enough to eat, I'd have done whatever it took to feed her and worried about the consequences later. So if it is in my power to do so, Judge, I would like to say that I give the man the watch and just let the whole thing be done with."

"Well if there is no victim, I don't see how there can be any crime," the Judge responded.

All the spectators smiled.

"But I still do have very grave concerns about the welfare of this child and Mr. Bloundin's ability to provide for her, at least in the short term."

"Your honor," Ross Potts said, standing, "may I be permitted to speak again?"

The judge nodded.

"If Mr. Bloundin would be agreeable, I would like to offer him a job in my plant. I would also like to take responsibility for seeing that he and my little angel have a place to live and plenty enough to eat until he can get back on his feet."

"Mr. Bloundin?" the Judge said, turning to Tommy.

"Yes, Your Honor. I'll do whatever it takes. I promise, this will not happen again," he said wiping his eyes.

"All right then," Judge Holliday replied, rapping his gavel on the wooden block on his bench, "case dismissed. You are free to go, Mr. Bloundin."

With the crack of wood-hitting-wood still hanging in the air, Tommy jumped up from his seat and ran toward Erica. She jumped up as well and met him half-way. He grabbed her, picked her up, and held her tightly in his grasp, closing his eyes, their tears falling freely to the courtroom floor.

"I missed you so much," Tommy said.

"Me too, Daddy."

After a short while Tommy opened his eyes and looked past Erica to Ross Potts. "Thank you," he said.

"It is I who is in your debt, sir," Potts replied, stroking Erica's head with the palm of his left hand.

"I think a celebration is in order, Ross," Alton Green, standing with Ms. Martha, Rebecca and Martin Nathan, said from behind.

"Indeed it is," Potts answered, "If you'll drive, Alton, I'll buy us all some lunch."

"La Reserve?" Alton suggested, referring to the most expensive restaurant in town.

Potts smiled, "Perhaps we should allow our guest of honor to decide," he said, looking at Erica who had raised her head from her father's wet shoulder. "Where would you like to eat, Sugarplum?" he asked her.

Erica smiled. "Well," she hesitated, having only ever eaten at one restaurant in town, "I know where they make the 'best darned hot cakes you ever tasted,'" she said, quoting Mackbone.

Alton and the others laughed aloud, entertained by Erica's

innocence, Potts, however, was taken aback, his smile faded.

"Do you like pancakes?" Erica asked, noticing his hesitancy.

"I used to," Potts responded, "a long time ago. But I promised someone once that I'd never eat them again."

"Never eat pancakes?" Erica asked. "Why would you promise that?"

Potts' mind raced back to the memory of the early days of his marriage. "I don't really know why, some silly notion I guess," he answered, his thoughts still back in time. "I did it at a time that I thought I was unhappy. But you know what?"

"What?" she asked.

"I just realized, that's when I really started being unhappy."

Alton placed a hand on his old friend's shoulder.

"And you know what else?" Potts continued.

"What?"

"I don't think that there is anything that I would like more right now than to be sitting with all of you nice people in front of a big stack of them, covered with butter and syrup."

"Yum, yum, me too."

"Where is this place that has the best darned hotcakes you've ever tasted?"

"Down where all the lights are," Erica explained. "Can we go?"

"If it's alright with your Dad."

Erica looked to Tommy.

He kissed her on the lips, smiled through his tears, "You bet it is."

"Alton?" Potts asked.

"You know Ross, just hearing you talk about them, I swear I can smell them now. I'm with you."

They all filed out of the courtroom, past the throng that had been made to wait outside, in search of the the simple pleasure of life itself, under the loving gaze of their own angel in heaven.

—THE END—

FRENCH QUARTER FOLLIES

Dr. Paul Rodenhauser

FRENCH QUARTER FOLLIES

MIME OF MATTER

Hounds shake off sleep with a vengeance. Flapping ears sound reveille even before the morning paper arcs over the balcony railing. The paper usually clips a hibiscus and slides into the shutters with a thud. The hibiscus shrugs. Shutters fling open Rockette style two by two on down the balcony, promising a cuckoo. But Fred appears instead, slowing down enough at the final station to be visible beyond hands and arms. The dogs—and the smell—agitate Fred in the morning. Even when French doors open slowly, they suck in the stench of stale beer puddled on the brick sidewalk below. Emily says, "banquette."

Were it not obviously early morning on the basis of other information, the absence of carriages and hoofbeats would confirm that the asylum of sleep had finally seized the tourists. Not so for the real night people, the other telltale sign of morning and the absolute giveaway of the real asylum. Fred always says that living in the French Quarter is like living in any other mental hospital, but no mental hospital can hold a candle to the French Quarter! Finishing up the night shift, some diehards linger, some depart, some forget where home is, or that they have one. A few limp bodies lie in grotesque postures, interrupting, almost counterbalancing the boxy symmetry of the Vieux Carré. They look like casualties from skirmishes among early settlers. Neighborhood regulars and residents spot them and sometimes call the police. Sometimes they step around them long after calling the police. In time, they all get up and stagger on anyway.

Garbage trucks and runners revisit yesterday's routes, wisely avoiding the mugginess of later daytime activity. Fred is neither a runner nor a connoisseur of activity. He clearly recognizes the need for energy conservation, especially in this soggy summer climate. The humidity and temperature were both predicted to be in the 90s again today.

Dispersing from their shift work, hookers are as conspicuously underdressed as they are over-aggressive. What bad taste! Especially the transvestites among them could benefit from wardrobe consultation. This apparently innate ineptitude might be a clue—actually, a sign, if you will—for the discriminating purchaser of services. Sartorial splendor and genital endowment might be inversely proportional in this population. There have been many surprises—quick trips around the block, reactions, rejections, and renegotiations all within minutes, all on the same corner. Love might be blind but this is not love.

Fred's corner spins with activity almost continuously. What the drug dealers on Dauphine Street lack is discretion and imagination. The surveillance accorded this activity is woefully nonexistent; therefore, no requirement for state-of-the-art ingenuity exists. The underground in the French Quarter is no deeper than the corpses in nearby Cemetery Number One.

The satanic underground is another story, however, claims a middle-aged street musician who suspects a pair of Doberman "Pinchers" with red bandana collars of responding to his presence with special messages. Their stare communicates these messages, he believes, and their eyes follow his every movement as he passes by their courtyard. The mimes and other figures playing into this curious network provide indisputable evidence that he is the target of "evil intentions."

Living in a burned-out house under a mattress without benefit of plumbing or electricity may have contributed to sleep deprivation and nutritional problems, but infirmity was not an apparent factor this morning. In response to passing the "Pinchers" one last time, the musician scaled a nearby balcony on Dauphine and bounded into the living quarters of two startled inhabitants. Fred and Emily were the hapless hosts chosen in this moment of unbridled desperation.

"Help me," stammered the crazed musician as he pushed his way into the living room wildly.

Contagious as they are, the panicky feelings were suddenly mutual. "Was I expecting you?" Fred fumbled for words.

"What's your name?" Emily choked.

FRENCH QUARTER FOLLIES

"The satanic underground has contaminated everything. I'm doomed. I've been drugged. I'm going to die!"

As if responding to a command, the harried threesome hushed simultaneously and peered over the balcony at an ominous figure fidgeting with her black cane, muttering inaudibly. The legendary "Bead Lady" in her Darth Vader garb was passing by Fred's place. Not even on the hottest of summer days was this image abandoned—the black helmet, black sweater, and long black skirt ensemble with the pinned-on black nylon umbrella covering, staves and all, as a breast plate. A black knapsack and sandals complete this living French Quarter cartoon. She sleeps fully clothed just six blocks from Fred's townhouse in a parking garage alcove. Unlike her bed chamber, which opens to a full view of Baronne Street, her psyche is almost hermetically sealed against external reality. A former debutante, they say, she trades Mardi Gras beads for money and food. Her continuous gravely conversation with hidden voices is another reason why people cut a wide swath in her presence. Many locals fear that this stealthy creature has the power to endanger their lives. The musician falls into this category quite naturally and he avoids her. He once saw her hand over a red bandana to a working mime. *A red bandana!* It was the acceptance of it that imbedded the everlasting terror in his mind. Never before had he seen a working mime respond. His imagination exploded.

"Help me," the musician cried, visibly shaken.

Fred recognized the pale and tremulous intruder as the classical violinist from the corner of St. Peter and Royal. Although Fred knew the musician sometimes dressed in women's clothes, a more memorable association was the odor of the greasy, grimy overcoat he was wearing again this morning. Ordinarily he was a relatively quiet fixture in the French Quarter, one whose music, apparently shielded a lot of fears,.

Last night, Fred soon learned, a wanna-be-but-can't-concentrate college dropout had freaked out the musician with a scary story. He met her at the local police station at Royal and Conti where he was protesting the new ordinance against after dark street music in Jackson Square, and she was reporting her newly acquired roommate to be a serial killer. Had the dropout not prematurely signed herself out of the psych ward at Charity and dis-continued her medication just recently, by now she might have managed to develop a different perspective on this young man. She'd had this belief about other men but this was the first live-in serial killer. They met several weeks ago outside a Decatur Street coffee house and, after a brief acquaintanceship established on the basis of three or four conversations, she invited him to share her apartment. Three more conversations after he moved in was all it took before her emotional upheaval reached orbit. Thus, her trip to the police station.

The musician was blown away by her story. *A serial killer!* Passersby might have noticed a certain pallor. "Does he own a pair of Dobermans?" he ventured to ask.

"No, only a cat." A cloud of smoke emerged from her mov-ing lips. "Only a spooky cat."

As the musician attempted to catch his breath in Fred's liv-ing room, his story continued to unfold in spurts. The idea of a cat seemed to be unsettling to Emily, but the pressure and pace of the musician's recitation soon accelerated and eventually over-shadowed any similar reactions. His tone intensified as if he were testifying on a witness stand with all the "I-swear-to-Gods" and "so-help-mes." The pitch of his voice climbed up the scale as he pressed on with his saga. Words couldn't come fast enough.

While telling him about her suspicions—the musician contin-ued his story in a staccato fashion, now short of breath—the dropout shared a cup of coffee she'd purchased from the nearby Haagen-Dazs store. The heavy chocolate flavor piqued the musician's inter-est. "This Darth Vader character invented it," she responded.

Lacking in the kind of imagination that translates to anything practical, but able to be histrionic to the hilt, the dropout mimic-ked the Bead Lady's demands that M & M candies—more and more—be added to the coffee. The dropout even remembered the dirty, wet, crumpled dollar bill in the Bead Lady's grimy hand and described that to the musician, too.

The Bead Lady always attracts attention. It would have been difficult to ignore her presence anywhere, let alone in an ice cream parlor. Was it the flavor or the calories that inspired the Bead Lady's ingenuity? Actually, voices instructed the Bead

Lady to do things like add chocolate to coffee. It would enhance her strength, claimed a voice, and confirm her special powers. The dropout seemed to get the message, too, somehow, about the Bead Lady. Beware!

"Drugs" the musician muttered, "that's the answer."

It seemed impossible to track the leap from chocolate to drugs so Fred let it go, but the musician clearly began to believe he'd been drugged! In his frenetic search for something to hold on to, he remembered once hearing someone say that if drugs aren't the answer, you're asking the wrong question.

"Does the cat wear a red bandana around it's neck?" he begged deliriously.

"How did he know that?" the dropout wondered. "Yes, the cat sometimes wears a red bandana and, yes, the cat is black and... ." If he can know all that, she thought, then his other ideas might also be true. Could he help her with the serial killer?

Their continued association reaffirmed some and ignited other fantasies. She, the dropout, now feeling that he was clairvoyant, looked to him for the solution to the problem with the serial killer and he, the musician, believing that the serial killer was an undercover agent through which the Bead Lady was assembling a voodoo entrapment, wanted her help in identifying the source of his destruction. As they went off together to try to cleanse their respective situations of their mutual villain, they encountered the Bead Lady on Chartres Street, sipping coffee (au chocolat) and mumbling incoherently, laboring as she did lately under the delusion that she was controlled by the voice of an alien power in the form of a mynah bird. With the assistance of antennae, the umbrella staves in her breast shield, the birds spoke to her—in French—through computer chips inside her helmet. A *very* quick left turn took the musician and the dropout past a pedestal supporting a mime in French colonial costume and white powdered peruke, his blue waistcoat handsomely embroidered in gold thread.

(C'est moi, your host and narrator for this strange tale— invested, if you will, with the magic and wisdom of local history.)

Propped against the pedestal was an open cigar box bearing a sign, "Mime Over Matter." Dollar bills cradled in the box, planted there of course, constituted the matter.

The musician's heart began to pound as if it would leap right out of his rib cage. Did the undercover agent, the serial killer, know that he once "borrowed" some of that matter? His vision faded—he later reported to Fred that his lights went out—as sweat began soaking his shirt under the heavy coat. There is power in pedestals! Try as she may, the dropout couldn't keep up. By now, the musician was running and gasping for breath. She remembered that his violin was left on the corner where they'd been talking and decided to retrieve it, only to encounter her roommate enroute. Wouldn't you know, she thought, confirming her familiarity with bad luck. The roommate had just avoided the Bead Lady by crossing the street. Decked out in a sequined white outfit, blue high heels and an orange polka dot silk scarf, he would have been unrecognizable except for his crew cut. It was 10:30 pm. Wearing Ray Ban sun glasses, he carried a blonde wig. Astounding! This scenario triggered a flashback to a movie she'd seen about a cross-dressing killer, a psychiatrist, if she remembered correctly.

Now the dropout felt convinced that the Bead Lady was following her. She headed for her apartment intending to lock herself in. Accelerating her pace, she first found the violin and moments later was stashing it under her cluttered bed. Before securing the lock on her door, however, she was seized by psychotic fear. The apartment appeared to have been ransacked. Clothes were strewn everywhere. On the floor by her roommate's armoire she found a crumpled sheet of writing paper bearing a handwritten poem. This misperceived "message" later accompanied her to a less private asylum.

> We live and die
> in a mysterious, misguided
> quaint and violent
>   checkerboard city
> like flightless birds
> encompassed by grandeur
>   and squalor
> endangered by isolation

and evolving entitlement
which has spawned, some say,
an unproclaimed civil war,
   a free for all
        between arm's length
victims of speciously different
        circumstances
in a self help/help yourself
        unpoliced city of holdups, handouts,
          hovels,
senseless slaughters,
   and mindless
disregard for human life.

In the morning, an early riser walking his two Dobermans discovered the dropout's barely breathing body on the last bench downriver on the Moonwalk. She'd dropped several prescription bottles nearby, but she was still clutching the crumpled poem. Back to Charity, by ambulance this time, and up to the Crisis Intervention Unit she went. Her delusion about her roommate had so seriously influenced her perceptions that she misread a very critical word in the note. Instead of "senseless slaughters," she'd read "serial slaughters." Otherwise, she might have avoided the fate of another hospitalization. The penmanship was not very clear, on the one hand. Nor was it her roommate's handwriting, on the other. The author, however, would have agreed that she ended up in the right place.

When her roommate was last seen, he was headed for Burgundy Street and the most profitable corner for pushers and prostitutes. He might have still been there the next morning finishing up the night shift when the exhausted musician scrambled up to Fred's quarters, were it not for yet another unexpected series of events.

The serial killer's naïve notion to study the activities of the underworld but not fully participate turned out to be a short lived intention. Based on a belief that he was chosen by God to convert prostitutes to Christian ways, the serial killer translated this messianic calling into a highly specialized mission. His interests were, you see, limited to heterosexual prostitution. Not even cognizant of the alternative, he imagined that his costume would help him get close to his subjects. Shortly, after his arrival, his destination became a maelstrom of unanticipated activity involving unanticipated participants. Neither he nor the ex-Marine in drag encountered on the corner knew about the smoldering animosity among various transvestite factions but when the better dressed ex-Marine began heckling a bevy of scantily-clad, high-heeled, made-over males about their attire, all hell broke loose. Boundary issues had been inflaming this particular faction, and this harassment by—in their minds—two competitors represented yet another encroachment on their territory.

Suddenly the serial killer and the ex-Marine found themselves on the same side of a full-scale transvestite turf war. Under cover of patchy darkness, the neighborhood seethed, then convulsed into skirmishes of verbal and physical abuse as local bars periodically released irate phalanges onto the street. Stones, high-heels, purses and you name it became missiles. By the time police interrupted the melée, the serial killer had been battered and defrocked, but not daunted. Now at least partially initiated into the society of transvestitism, he colluded with the bloodied ex-Marine in adopting a new mission, a campaign against violence—unspecified violence. The decision to go generic consumed a lot of discussion time. This experience and other signs from God, like seeing women in threes as the Holy Trinity, clearly explained, he thought, his early morning appearance on Bourbon Street in the nude carrying a placard and railing against violence. This behavior and a few words about his special purpose to the police earned him the privilege of preceding his unsuspecting and, in fact, unconscious roommate to their new address.

Fred and Emily were still listening in amazement as the musician went on. He switched topics and shared a loosely woven tale of the horror with which he lived on a daily basis. His best friend in childhood was a dog, he explained, as if he were asked to discuss his early childhood history and as if he knew that Fred is a psychiatrist. Fred always felt confident that he could talk down someone in this condition except for the possibility that drugs were contributory or that unforeseen events would further antagonize the frenetic subject. Fortunately, the musician didn't notice either the neighbor's leashed Doberman on its morning walk or the Bead Lady's second appearance, tapping her way along St. Louis as she criss-crossed the French Quarter. Nor did he see the mime walking to work.

What hindered a smooth disposition, surprisingly, was a glimpse of a neatly folded red bandana on the bookcase in Fred's living room. Fred alerted the police to the fleeing musician's crazed state, but by that time he was approaching the river six blocks away. The muddy water, now reflecting the sunrise instead of last night's full moon, produced a blinding glare, disturbing in its own right. Shocked momentarily, the musician suddenly remembered a curbside conversation he had had way back when with a local psychiatrist who had recommended then that he get some help.

Charity Hospital would be his refuge. The musician's admission was expedited by none other than Fred, the psychiatrist on duty that morning, who already knew the patient's history and could have written it into the hospital record even before interviewing him. Ironically, the musician remembered Fred only as the psychiatrist he'd met at curbside some years ago. Fred had no question about the musician's current mental impairment and grave disability. By the time he'd finished interviewing the grateful musician, the thoroughly confused serial killer, and the half-conscious dropout, however, Fred's mind was spinning with questions. Was this a folie-à-trois? Or, just the product of three French Quarter follies? He never did figure out how his one-sentence poem, an emotional reaction to the recent murder rate in New Orleans, ever became the property of the dropout. Nor did he want to risk being incorporated into a delusional system by asking about it. Could the woman with the baby carriage who rummages through the trash bags on Dauphine Street somehow be the connection? Any explanation based on the supernatural was, of course, incompatible with Fred's world view. That idea didn't occur to him.

Late that night on Fred's block of Dauphine Street, the Bead Lady was heard shrieking uncontrollably. Her only intelligible words sounded like "dead bodies." Fred, whose activity was fully visible through the panes of the second story French doors, was covering Emily's cage at the time. Emily would have been more appropriately named Emile, but misspellings, mispronunciations, and malapropisms are not the exceptions in New Orleans. The local breeder, who convinced Fred that male mynah birds are better talkers, had named him Emily!

The redness of the bandana covering Emily's cage penetrated the night as did the silence which followed the Bead Lady's mysterious disappearance. And the next morning, like the black garments limply draped over a black helmet and cane on the banquette below Fred's quarters, Emily's cage was empty.

FRENCH QUARTER FOLLIES

CHARITY

Never underestimate the power of a mime. The scuttlebutt on the Charity in-patient ward particularly affected the musician, not that he wasn't already one of the most relieved and obliging patients ever to cross the threshold of this venerable institution, let alone the psychiatric ward. According to hospital folklore, the skid marks from recalcitrant rubber-soled shoes at the entrance to the psychiatric ward represented the usual attitude toward admission. But for the musician, being on a locked ward was nirvana—no Bead Lady, no Dobermans, no mimes and, as they say, three hots and a cot! He listened intently to the news about Bead Lady's disappearance but he was less puzzled than ambivalent about this turn of events. On the one hand, he might never again have to encounter her presence and all the baggage connected with her being. On the other hand, there could be a worse alternative. Could someone have a power greater than hers? Her mysterious departure had to be the work of a special intervention. *Somebody* was responsible for this! It must be a mime, he concluded.

It happens that mimes are magnificent figures for divesting personal conflicts. Almost any thought or emotion can be disowned and projected onto an unsuspecting, mute, motionless but living being without risk of contradiction. The greater the conflict, the greater the temptation to unload it. It seems therapeutic to wonder out loud whether anybody ever thinks about the private lives of mimes. Who wonders what they think and feel? Do they have hobbies, families and friends? Or, are they simply fixtures on the landscape, empty shells placed to provide entertainment—for some, comic relief; for others, tragic remembrance or its avoidance.

The musician's world had turned inside out. Never in a hospital before this, he had always been a drifter and, since college, the drift was one of steady decline. Neither belief nor disbelief registered on the faces of those to whom he announced his college successes in music, not to mention his graduation *cum laude.* It was possible, mused most listeners, but beyond music, the demands of the curriculum must have been minimal, they thought. Actually, he had little interest in anything but music, including people. Growing up was an experience in fantasy, music and solitude. Since a very early age, he believed he possessed special powers, magical control over situations and even people. He preferred the non-human environment, however. Animals were his friends. Is it significant that he now lives like one, in an abandoned, burned-out house without electricity or water in a crawl space underneath a propped up mattress? Although he seems to notice the irregularity of his lifestyle, a kind of acceptance—more like expectation than resignation—describes his attitude. No signs of disappointment were evident. No problem! Maybe it's denial, but his interests always clustered into a singular pathway. First and foremost, he is a musician, a performer. If this pathway were frustrated, he would most likely be paralyzed with panic.

But not even worry was an option for the musician today. He was still basking in the benefits of his decision to seek refuge at Charity and congratulating himself on using sound judgment, a term he heard bandied about on the ward several times this morning. Unlike the dropout and the serial killer, he was a "voluntary admission." Although he had seen the dropout yesterday, their first day on the ward, she was too dopey and distracted to talk. This morning, however, they compared notes about the Bead Lady and serial killer, their respective nemeses, neither seeming at all surprised about the other's presence on the ward—an interesting situation considering that neither previously questioned the other's mental health. Nor did they now! One thing just leads to another. That's how it is, life in the French Quarter! About themselves, however, they each had a few secret doubts—regarding recent events, at least. If nothing else, they recognized the relief from the terror they'd been feeling. Although awareness of this contrast nourished those seeds of self-doubt, still all of it could have been true! They both thought a lot about their experiences privately, and both surely hoped that their stories would be validated somehow.

FRENCH QUARTER FOLLIES

Sitting in the day room as they were, chattering away with their backs to the hallway, the serial killer's entrance went unnoticed by the two collaborators. The serial killer was still nursing some painful cuts and bruises from the transvestite turf war he and the ex-Marine fought with no cause save self-defense, thus his new thing about violence. He might have been overheard this morning insisting on an explanation of why the ex-Marine was sent to jail. Completely confused about why either he or the ex-Marine should be detained, he expressed total outrage when told that the police considered him unstable if not outright mentally ill.

Denial was still casting a long shadow over the prognosis for this young man who grew up in a fish bowl in Omaha, a land known for turf not surf. For him, contradictions in terms were not only significant in their own right, they were also symbolic of the many double binds and double messages too powerful and too painful to remember, let alone reconcile. Unlike the mimes who are only perceived that way, this lad *was* an empty shell. Neither rescuing prostitutes nor recoiling to the martyr role and parading in the streets would ever relieve the pain let alone address the underlying injuries.

Shortly after their admissions the previous afternoon, the musician and the serial killer had a drifter to drifter conversation in the day room about their convergence on New Orleans. At the time, neither had any inkling of their linkage, imaginary as the basis might have been. The musician, who was born and raised on the outskirts of Baton Rouge, had little to say, but sustained considerable curiosity about the young man's beliefs that God instructed him to travel to New Orleans after graduation from college to find a new life and friends. During the spring of his senior year, he'd become infatuated, then morbidly despondent, when the woman he idolized, a classmate, showed no interest in him. It wasn't clear actually whether he'd ever approached her or whether the loss was based on fantasy alone. Suicide was an option if it could be "accidental," but none of his risks succeeded along these lines, not even the ninety-mile-an-hour motorcycle marathon on winding country roads. Instead, out of the depth of his despair, God's voice emerged and, simultaneously, so did hope! His grasp on reality has been tentative ever since. The hefty dose of Haldol, an anti-psychotic medication, helped loosen his tongue enough to at least communicate, if not develop some semblance of a relationship. Had the musician known the identity of this young man, Dean, to be that of the "serial killer," his reaction might have been distinctively different from one of listening so attentively.

This morning, Clarissa, the college dropout, was recounting to the musician what she could remember of the evening after she'd lost sight of him and found the crumpled poem. She did, in fact, recall that she'd located his violin. This pleased and reassured the musician immensely. She did not remember anything about the sequence of events thereafter. A throbbing headache reminded her of the interruption of consciousness and filled the gap to her satisfaction. It's easier to talk about headaches anyway. Obviously still fixed on the serial killer idea, she also revealed her weak grasp of the passage of time. While she was expressing the feeling that weeks had gone by since their last conversation, she was shaken into the present tense by a glimpse of Dean. Hallucinations were not part of her mental life to date, nor would she have been likely to admit to such experiences. No such alibis were available, however, not even something like an apparition which, in the French Quarter, would be considered a lightweight one. She fled the day room. Dean did not see her because he was talking to the nurse about his wish to leave and because the tears in his eyes blurred his vision. Depression was breaking through—a good sign, particularly this early in his treatment. Not only did he have no idea of Clarissa's presence on the ward, he had no idea whatsoever about her belief that he is a serial killer and, therefore, the reason why she never visited or slept in her apartment after he moved in.

Sounds of shattering glass and desperate pounding at the end of the hall alternated with blood curdling screams and rushing foot steps. The entire ward shook. Screams gradually gave way to plaintive sobs.

Was it Clarissa's initial attraction to Dean that created this catastrophic sequence of events? Does she mostly fear the attraction or the rage that might be emerging to shield her fragile feelings? This scenario has played out several times in the past. Given that paranoia has its roots in early reality, the hospital staff would become deeply invested in helping her discover the identity of the original culprit as well as the basic emotions she associated with that relationship.

About this time, Daddy called from New Jersey, having just learned of his daughter's fourth hospitalization. A social worker had left a message on his answering machine. His call came when the psychiatrist, Fred, and the entire nursing staff was involved in the emergency situation. Otherwise, an interception of his call would have been impossible. Now, who could have been responsible for that? *Moi?* No, she wasn't physically hurt, he was told, and he agreed to call back the next day. What an uneasy character he seemed to be!

A whole week went by before Clarissa would emerge from the darkness of her room. The musician's condition was improving to the point of questioning his recent version of reality, although he waffled periodically. "Where did I ever get that idea?" he would say, shaking his head.

He could also begin to imagine that Clarissa had "a problem." And, furthermore, he was beginning to understand Dean. Here was a man driven to fulfill a mission and willing to risk his well-being in the process. Dean's odyssey sounded plausible to the musician, having heard many stories in the French Quarter of similar caliber. But, no one understood the dynamics of the case, least of all Dean, although he held the key to everyone's enlightenment. There was no doubt of a massive injury to his fragile self-esteem. He'd experienced rapid slippage away from success and independence to a marginally functional state of disturbed thinking. Except in the abstract, the musician didn't understand much about the dynamics of rejection or attraction but he could at least figure out that Dean and Clarissa found each other for some reason, maybe even one with some promise for their future welfare.

The struggle between the *anti*psychotic effects of medication and the *pro*psychotic effects of rejection for control over Dean's mind became visible during the first hospital week. He seemed to be waffling, too, like the musician, under the weight of these forces but his struggle might also have been explained in terms of shifting priorities. The women of recent significance in his life, like the classmate or even the prostitutes, became dimmer figures as childhood memories surfaced. Among these memories lurked the ultimate rejection. The locked ward simulated this all too familiar experience, but this time he wasn't alone and the ward wasn't a dark closet.

The female medical student who befriended Clarissa during her week of self-imposed seclusion reported that Clarissa could now express hatred without losing control. Therefore, by the time Clarissa emerged from her room, this dark stormy morning, into the community meeting already in progress, this preceding news imparted a certain confidence to the staff and, through osmosis, to the patients. The student, who worked with Clarissa twice a day, was able to elicit some memories which might explain some of her twisted perceptions. Clarissa had begun to perceive her emotions to be the source of danger, and no longer insisted that the targets of her feelings were the source of her problems. It was once entirely the other way around, sadly.

The depth of her recently exposed shame about past relationships and experiences, which far exceeded any current embarrassment about her behavior on the ward, caused Clarissa considerable pain. That's not to say that recent events weren't also on her mind. She'd been wondering about her previous interaction with the musician and felt a need to clarify some things with him. She found it difficult to sort out their respective distortions. Clarissa hoped to speak with him soon and began to ask about the possibility. The musician, Maury, at forty-eight, was a generation older but hardly a father figure. He reminded Clarissa more of a clown. This could have been an advantage, considering the realities of her relationship with her father. Back to feeling comfortable as a loner, Maury's interpersonal distance always allowed the other's thoughts and feelings to safely fill the space between him and the person in his company. At this point in her recovery, this attribute of Maury's might also be beneficial to Clarissa. For the moment, Dean seemed to have lost his importance to her but Clarissa could only take one step at a time. She was truly and completely exhausted.

Events leading to Clarissa's self-seclusion were still haunting staff members, but their distress was a well kept secret.

FRENCH QUARTER FOLLIES

While running down the hall to her room a week ago after flee-ing from the day room at the sight of Dean, Clarissa was sobbing, yes, but to this day, the source of the screams, shaking, and pounding remained unexplainable to staff. Every glass pane in one window near the nursing station had shattered spontaneously at the moment of Clarissa's flight. Then the wind whistled omi-nously across the jagged edges of shards still embedded in the window frame. One nurse's aide became so terrified that she fled the ward and never returned. A nurse later resigned her position. Although he appeared to be only mildly preoccupied to his friends and coworkers, Fred, the staff psychiatrist, was deeply troubled about this incident, never having recovered from the mysterious disappearance of his valuable mynah bird the night after these three French Quarterites were admitted.

Community meetings frequently become a way of life in psychiatric hospitals, and Charity is no exception. Today's ses-sion, however, ended abruptly, soon after Clarissa's return from hiding.

"We're glad to see you, Clarissa." A chorus of patients and nursing staff greeted her. Sitting together, Dean and Maury were among the more sheepish members of the chorus—that is, until Clarissa came into their direct line of vision.

As Clarissa finally appeared in full view, she said, "Thank you," to the chorus in a perceptibly weak and gravelly voice.

She was dressed entirely in black. A long sweater and skirt ensemble covered all but her hands and feet. She wore sandals and the three strings of Mardi Gras beads around her neck added an eerie touch of color. The periodic giggles of a manic patient only intensified the drama. Clarissa's vacant stare, periodically illuminated by the flashes of morning lightning, assured Maury that she was possessed—a reincarnation of the Bead Lady. He had *no* doubts!

Dean froze, his grasp on reality being far too tentative to rec-oncile this transfiguration. Despite his apparent improvement, he'd remained extremely vulnerable. There was no escape from the terror. He fell mute and motionless, and so he stayed, sealed off completely from this horrifying situation. In turn, his waxen image horrified all who laid eyes on him. Maury thought of Dean as a mime but surprisingly he did not experience the familiar panic. Maury had never known a mime personally. He'd always kept a distance. Here stood Maury, more or less alone, on a locked psychiatric ward with the Bead Lady incarnate and an involuntary mime. Wasn't this where he came in? Was this his therapy, getting to know the mime and the Bead Lady? Was this desensitization the equivalent of getting to know himself? Whoa! *This is too heavy,* he thought. *Who needs this?*

A woman screamed. Footsteps rushed to the nursing station where hundreds of unstrung Mardi Gras beads had suddenly cascaded onto the shiny, waxed floor. Several staff members slipped and fell. An aide sprained her ankle. In the chaos which followed, many patients rose to the occasion and helped the staff. The confusion surrounding this situation, particularly the need to have several staff members carried to the emergency room in wheel chairs, allowed Maury, a voluntary patient, to assume the role of doorman for door after door after door. Jogging down Bienville Street during his escape into health, he could have sworn he saw Dean, the erstwhile serial killer, being carried into the Wax Museum on a chair by two men in white coats.

FRENCH QUARTER FOLLIES

CATAHOULA and PATAGONIA

Maury heard a rumor. Actually, he confused two stories and came up with his own version. One story involved a description of a schizophrenic man by his psychiatrist who referred to him as a committee of the minds. The other related to proposed regulations in the French Quarter regarding street performers about which the mimes were particularly exercised. Thus, Maury told his cronies in the French Quarter about the committee of the mimes, a concept of considerable emotional consequence for Maury. The idea of even one agitated mime presented difficulties for him. No wonder his mind twisted these tidbits of information. As a street musician with seniority in the French Quarter, he had concerns about any and all regulations affecting performers, but his concerns in this case fixated on what this committee of mimes might do. Weren't they powerful enough individually without ganging up?

It's true that Maury's treatment in the Charity psychiatric ward some two months ago effected a significant change. He no longer panicked around mimes. He didn't have to avoid them, nor did he believe they conspired with the Bead Lady to trap him in a voodoo spell. But he'd remained cautious, and this idea of a committee of mimes rocked his boat with great impact. He had neither the presence of mind nor the administrative talent to entertain the possibility of a counterforce in the form of a committee of musicians. Noticeably more social than usual, and more animated than ever, Maury kept very busy since his clever elopement from Charity. How ecstatic he felt to be over his fears and still no trace of the Bead Lady or her incarnate, Clarissa. Amen, he thought, but the uncertainty was unsettling. Luckily he was able to retrieve his violin from Clarissa's landlord, who knew Maury. His instrument had become his confidant, his livelihood and his security.

DR. PAUL RODENHAUSER

Clarissa's father was retaining her apartment, Maury learned, but no one had any word of her whereabouts. He assumed she was still on the ward at Charity or, for all he knew, she'd been shipped to the long-term state hospital in Mandeville. Secretly, he always thought the Bead Lady belonged there but he feared saying the words. The jury was still out on Clarissa. Even if she is the reincarnation of the Bead Lady, who vaporized on Dauphine Street not so long ago, she might be less menacing.

Now Maury was equally concerned about Dean, another Quarterite with a quixotic history, but from a different point of view. Everytime Maury passed the Wax Museum on Iberville, he checked the lobby through the window to see if Dean might be visible, wondering whether he'd ever snap out of his motionless state and get back to the way he was before that god-awful day at Charity. That was the day Maury first heard the word catatonia, but he'd subsequently confused it with Patagonia. No doubt his wires got crossed when he heard about the new clothing store opening in the RiverWalk. Still believing he saw Dean being carried inside the Wax Museum, Maury more than once asked the Ticketmaster at the Museum the names of the waxen figures most recently acquired. Among other factors, lack of funds prevented a personal reconnaissance.

Don't assume that distractions weren't abundant for Maury these days. The French Quarter was mobbed with tourists from this convention and that. At one point, there were 20,000 in town for one convention—orthopedic surgeons, if Maury remembered correctly. He kept track of the local goings on partly for business purposes, when to be on his corner regularly, versus when to slack off. Another distraction besides this mime business was, of course, the unsolved mystery of the Bead Lady's disappearance. The grapevine was humming with speculation and some trepidation, the former about her departure, the latter about her possible return. Maury was mostly in the trepidation camp; that's why he had been dressing for performances as a woman lately. Incognito, he thought. After all, he had good reasons on which to base his decision to take such precautions and, of course, he credited himself with sound judgment. Of all the Quarterites, wasn't he the one to witness a reincarnation and survive? He had the inside story and yet it remained an untold story for the time being—for obvious reasons. She'd be back one way or another, that Bead Lady. It was only a question of time, he thought.

A few weeks ago, Maury had mistaken Sophia for the Bead Lady, sans helmet, of course. Sophia lived in a ramshackle dugout across Rampart near where the mules are stabled. She adored the mules and helped care for them and their carriages. Sophia didn't wear a helmet but she resembled the Bead Lady in other ways, mainly her dark image and slow gait. The darkness in Sophia's case was not a product of black dye intentionally applied to cloth and chosen as apparel, however, but of layer upon layer of ground-in dirt. She smelled of manure, mostly. Sophia and Maury were two of a kind, not soul mates by any stretch of the imagination because neither really understood relations outside the non-human environment—Maury connected best with dogs and Sophia, with mules—but they had other common characteristics, including superstitions and an intense aversion to personal hygiene. Their chance meeting set the stage for a conversation of future consequence. Sophia, who regularly rummages through the trash on Dauphine Street—in fact, survives on that basis—told Maury about some of her recent discoveries, including news about Clarissa.

Clarissa was indeed alive and, if not well, at least much improved. Her transition from the hospital was a slow one with frequent furloughs. She was hardly recognizable—more stable, if not self-confident, and more reflective, if not insightful. These were some of the words chosen by Fred, her psychiatrist, to describe her condition upon discharge. A remarkable improvement, all the psych staff at Charity agreed. Now that her mood is so much brighter, so is her wardrobe. Everything dark, particularly black, has been discarded or given away.

Most pleasing to Clarissa, her new found ability to concentrate on the here and now allowed her to succeed as a waitress in a small but busy bakery and coffee shop on Ursulines. Maury couldn't believe his eyes this morning when he purchased his daily dose of caffeine. An impostor, a double, he assumed. As promised—he was testing her—she stopped by his corner on the way home from work. Maury was reassured that she had improved but he was not convinced about her identity. He still suspected she might be the Bead Lady.

"We worked some things out," she told Maury during their conversation on his turf.

This time, unlike her previous hospitalizations, her father got involved. She shared with Maury the peculiar message her father received when he first called the ward. An unidentified garbled voice told him to get his ass down here and take some responsibility for his daughter. He did. He flew down and stayed with Clarissa for several weeks. This changed her life, she said. Clarissa admitted to Maury that now at least she doesn't feel as much guilt about being born, the event that took her mother's life—a small step for some, but not for Clarissa.

Maury didn't asked about Dean but Clarissa told him anyway what she'd heard about Dean's very recent transfer to Mandeville, the "long-term facility," as the nurses called it. Her tone of voice revealed her concern. Maury thought he saw a tear. A nurse's aide, a regular coffee shop customer, had informed Clarissa of this turn of events. "Then who was that being carried into the wax museum?"Maury pondered out loud. Hearing this, Clarissa's newfound ability to follow her instincts told her to keep a distance. Throughout the remainder of her hospital stay, Clarissa had succeeded at keeping a distance from Dean, although she couldn't help observing his motionless state. Actually, she was more distrustful of her own than of his emotions. Still a long way from being comfortable with her feelings, she could now at least talk about Dean. As for Maury, even his fleeting glimpse of the immobile Dean clearly engendered alarm on his part, but during this conversation, Maury felt compelled to expound on his ingenious elopement from the ward which occurred just moments after the big freeze. Clarissa seemed uninterested. Considering himself the Houdini of hospital escapees, Maury's disappointment registered visibly.

Another distraction for Maury these days was the blue-eyed, female Catahoula puppy, a demure but feisty little thing, owned by the custodian for the gallery on Governor Nichols. Maury loved that puppy. No one had known him to be more connected with another living creature. She became part of his daily conversation. With his brown eyes as sparkling as her blue coat was speckled, he told stories about Catahoula hounds he'd known in Baton Rouge. In fact, he'd owned one as a child. To this point, Maury was unaware that Fred, the psychiatrist on Dauphine, had a pair of Catahoulas, but the subject came up in conversation with the custodian.

"Really?" Maury shook his head. Now how did he miss that? Surely he knew most everything about the French Quarter.

With informers like Sophia, Maury was a virtual repository of information. The French Quarter's culture, which rests on an infrastructure steeped in the occult, is incredibly complex, yet gossip and folklore have always managed to record, dramatize, and perpetuate its essence. Thus, stories are embellished—more likely distorted—and passed on by vintage Maury characters like the one about the young man suddenly stricken with Patagonia. Or, the one about the committee of the mimes. Or, the one about the Catahoula hounds in Baton Rouge so endowed with special powers that they could read his mind.

Today on her rounds, Sophia told Maury of Fred's infatuation, if not fetish, for mimes. The young staff psychiatrist at Charity's personal life was well known to Sophia. What better source of personal information than someone's trash? She knew his income, his Visa card number, and even his brand of condoms. Based on his experiences during his brief stay at Charity, Maury gave Fred a lot of credit as a doctor, although the events of that week were still unexplainable, even to Fred.

"An infatuation with mimes," you say.

Maury had begun to struggle with the differences between the natural and supernatural, and between the psychological and the parapsychological, at least the precepts. These were not terms in Maury's vocabulary. Beyond the medium of music, he often could not articulate what he could formulate in his mind—a little like an idiot savant, Fred thought, in his analysis of Maury's makeup. Maury could sense a power struggle of sorts between these forces, but damned if he could figure out which side he was on! Whether or not he possessed the ability to sort it out would not likely become an issue. Maury clearly had more important matters on his mind.

Today's conversation with Sophia under a smelly and

smudged red umbrella also helped Maury make a connection between Fred and the gallery. Was he the mime artist? Absolutely—and the hounds, yes, another connection! In many ways, Maury and Sophia decided, psychiatrists and mimes are interchangeable. Both used silence in their work, mimes even more so—and mimes certainly enjoy more anonymity, thanks to Sophia, whose rummaging was limited to Dauphine Street where no mimes lived currently. Little did Fred know—nor will he ever know—the amount of evidence he'd already captured on canvas to explain the recent chaos in his life. Strange how minds—and mimes—work!

Mardi Gras, the tumescence of tourists, and the clutter to prove it, came and went quickly again this year. Clarissa, while still working at the coffee shop, had recently started classes at the University of New Orleans. For the sake of her own stability, she saw to it that her path and Maury's rarely crossed. Unfortunately, the risks of having to struggle with his version of reality were greater than the benefits of their acquaintanceship. Fortunately, her successes in school, and particularly her busy work and study schedules, absorbed almost all of her time and attention and, therefore, served to reinforce her resolve to keep her boundaries intact.

As usual, this year's influx of Mardi Gras visitors resulted in a residue of "party hounds" and "crazies" looking for a Mardi Gras way of life. While the sifting and sorting of these hangers-on continued—but many wised up quickly—word got out about a figure quite unlike the others, a striking young man with definite class who strolled through the French Quarter each morning on the same trail blazed and worn by the Bead Lady. Wearing the uniform of an early 18th century French lieutenant, sword and all, he greeted passers by with the grace and confidence of a Founding Father. Rumor also had it that he was the spitting image of the wax figure of the *Duc d' Orleans* in the infamous—á le Maury—Wax Museum. Maury rubbed his eyes. He could have sworn it was Dean, the Patagonic young man from Charity, the suspected serial killer, the former innocent transvestite martyr, the boy from Omaha with no identity. The empty shell.

"My God!" Maury muttered under his breath. "My God!"

Convulsing with emotion and too wobbly to either remain

standing on his corner or to run, Maury, as if for show, performed a kind of reverse swan dive and accidentally struck his head on his dollar-bill laced cigar box.

Maury saw stars. Sometimes it takes being hit up 'long side the head, they say. And this is how the truth became known to him. Suddenly, while still under the influence of the stars, a deep voice spoke to Maury.

C'est moi, Maury, the chairman of the committee. Which committee, Maury, the minds or the mimes? It is Catahoula or Patagonia, Maury? Dobermans or catatonia? And what does it matter? The Duc is one of us, Maury. The French Quarter is our refuge. We'll all make it one way or the other with a little help from charity. Tell folks to keep those dollar bills coming.

DR. PAUL RODENHAUSER

METAMORPHOSIS

Recent experiences rendered Maury, the preeminent street musician, nothing short of flabbergasted. From his vantage point at St. Peter and Royal, he held court nightly over cigarettes and whatever spirits were available—between performances, of course. His head injury, from which he recovered quickly, required seven stitches but the number frequently changed—always inflated—from one to the next version of his recent revelation. Never in his life had his version of reality been so unequivocally validated. All this, mind you, based on two recent but fleeting before and after glimpses of Dean. Of course, the two scenarios were related. Of course! The transformation occurred in the Wax Museum. Clarissa was obviously not as well as she appeared to be the last time they spoke or she wouldn't have been so adamant about Dean's transfer to Mandeville, he thought. This clearly had not been his fate.

Maury wallowed in his righteousness like a Catahoula hound on shag carpet, one of Maury's favorite expressions. Fear and excitement were intertwined. He could hardly contain himself. Both emotions pertained to his no longer secret redemption, a sorely needed reprieve from this, the darkest year of his life. As scared as he was of the bygone Bead Lady, he was now equally elated that Dean had materialized in the French Quarter. Fearful, too, yes again, but this time of his own prowess! Had he not been certain he saw Dean being carried into the Wax Museum by two men in white coats some months ago, and equally certain he saw Dean dressed as the *Duc d' Orleans* a recently as two days ago, this glorious chapter in his life would not exist.

Sophia spread the word of Maury's clairvoyance. The custodian at the gallery heard about it from the clown who makes balloon animals and hats on Jackson Square, who heard it from the old man who feeds a number of stray cats on Orleans Street. He heard it from a carriage driver from Sophia's neck of the woods. Maury must be smarter than he looks. Despite being unaware of these recent newsworthy events, tourists wondered more than usual about the violin virtuoso's background and could be heard commenting on their intrigue with his full bodied inflection, the confidence behind his performances, his bemused expression.

Simultaneously, local curiosity about the Duke's arrival began mounting. French Quarterites clamored to see the Duke, whose background was virtually unknown outside the circle of Charity Hospital confidentiality. Even there, the available history was sketchy and of questionable reliability. Of the potential resources, only Dean's alcoholic father responded to staff attempts to gather background information and, as might be expected, he reported none of the abuse he inflicted. Staff wondered if he would have responded to phone calls at all if he had been sober.

How far does one have to travel to get away from Omaha? Dean's odyssey to this time and place had passed through several distinctly different permutations. His migration to New Orleans germinated from unhealed wounds of rejection, a recapitulation of every stage of his early years. So conditioned to disavowal was he that his infatuation for a young coed turned inside out and against him before he could even muster the courage to approach her. From beginning to end, the romance had all the characteristics of being auto-erotic. Sadly, these were the strongest and last true positive emotions he felt. The depression which followed might have been shorter lived had his attempts to end his life not created additional entries on his list of failures. By the time Dean miraculously reached the French Quarter, another transfiguration occurred, this one mightier than the first. Depression became omnipotence. He shouldered a gallant struggle against a special form of debauchery—and lost to a gang of outraged drag queens. Rechanneling his efforts into a zealous campaign against violence then resulted in involuntary commitment to an infamous public psychiatric ward. Only the staff at Charity knew any of this history, however.

Sometime during Dean's "antebellum" tenure in the French

Quarter, Clarissa, the only local resident to befriend him, rather summarily decided he was a serial killer. Poor guy! This was one piece of information most hospital staff didn't know. The medical student who treated Clarissa kept that confidential out of concern for the well being of both Clarissa and Dean. While Dean and Clarissa were both patients at Charity, Clarissa's inadvertent and momentary resemblance to the legendary voodoo queen, the Bead Lady, instigated Dean's realization that the only thing left to lose was himself—or maybe, from a therapeutic perspective, that he had a self to lose.

So, as a result of this revelation—or, if not, at least coincident in time with the Bead Lady's reincarnation, Dean adopted the ultimate defense, one employed by many members of the animal kingdom, and became immobile. He was a long way from feeling at home.

Professionals wondered if this lad could ever be fixed, but others—*moi, par exemple*—would have argued he wasn't broken, just incorrectly situated. Perhaps it's the environment that requires adjustment, not the patient. Maybe the twentieth century isn't his cup of tea!

By being so far behind the times, counterparts in psychiatry like Fred—the Charity psychiatrist, poet, artist, French Quarterite, Catahoula owner—haven't begun to appreciate the concept of situational problems like Dean's and the unlimited number of adjustments available. Regression to them is a personal problem, a defense, a flight from the present with nowhere to go but back up the developmental scale.

Change the environment, stupid! The French Quarter can fix it. Touché, shrinks!

At this moment, Fred wasn't looking for additional challenges. His personal and professional lives, entangled in more ways than could be explained by coincidence, were both too complicated for comfort. Their embodiment in one functional person allowed no escape from one to the other. The simultaneous disappearances of the Bead Lady outside Fred's townhouse and his pet myna bird from inside remained unsolved and unsettling. The conditions surrounding Clarissa's hospital crisis and Maury's elopement were still under investigation. Concern about

FRENCH QUARTER FOLLIES

Dean and Clarissa when they were still in the hospital forced Fred to develop a habit of spending a lot more time on the ward, thus adding even more stress to his life. Fatigue, the likes of which he hadn't experienced since his internship, compounded Fred's problems and sent him into a state of existential despair.

In spite of the best efforts of psychiatrists like Fred, Dean succeeded in accomplishing some psychological work during his protracted period of immobility. He grew aware that no one hurt him, that negotiations for personal space, albeit limited, were not necessary, and that boundaries were honored even when he couldn't imagine having any of his own. So this creative lad began thinking of himself as being locked in a closet with clear plexiglass walls, safe and secure, but no more isolated than he needed to imagine himself to be. Up to this point in his mental life, a closet meant an abusive mother, the impact of his body hurled against the wall, pain, the turn of a key, darkness and panic. Bruises appeared later in the process. This new invention, his own invisible closet, became a protective chariot illuminated by the life surrounding him and the possibility he might someday be a participant. Brilliant! Absolutely brilliant. Dean clearly had the ability to turn himself around.

Actually, Dean did not go to Mandeville, the long term psychiatric facility, as Clarissa had been told. She'd been misinformed by the nursing assistant who recognized her in the coffee shop. The assistant was obviously outside the information loop, or maybe she was deliberately misinformed in order to conceal an "incident", as staff blunders were officially labeled. More on that later. Clarissa and Maury would both have benefited from enlightenment regarding Dean's whereabouts, but for the moment they remained in the dark. Meanwhile, Maury's confidence in his beliefs continued to gather momentum.

Mobile had been Dean's destination, not Mandeville—and not the Wax Museum on Iberville as Maury had declared out loud in Clarissa's presence, unfortunate for their relationship. Not incidentally—actually, a *very* important piece of this story—it turns out that The Ticketmaster at the Wax Museum was predisposed toward gullibility, perhaps an occupational hazard or — who knows—a prerequisite. Maury's visit had triggered The

Ticketmaster's imagination, and not just a little. Well before their unusual conversation about the possibility of Dean's residence among the museum figures, The Ticketmaster couldn't stop thinking about the figure in the back that keeps on "breathing," the one leaning against the tree on the battlefield. After his conversation with Maury, he began checking the other figures for signs of life. The Ticketmaster could not refrain from this activity. One night after closing, the museum's manager dropped in only to find him palpating the chests of those gathered in Jean Lafitte's Tavern. The manager also thought he saw a stethoscope bulging in The Ticketmaster's coat pocket. Our Ticketmaster-doll doctor had come a long way beyond gullibility!

Meanwhile, back at Charity—toward the tail end of Dean's hospital stay—the staff had decided in favor of a pre-Mardi Gras pageant quite different from the usual ward celebration. This one would be designed—in their characteristic way of rationalizing—for the benefit of the patients! Plans this year called for stationary, historic scenes—similar to those in the Wax Museum, actually—to be staged instead of the traditional Mardi Gras parade and presentation of the court. This annual event on the psychiatric wards at Charity attracted family, friends, city officials, and other voyeurs to watch the disbelieving and confused patients paraded in costume to their designated place on the bigger-than-life dais. Although any departures from this routine, like the innovative but less demanding plan for this year's celebration, were justified as helping prevent staff burnout, any informed patient might have been greatly relieved, regardless of the rationale, not to be expected to go through the parade and presentation rigmarole.

The nursing supervisor's uncle, who happened to own and operate a Mardi Gras float construction business in Mobile, offered to supply scenery, props, costumes, and a few mannequins to complete the display because of the limited number of patients able to participate this year. Despite his inflexibility, Dean was actually considered to be among the patients eligible to take part in the pageant. Indeed, he fell into the category of those thought to be in need of stimulation and this activity certainly qualified. Dressed in an 18th century French Lieutenant's costume, hat, sword, and all, Dean had the dubious honor of becoming the *Duc d' Orleans* in a scene depicting the signing of an important land grant treaty. Little did anyone who participated know what a landmark occasion this would be in the history of Mardi Gras spirit at Charity!

Speaking of being in the dark, the next day the Duke experienced overwhelming fear, confined as he was to a tiny space in the back of an enclosed, speeding moving van. The hired hands responsible for returning the borrowed display materials mistakenly loaded the immobile *Duc d' Orleans*, chair and all, and trucked him, along with the load of costumed mannequins, back to the warehouse in Mobile. Not only was this kind of oversight unprecedented in the history of this or any other charity institution, it went unrecognized well beyond the time it took for the Duke to rally.

The admission of an anorexic young woman on roller blades, her head and body wrapped in sheer pink chiffon with long veils trailing in the wind, distracted the staff for several hours, particularly because of her refusal to stop skating back and forth on the ward. Her futuristic image and frenetic behavior contrasted sharply with that of the missing patient. Security officers and staff later began their search for Dean by lifting all the false ceiling tiles in an area where a patient had climbed and hid for several hours the week before. Doesn't it seem odd to look for a catatonic patient in the ceiling?

DR. PAUL RODENHAUSER

IMMOBILE IN MOBILE

Unlike the Duke, who wanted only a familiar, predictable environment, Clarissa yearned to be able to travel. Although the hospital staff thought it might prove to be for the better in the long run, Clarissa's world caved in, completely, once she arrived in the French Quarter two years ago. Her therapist thinks this resulted from the distance she finally established between herself and her troubled family ties, her father in particular. The absence of that struggle which kept her so entangled created in her a need to grow up again. This time, a forgiving environment cradled Clarissa, thankfully. For Clarissa, such a move represented a strong statement about her need for clearer definition and this took all the energy she could muster. Unfortunately for her, the separation had to be abrupt and her personal boundaries, therefore, emerged as extremely ragged once she'd torn herself away.

Clarissa had never had the luxury of a slow, gradual process in which to develop as an individual; a process which brings with it the benefit of countless opportunities to learn from experience, to integrate thoughts and emotions, to love and be loved, to have realistic expectations of oneself, and to achieve on a step by step basis. Independent of her inability to cope with all the other issues in her life—if it were possible to compartmentalize them—Clarissa could hardly manage the chores involved in everyday living even before her departure from New Jersey. Left entirely to her own devices, she was overwhelmed with impulses, twisted thoughts, distortions of her environment, and hurtful memories—internalized ghosts, her therapist called them.

Life in the French Quarter was truly a learning experience for Clarissa. She'd never ever imagined the amount of emotional baggage that was to accompany her. She could barely have made ends meet even if she could control her impulses. She could barely hold a job because it was so difficult to concentrate. Her intuitions about people were anything but accurate because her needs so overwhelmed any remnants of judgment that may have been accessible. Furthermore, she constantly struggled with the fear that if she couldn't trust herself, the chances of finding trustworthy relationships were nil. Since her arrival, she'd been hospitalized three times, all at Charity, where not being able to pay for services doesn't prevent one from getting help. If nothing else, her first hospitalization in New Jersey led to recognition of the need to relocate and enough courage and professional support to do so. She floundered badly in the weeks following her departure from Princeton where she grew up, and where her father still taught high school. Her next two hospitalizations were ignored by her father and other family members for reasons related to their need to be right about her staying close to them. All alone in the French Quarter, she quickly became a lost soul. Charity could only help her through the crises. Afterwards, community mental health centers offered her medications. She treasured the occassional encouragement to take her pills faithfully. The professional staff were as hard pressed for time to provide her with a supportive emotional experience as she was to find a means to pay for her treatment.

Clarissa's fourth hospitalization was very different, mostly because her father did not limit his interest to a few long distance phone calls. He got involved personally in her therapy and, fortunately, she was able to hook up with a social worker at Chartres Community Mental Health Center who took a special interest in her. If all aspects of Clarissa's life had been normal otherwise—and they clearly were not—growing up without a mother would still have been a lopsided and challenging experience. Housekeepers couldn't really fill the void, and her father, who had many problems of his own, never remarried. All her relationships were severely affected, it seemed, even those with her many therapists, but this one clicked. Maybe it was the right time and place and distance from her origins, maybe the product of her newfound neediness, or maybe the result of what she learned from several hospitalizations, but finally, for the first time in her memory, but especially since puberty, Clarissa could feel a semblance of stability, or at least predictability.

Clarissa and her therapist were both impressed with how far she'd traveled, geographically and emotionally, to get away from New Jersey. Both remembered how important it was, originally, to stay put for awhile. Nowadays, however, Clarissa felt ready to venture beyond the French Quarter and the St. Charles streetcar route which she'd recently mastered without panicking—well, at least without throwing up.

Her employer's second invitation to join him and his wife on a day trip to Dauphin Island turned out to be very well timed with her work in therapy. She had to decline their first invitation because of physical symptoms, mainly nausea, when she ventured too far from home. Feeling obliged to disclose the real reason rather than make excuses, Clarissa experienced considerable embarrassment, but this benevolent couple not only understood but empathized with her situation and readily agreed with her therapist's plan that she be dropped off at a safe spot enroute if she became too anxious. They'd simply stop for her on the way back. Very much reassured by these arrangements, Clarissa accepted the invitation.

She made it as far as Mobile! Everyone recognized this as a major achievement. They would celebrate back in New Orleans. This much success offset the disappointment of not having a day at the beach house with her newly adopted family. It was too cold to swim, anyway, but walking the beach would have been a treat. Instead, the park in the Mobile historic district became a home away from home for Clarissa. The weather was particularly pleasant for February.

Clarissa smiled inwardly and it showed. She cherished this opportunity and accepted it as a challenge, another major step in her journey. That's not to say she felt particularly comfortable. As usual, she experienced struggles of many kinds. Everyday life brought everyday challenges even in Mobile, but this day had special meaning and brought not only a special sense of freedom, but the promise of more. She'd arrived late in the morning and expected to leave by late afternoon, so she had ample time to explore parts of the historic district, the nearby shops and, of course, the park. She particularly enjoyed parks as evidenced by the amount of time she spent on her favorite bench in Jackson Square.

Back in the French Quarter, the garbage from Mardi Gras littered the streets, the clean lines of the curbs obliterated with layer upon layer of sooty, soggy, trampled go-cups and condoms and who knows what else. Cleanup, especially on Bourbon and Royal Streets, required shovels and a lot of muscle. Mardi Gras had been stressful for Clarissa and her employers, as it always is for residents of the French Quarter. The energy from the twenty-four hour a day revelry quickly becomes tension. This, plus the sleep deprivation from noise, adds up to irritability at best. Although disappointing to the locals, the bakery and coffee shop had been closed all week to avoid the chaos and its inherent risks. For the first time, the windows were boarded up this year as a safety precaution.

What an opportune time for Clarissa—and her employers— to spend a day outside the French Quarter. Although Clarissa thought about some of her neighborhood regulars at the shop and some classmates from school, on this glorious occasion she had no special need to reflect on those relationships. To her surprise, however, she thought about Maury, the street musician, periodically, whom she knew mostly as a fellow Charity psych ward patient. She remembered him mostly as a man obsessed with French Quarter mimes and the Bead Lady, the alleged voodoo madame.

This special day gave Clarissa a lot of uninterrupted time to think about the continuity in her life, or lack of it, and her interest in being authentic. Being in touch with her feelings, and having better congruence between how she felt and what she decided to communicate, constituted her major goal for herself in therapy, a big order considering the hole in which she started just two years ago. As she wandered through the historic district, Clarissa enjoyed several hours of reverie. The architecture and construction of the many 18th and 19th century homes inspired confidence that they'd be there indefinitely. The quaint shops clustered here and there fascinated her. She bought a few things—book markers, refrigerator magnets—only small, affordable items—and had lunch in a beautifully restored Victorian home which housed a small deli with special coffees. She'd become infatuated with the menu in the window—seafood, naturally.

So far, so good, but enroute back through the historic district toward the park, Clarissa almost lost her lunch, not from feelings about the distance from home, although they played a part, but from fear on a more realistic basis. This fear didn't qualify at all as neurotic, she thought. Crossing her path a block away, she saw a figure draped from head to toe in black, wearing a black helmet and tapping its way along with a cane.

Clarissa had suspected that the Bead Lady, who disappeared months ago, might have been the victim of one of her own kind if, in fact, she was a voodoo queen as everyone believed. Clarissa, who, unlike Maury, never expected to see the Bead Lady again, sincerely hoped she was laboring under an illusion. Could it have been a *déjà vu*? Her impression of the Bead Lady had been deeply ingrained. A memory so alive with emotion—as this one was—might have surfaced momentarily, especially considering her uneasy feelings about strange surroundings. She tried to convince herself of this possibility. Or could it be the lunch? Although she had the presence of mind to pursue the image, she could not find any likeness of the unmistakable Bead Lady among the many pedestrians in the area. According to Clarissa's understanding, the Bead Lady spent all her adult life in the French Quarter. How could she appear here? And then disappear? All of a sudden, Mobile felt unsafe. Clarissa's heart began pounding out its familiar warning. Danger may be lurking. Be prepared to run, her heart told her.

When Clarissa turned to go back to the park, she encountered yet another shocking image. Some distance away, a handsome young man, wearing the uniform of an 18th century French lieutenant and carrying a sword, sat in the middle of the park on a bench facing her. Clarissa's doubt about her perceptions and her stability increased, yet she approached the young figure. His posture seemed almost too rigid to be explained on the basis of military training, and he bore an uncanny resemblance to her former acquaintance—in fact, roommate for three days and later, fellow patient on the Charity psych ward. Furthermore, this was the young man who had unknowingly been the recipient of her projected anger. These emotions were uniformly directed to other men in order to preserve her relationship with her father whom she believed she needed in order to survive. Psychiatric people called it displacement—with some projection thrown in.

Clarissa once saw this innocent man, Dean, as a serial killer when indeed her father was the one who'd been violent. As a result of this relationship, she never learned to deal with her own anger. If she ever got angry, her father would get angrier, thus the confusion resulting later, and the projection. She couldn't differentiate her anger from his. The boundaries of her own emotions were, therefore, never clear. Attraction to any man became cluttered with unbearable emotions and distortions of even delusional proportions at times. Even though she'd learned to stop projecting, men were objects of ambivalence at best. Such was the case with Dean, who, dressed in an historically significant outfit, now sat conspicuously before her on a park bench in the middle of the Mobile, Alabama, historic district, motionless, mute, and vulnerable.

Clarissa cried, first for herself, then later for Dean. She had seen Dean this way before but in jeans and tee shirts on the psych ward. She'd purposely avoided him to protect herself from unmanageable emotions. Wasn't this where she came in? Between memories of Maury's obsessions about mimes and the Bead Lady—and his subsequent delusions about Dean and Dean's mime-like immobility—and all of her own problems, wasn't this scene also something that should be avoided? She had to take a moment to reconsider her own needs. On the other hand, she figured dealing with this might be a part of getting better.

Not many but some choices were available to this fragile, young woman, now alone in an unfamiliar city, but Clarissa stayed with Dean, bought him food and talked to him. Tears flowed off and on throughout the afternoon, mostly, but not exclusively, Clarissa's.

*   *   *

Some would call it rehab, but the metamorphosis of this toy soldier (a.k.a. Dean, the serial killer, martyr, protester, once an empty shell and now the Duke), like his guidance back to the French Quarter from Mobile, must have been as much a product of something like supernatural intervention as his original journey to New Orleans. Surely he had no handle on it. If the word Omaha describes those who go upstream or against the wind, then the Duke must have been walking with his back to the wind from the get-go. He, no doubt, caught a tail wind in the process and got blown all the way to New Orleans. He'd come a long way from Omaha and a long way from Charity. Transplanted to the South, to New Orleans, to the Vieux Carré, and reduced there to a generic state of mind, he found himself now back in his adopted neighborhood but situated in the early part of the 18th century. All of this happened after a side trip to Mobile. The French Quarter would remain his niche, he hoped. He belonged here, no doubt about it!

Dean was no dummy. It didn't take him long to fit into a routine even if he didn't understand what inspired it. In particular, he was unaware of the visual impact his handsome features, lithe physique, and 18th century uniform had on his surroundings. Because his grasp on reality remained so tentative and his defenses so porous, he responded to social stimulation on a reflex basis, almost like an infant. Due to the fact that the circuitry for these reactions required functions not much higher than the brain stem, his social responses bypassed whatever inhibitions his emotionally challenged personality might try to impose. The Duke mimicked his environment exceedingly well. If people smiled, he smiled in return. If they spoke to him, he spoke in return, frequently using the same words, his capacity for improvisation quite limited at this point. With his characteristic vulnerability working this time around as a vehicle for growth, the Duke became a walking, talking, antique Ken Doll dressed to kill.

And so the neglected boy from Omaha became affectionally known as *Le Duc d' Orleans*, or "the Duke" for short. Although he mirrored the behaviors of his French Quarter environment amazingly well, his repertoire of responses did not yet include affection in turn, thus, the emptiness in his life. To the degree he was experiencing feelings these days, wonder-stricken might have best described them.

Tourists, Parisians, and French Canadians in particular, found the Duke irresistible. But his charm and shyness endeared everyone as he made his daily rounds back and fourth on Royal and Chartres and around Jackson Square. *"Bonjour, monsieur."*

"Bonjour, mesdames et messieurs," he answered softly.

"Comment ça va, aujourd'hui, monsieur?"

"Tres bien, merci, et vous?" he responded, enroute to the coffee shop and bakery where he was becoming accustomed to having his breakfast each morning. The owner took great pride in his new customer and, being a very generous man, he charged not a penny. The Duke enjoyed an open invitation to breakfast on a daily basis as a guest of the establishment. True, the Duke's presence benefitted the business, but the gesture had other origins. Being European, it felt natural to the owner to include the Duke in the company of his establishment and, furthermore, the owner had a certain investment in being a matchmaker. He suspected Clarissa might have developed an interest in this debonair young man.

By this time, Clarissa's recovery seemed secure. Her visits to the community mental health center were now less frequent and her markedly improved ability to manage her emotions, and imagination increased her confidence. At work, she enjoyed the safety of camaraderie with her familiar customers, especially the neighborhood regulars, and her college courses held her interest. She talked a lot about her studies. Languages interested her most. The occasion of a former therapist's return from working in Guyane, and her recent trip to New Orleans to visit with Clarissa, conveyed a sense of support and renewed the resolve Clarissa desperately needed to continue her personal work. The boost to Clarissa's self-confidence derived from that visit—coupled with her dogged determination to overcome her inhibitions—had a lot to do with her ability to travel as far as Mobile.

While her employers especially, but also a few patrons and college professors, provided Clarissa with a lot of support, interest in the debonair young duke was fast becoming a universal phenomenon in the French Quarter. The Wax Museum Ticketmaster, a collector of toy soldiers, responded with intrigue to rumors of this rakish aristocrat—an anachronism, he was told, if such a term could be applied with any meaning in the French Quarter, where acceptance of any behavior or manner of dress is the norm. Actually, the Ticketmaster heard about the Duke from Sophia, who gave him a copy of a crumpled poem as she tended to do from time to time for no apparent reason. Although she fashioned herself as the communications maven of the culture she lived in, some of which consisted of mule manure, Sophia's contacts were limited to those neighborhoods must generous with their trash—that is, where the value of the harvest exceeded the time and energy required to retrieve and redistribute it for either barter or cash. Fortunately, the Ticketmaster worked and resided on Sophia's rummage route. They got along well, most of the time.

Exhausted from recent adventures, but grateful, like Clarissa, for his ability to manage the basics of everyday life, the *Duc d' Orleans* settled into a routine. Finally, as a result of a long and torturous journey, he found his niche, a *raison d' être*, and a home. True, he would not want to venture beyond its boundaries—the world outside the French Quarter seemed quite risky—but who would have predicted this much progress even several months earlier? Everything fit together for him, even when conditions were more uncertain than usual. For example, occasionally, when the Duke would succumb to surprises or uncertainties on other bases with seizure-like immobility, those moments were prized by tourists and the fear went unnoticed. After all, regardless of what instigated them, pauses were always appreciated as photo ops. In many ways, from photographs to autographs or just glimpses of him, the Duke was fast becoming a collector's item. He, too, was collecting, however. Dollar bills and fives filled his pockets. The mimes and musicians scratched their heads in wonderment, although Maury had to be careful of his fresh scar.

FRENCH QUARTER FOLLIES

"LAISSEZ LES BON TEMPS ROULEZ"

Like everything else around New Orleans, French Quarter horses move slowly. Sophia had arranged to have one of the mule-drawn carriages at her disposal for a few hours this summer evening as payment in kind for her work around the stables. The custodian at the gallery, the Ticketmaster from the Wax Museum, the clown from Jackson Square, and Sophia's new friend, Ginger, a local prostitute, were all at their predetermined stations awaiting to be picked up, so to speak.

This long anticipated evening of revelry would have been far less entertaining without Maury, the street musician. That's one reason why Sophia included him on the invitation list. Another had to do with the wish to show off to Maury, and another, the need to give the appearance of having many friends, at least more than a few. None of these Quarterite peasants had any particular bonds or even common characteristics, with the possible exception of their creativity in the process of blurry reality with fantasy, then defending themselves against the social repercussions that seemed to be the result of their success in that regard. To say that the overlapping versions of reality on which they agreed were based on superstition is to be generous. For this group, superstition is the highest form of thought.

As usual, Sophia got started late, so each member of the party waited a long time. Each quite naturally assumed no other guests would be present. With a bottle of rum under his arm, Maury stood on his corner at St. Peter and Royal talking with a man who said he was Michael Jackson and an impersonator. It wasn't ever clear to Maury if this man was the Michael Jackson or an impersonator of Michael Jackson. The possibility of neither hadn't occurred to him. After a long, drawn-out conversation, it seemed to Maury that the Michael Jackson character wasn't clear about that either.

DR. PAUL RODENHAUSER

Due to a sixth sense of wariness, Maury was reluctant to tell too many people, including his new acquaintance, Michael Jackson, about his special powers and how he correctly predicted the coming of the Duke to the French Quarter. Of course, he had not really predicted the Duke's arrival, but his penchant for hyperbole had taken it to that level. And, not only was he his own best listener, he believed everything he heard. It did seem ironic to him that so many people in the French Quarter thought they had special powers, including this Michael Jackson character.

Maury's mental life meshed tightly with the world of the supernatural as did that of the others' in Sophia's little congregation, but his ideas about the Duke were no doubt going to be unique. Almost all his views were guaranteed to be entertaining. Thoughts about the Duke consumed most of Maury's waking moments, lately. Sophia had already told Maury she believed the Duke to be a resurrection of an 18th century lieutenant killed in battle under Lafayette's leadership. In fact, she feared this roaming officer would rally others to rise from the dead and reenact the battle in which he was wounded in order to rectify the outcome. At night she could visualize them in full uniform crawling from their graves, stretching, then running for cover. The proximity of the dugout in which she lived to Cemetery Number One kept many such images very much alive. She figured the Duke died of infection. She'd woven together an elaborate story to explain the Duke's existence. Others of his ilk were already in the community, she was certain, but incognito. Sophia was determined and streetwise, therefore, always cautious. Harm was just around the corner. Any day now, she expected the reenactment would take place, led by the Duke. Her beliefs and dreams instructed and protected her, thank goodness! Frequently she confused her dreams with everyday life, however, in either case, Sophia felt prepared for this upcoming battle. She had a plan.

On her way into the French Quarter from Basin Street, Sophia passed through some congestion related to activity at the Municipal Auditorium which reminded her of a high school graduation, but it was a sports awards program, she learned. Education, she thought, was a waste of time. She hadn't yet developed an opinion about sports. Her slow progress through the crowd allowed an errant youngster to catch a ride, a pink-haired hiphop rapper headed for the end of Decatur Street in the lower French Quarter, the ghetto for this special sect. Some called them gutter punks. Here was a living example of an everyday experience easily confused with a dream. This rapper's visual impact would register as the epitome of living and breathing surrealism for even educated and so-called people of culture. (That's one of Sophia's descriptors for the elite.) Although Sophia, herself, was used to this image in the landscape, being up close made her feel spacy and confused. The mule was skittish and the surrounding commotion, quite unusual, Sophia thought, between mental fade-outs. This strange pair headed down Toulouse, clippity clopping toward swarms of pedestrians with a different purpose.

After a lot of soul searching, the Ticketmaster had concluded that the Duke was indeed a former museum figure. Actually, he happened to believe—off and on—that the wax dummies were living people whose vital functions were suspended for limited periods of time. How, he wasn't sure yet. In his way of thinking, this physiologic state provided mutual benefits. It allowed them to rest while they simultaneously educated the unsuspecting public.

This was one of those "on" times for the Ticketmaster. These people were living! Because he knew about duplicates in the warehouse, he had no difficulty reconciling the museum's uninterrupted operation while the Duke departed for greener pastures. He admired the Duke and all the Duke's fellow museum aristocrats, but also the commoners, for whom he felt particularly sorry. Like the Ticketmaster, they had no status.

The Ticketmaster was standing outside his apartment on the corner of Conti and Dauphine where beaucoup activity reigned this evening. The local chapter of The International Society for the Study and Enactment of Anachronism had scheduled a business and social meeting for 7:30 that evening at the Prince Conti Hotel. The members were all to arrive in costume. Cameramen stood by. A few of these living history buffs arrived early, dressed in Revolutionary War uniforms. Later, some came in Civil War regalia. A group from a Civil War hospital battalion particularly impressed the Ticketmaster. Next, he saw LaSalle alight from a Ford Explorer and a few Elizabethans pulled up in a Plymouth

DR. PAUL RODENHAUSER

Voyager behind him. This scenario fascinated the Ticketmaster whose knowledge of three-dimensional representations of history heretofore centered only on toy soldiers and wax museum figures. As if forgetting why he was standing there on Conti Street, he decided to attend the meeting and soon disappeared into the growing number of anachronisms.

A parade on Bourbon Street delayed Sophia even longer. "Son of a bitch," she muttered, unaware it was Bastille Day. "Is there ever a day in this city without a celebration?" She asked the rapper if it might be the Queen's Birthday. Soon they reached Maury who brought Michael Jackson with him, then Jake, the custodian, hopped on with his full-grown Catahoula hound in tow, then Ginger from the lower end of Burgundy, but no sign of the Ticketmaster as this unlikely group traveled down Conti from Rampart in their wobbly, old black carriage. The newer carriages are white or pink and pretty spiffy, but Sophia made up a reason why hers had special character. More celebrities had ridden in it than any other.

Very little additional time passed before they all agreed that the Ticketmaster must have been kidnapped. In case they needed a common cause, they now had one. And they also had two common bottles already tapped, one rum, one tequila. Overflowing their container, this almost asocial entourage now included Sophia, the bag lady, Maury, the street musician, Jake, the gallery custodian and his Catahoula hound, Glendale, Ginger, the prostitute, Michael Jackson, the impersonator, and the rapper named Vincent. This wagonful of merrymakers looked like a band of gypsies as they took off down Conti behaving like children in parallel play. Each had a distinct agenda and their agendas just happened to overlap enough to keep them together. For example, if it weren't for the organizing principle provided by the mystery of the missing Ticketmaster, each might have offered a different reason as to why they were going forward. Their overriding mission to find the Ticketmaster consumed them, however, and they, hell bent toward early burnout, consumed the most available propellant, alcohol. Unimpressed by this self-absorbed downward spiral, the mule, partly by default, became their leader.

Interest continued, however, about this Duke fella, as Ginger the prostitute phrased it—another overlapping concern. The *Duc d' Orleans*, a prominent figure almost three centuries ago, who reappeared in the French Quarter just after Mardi Gras as the crowds were thinning, intentionally or not succeeded in captivating the attention and the hearts of locals and tourists alike. Never in the collective memories of this motley crew was the French Quarter so alive with titillation. The Duke's tendency to keep a distance only served to accentuate the intrigue. He was fast becoming an icon in iconoclastic times. This youthful founding father roamed the French Quarter appearing sometimes pleased and sometimes puzzled, as if he were assessing the progress of the French Quarter over the past three-hundred years. All of this, of course, was ascribed to him, but not confirmed. No one knew what the Duke thought or felt. His visage served as a blank screen. Information ran rampant, albeit all projected, assumed, invented, and none of it accurate.

In reality, the Duke was an undetected, involuntary escapee from the psych ward at Charity. No one who knew him now would have guessed that at the time of his assisted elopement— when he was hoisted in a chair to a van while in an immobile state—he would not have had the wherewithal to plan or carry out an escape to the outside world if left to his own devices. He had retreated instead, assuming an immobile stance as a paradoxical but effective escape, a particularly understandable choice in the absence of a support system. Waxy flexibility best described his posture. If he thought anything, he thought he'd be harmed, if not killed. If he felt anything, it was terror; otherwise emptiness prevailed. What a significant achievement it was that the Duke now had the ability to begin to reflect on all of this, constructively!

Maury referred to the prostitute as Blondie. Only Sophia among them knew that the stimulus for this sobriquet was not authentic. She wouldn't say anything, not Sophia, partly out of an intuitive need to protect Ginger. Maury's track record with confidences hadn't been stellar. She also knew better than to contradict Maury. He was always right, although with immediate proof at hand, Sophia this time felt the urge all the way to her lips.

Ginger's pimp was under the illusion that she felt feverish and couldn't work this evening. God forbid he should recognize her on this, her only night out in months. The pimp was brutal. She needed the night off, she told Sophia, but she figured she wouldn't be able to enjoy herself because she was so scared she would be discovered. Sophia offered her a blonde wig found months ago in the trash following a transvestite uprising on Burgundy Street. Sophia had already worn out the blousy outfit she found with it. She'd given away the shoes. They were huge, she said.

Having begun the conversation about the Duke, Ginger's version of his significance came forth without an invitation. She had no doubts he was a Hollywood actor doing a publicity gig for an upcoming big-budget, historical movie. He'd be gone in a short while, she assured her carriage mates. Maury nodded. Furthermore, she perceived him as an aloof and arrogant hunk who, like all men, needed to be brought down to size. This, not incidentally, was the sole challenge motivating her choice of professions. If the Duke were to become one of her conquests, she'd have to work quickly, she sensed.

Not surprisingly, Maury's convictions about the Duke were deeply imbedded in the culture of the French Quarter. frequently wrong but never in doubt, his confidence in his beliefs was such that he declined to discuss them despite several inquiries. Not even the rum dislodged the information. In particular, he didn't trust this Michael Jackson character, especially when there'd already been a suggestion about the entertainment industry invading and exploiting the French Quarter. That irritated Maury for some reason and increased his characteristic suspiciousness. Suspiciousness had already come into play in a big way regarding the Duke's true identity.

Michael Jackson and the rapper, Vincent, hadn't heard of the Duke, but the gallery custodian, Jake, imagined that the Duke was a sort of mime, a new breed, maybe, a roving entertainer, an actor, but one more inclined toward pantomime. Maury looked nervous—mimes, again. Jake gathered his assumptions from the prints and paintings of professional and amateur artists who framed or hung their work in the gallery. Some were for exhibition and some were for sale. Fred, the psychiatrist and amateur artist from Dauphine Street who'd specialized in mimes, seemed to be especially fascinated with the Duke as a model, Jake told this *corps du jour*. Fred's original interest in mimes gave Jake the notion that the Duke might be some kind of mime. Jake had the good sense not to share with the group his infatuation with one of Fred's paintings of the Duke and how it required a lot of self-control not to take it home. He'd stolen before, but never at the gallery where he almost enjoyed his work—and besides, the income helped him keep Glendale healthy. The *corps du jour* even had a conversation about Glendale's reaction to the Duke.

Jake spoke for him. "Zilch," he said, as Glendale barked at a big tomcat skedaddling across St. Ann Street, near the Cathedral.

Dukemania had seized the French Quarter, Maury concluded with some noticeable trepidation in his voice. Until his brief psych hospitalization at Charity less than a year ago, Maury's fear of mimes was exceeded only by his fear of the infamous Bead Lady and her voodoo powers. His therapy, there, helped considerably, but would it have long lasting effects? He began to wonder, especially considering his beliefs—increasingly strong beliefs—about who the Duke really is. A double shot of rum would help Maury digest all this information, he thought.

This *corps du jour* comprised of six unlikely companions and one best friend, Glendale, rattled through the French Quarter looking for the Ticketmaster behind their half-horse, half-ass. Maury quipped that the front half was horse because what they were facing was clearly the other. Luckily the mule knew his way around because as they continued their antics, he became more engrossing as well as more noticeable. The doors of the museum were locked, they discovered. No one answered The Ticketmaster's studio apartment buzzer. Unaccustomed as the members of the corps were to using telephones, Ginger allowed herself to be elected, but no one by the name they concocted from their frazzled memories and agreed upon was listed in the directory. They checked the Moonwalk, the coffee houses, all the places locals congregate. No one had seen The Ticketmaster. A considerable amount of time had passed so far in awaiting, let alone enduring this buggy ride. None of the *corps* took that or their empty bottles as any possible indication of inebriation. Having been unsuccessful in their attempts to determine The Ticketmaster's whereabouts, it seemed only logical, once they'd exhausted their resources, to summon the help of the police. To the station, ho! Sophia snapped the whip and off they went. Was that mule getting pissed, or what?

As the *corps* rattled onward in yet another new direction—and toward a new agenda—The Ticketmaster had begun unraveling the mysteries of modern history. Of course, in his way of thinking, he would have the whole scheme down pat by midnight. In actuality, The Ticketmaster himself had begun unraveling. In his expansive thinking, the Confederates, the Revolutionary soldiers, the Elizabethans courtiers, the Union Army's hospital personnel and all the others he'd observed this evening were joined in a grand enactment. A living and breathing pageant depicting every stage in Western history since Romulus and Remus had unfolded before his very eyes.

In a matter of minutes, The Ticketmaster's entire world became one massive panorama of historical landmark events, international stalemates, conquests and the battles fought in the process. He saw Caesar murdered, Jean d' Arc burned at the stake, Anne Boleyn beheaded, Lincoln assassinated, American Revolutionary war soldiers gored with bayonets, Civil War confederates blown to pieces by Union cannon fire, flashing semaphores, flares lighting the skies, bombs bursting, the Star Spangled Banner, and the answer! The answer was education. The public had both a right and need to know its bloody history, he concluded. They shouldn't have to pay to learn about their history. The Society for the Study and Enactment of Anachronism doesn't charge for its educational benefits, but they can only do so much. He must do his part. With his connections, he can make major contributions to the cause!

The frenzied Ticketmaster rushed back to the museum in the dark hours of the night to talk to his friends, the wax figures whose vital signs were—in his mind—only temporarily suspended. This cause would rally them. His blindly driven mental state only gathered momentum once back in familiar territory. Over the next several hours, he worked harder and faster than ever before in his life. He felt superhuman. Nothing could stop him. He had unlimited capabilities and unlimited energy to carry out his mission.

FRENCH QUARTER FOLLIES

So absorbed was The Ticketmaster in the planning stages of his massive undertaking, that he completely missed the excitement on Conti Street. A loose mule still in harness caused quite a commotion gallavanting up the street toward Rampart. Crowds of wide-eyed tourists gathered on the sidewalks and filed into the street as the mule passed by. Since traffic on Conti travels in the opposite direction, toward the river, the mule encountered a ready-made obstacle course of moving cars and pedestrians. The crowds following behind provided the same for those in pursuit. What a scene! Galloping hard and fast once he reached Rampart, the mule found his way to the stables long before the entanglement on Conti Street could be dislodged.

Before the *corps du jour* found the police station, the police found them. They lay in a heap on the corner of St. Peter and Chartres, half covered by their once rickety and now fractured, muleless carriage, the one once ridden in by countless celebrities. By the time the accident occurred, the entire group collectively could not muster the faculties to become one functional driver and the mule had had enough. Traveling at a rapid speed around yet another corner on their way to the police station, they clipped a street sign post with their right rear carriage wheel, severing it completely and doing considerable damage to the sign post and the adjacent, illegally parked automobile it hit. The sensible mule took off before someone blamed him and there they lay. The Duke, who observed the accident from a distance, wanted to help, but because anxiety interfered, he hesitated. He noticed how Vincent protected the shaken Catahoula hound, Glendale, from the impact of the fall.

It took forever for the police to untangle this ensemble of vagabonds, not to mention their story about The Ticketmaster's disappearance, their belief he was kidnapped, and their valiant efforts to find him. With the exception of the rapper who was a minor, the whole group was held responsible for the street sign damages and Sophia was cited for a moving violation. The police showed no interest whatsoever in the whereabouts of The Ticketmaster despite the lively protests of the *corps du jour*. Little did any of them—the police or the vagabonds—know why that would have been a good idea. The party broke up as they all set out to play Capture-the-Mule.

Their preoccupation with the little band of gypsies prevented the police from carrying out a number of their usual duties, patrolling the streets in particular. Which is one reason it took so long to restore order on Conti Street. Furthermore, capturing—well, actually locating—the mule took additional time and energy. What confusion! All the while—and it took hours to locate him (actually the entire night)—the mule must have been standing outside the stable doors, still pissed but waiting patiently. Smart, that mule! Sophia's friend, Squeaky, found him there when he reported to work at six in the morning. Not a soul thought of checking to see if he might have returned to the stables.

Sunrise came all too soon for the weary revelers. They were still picking up the pieces of their carriage and their personal belongings, muttering about how hard it was these days to make a living, how nobody allows them to have a good time and how the police seem to have it in for them. Sunrise also revealed to these and other early-bird Quarterites the whereabouts and workings of the missing Ticketmaster. How different this evening might have been were it not for the meeting of the local chapter of The International Society for the Study and Enactment of Anachronism. While members of the corps were playing Capture -the-Mule, The Ticketmaster was playing let my people go! There they were in all their splendor. The entire cast of every scenario at the Wax Museum now resided inside the park in Jackson Square. And right in the middle, in front of the statue of Andrew Jackson, sat the *Duc d' Orleans*!

FRENCH QUARTER FOLLIES

EMPTY HANDED

As the bewitched Ticketmaster feverishly arranged his open air diorama under cover of darkness in Jackson Square, he mumbled constantly but incoherently. "Never again" and "my people" would have been audible were all his subjects not hearing impaired. All the historic figures from the Wax Museum on Iberville found themselves appropriately, if not artistically, grouped and on display in new and natural surroundings. "The public will be properly exposed," he'd mutter, the words bubbling through the sweat pouring down his face across his lips. If not the public, the wax figures were surely becoming exposed! After completing his masterpiece, The Ticketmaster stood way back, smiled—despite the fact he could barely see the fruits of his labor—then quickly hid in the bushes to watch the facial expressions of the thousands of spectators he expected. Exhaustion was irrelevant.

The Ticketmaster's lunatic efforts attracted some attention, yes, but ever so slowly since the figures were so lifelike. As the unlikely ensemble of French Quarterites involved in last evening's carriage accident on St. Peter succeeded in corralling their runaway mule (that's how *they* told it), finished picking up the pieces of their carriage, and recovered their meager belongings, they began their diaspora on foot. The first of that discouraged group to pass by Jackson Square was none other than Michael Jackson, the impersonator. All the others, with the exception of Maury, headed for destinations in the other direction. Maury decided to clean up his wounds in the City's watertrough for mules on Decatur Street before making his way back to his less than humble abode. He'd heard that mule saliva had medicinal powers. Some of his abrasions required attention, at least cleansing, he figured. Otherwise, he wasn't hurt.

DR. PAUL RODENHAUSER

The Michael Jackson character, as Maury thought of him, never noticing the ticket master's splendid display of characters, walked on over to Canal to catch a sturdier carriage than the one he just left—an RTA bus. Maury, on the other hand, did notice—did he ever—despite his fatigue and fiery brushburns, and he immediately identified the central figure in the park. The Duke had been the focus of Maury's attention since his arrival in the French Quarter in the aftermath of Mardi Gras, although Maury's disposition regarding the Duke was changing over the course of time. While Maury's celebration of his own genius in predicting the Duke's arrival in the French Quarter had been declining, suspicions about the Duke's persona as a cover for another identity steadily increased. Then, just last night, it came to him!

What Maury hadn't discussed with anyone to date, not even with his friends *du jour* who'd just departed, involved a great deal of detective work on his part, which he figured must have been brilliant. Why otherwise would he experience so many headaches these past few months? The discussion last evening by his carriage mates clinched his theory, particularly Jake's belief that the Duke is a pantomime artist, but also Ginger's hunch about Hollywood. Maury's previous preoccupations included mimes and the Bead Lady, primarily. His desensitization to these figures as a result of his therapy at Charity afforded him a period of quietude. When the Duke appeared, however, a more rarefied version of earlier paranoia materialized and smoldered but only as skepticism. As coincidence would have it, the waxen likeness of the *Duc d' Orleans,* who'd taken up residence in Jackson Square today, could not have been a better replica of the living *Duc d' Orleans* who took up residence in the French Quarter several months ago. Identical twins are less alike.

Maury seemed spellbound at the sight of the Duke. He, himself, became immobile for a brief time. First care for the brushburns, he thought. Later, he'd carry out a strategic plan to once and for all solve the mysteries lurking in the dark nooks and crannies of the French Quarter. Day by day, Maury was feeling less fearful of coming to terms with his own extraordinary capabilities—in a word, his brilliance.

Like Maury, Clarissa knew Jackson Square well. Because she

now lived on Decatur Street in the upper French Quarter, it was natural for Clarissa to walk around or through the park on the way to and from work. For the past several months, she'd been seeing more and more of the Duke. Because her employer, who obligingly and carefully brought the Duke along when they all drove back to the French Quarter after that emotional day in Mobile, also provided him with food, Clarissa and the Duke had occasion to meet at least once a day. Her self confidence, her interest in her appearance, and her mood improved so noticeably since their reunion that heads now turned to appreciate her wonderful, vibrant beauty.

On that bittersweet afternoon in Mobile, the Duke's emotions began to thaw slowly. How could he not have felt something, if not elation, to be found in a strange city by the only local person who tried to befriend him? Those same feelings not being tapped were the irrepressible needs initially responsible for drawing him to the French Quarter. These days, he talked to Clarissa and—except to satisfy his public with rote phrases—only to Clarissa, albeit haltingly. Though his physical immobility had disappeared completely, his voice still faltered when emotions invaded. Clarissa had earned his confidence. Although both tended to withdraw from any physical expression of tenderness, they actually touched more often than accidents would have allowed.

This soon to be even more eventful day turned out to be anything but sunny, but the heat could take its toll. It took more time than usual for the French Quarter to rev up energy this morning. The park's nearsighted caretaker didn't oversleep today, so he unlocked the gates well before the shroud of haze lifted high enough to illuminate the waiting surprise, the gift to the American public designed to educate them about history. The waxworks waited patiently.

Eager to meet the Duke early for breakfast, Clarissa cut through the park this muggy morning. Excited and emotionally vulnerable vis-à-vis recent developments between her and the Duke, she was totally unprepared for the disarming experience which followed. The unrecognizing gaze of an immobile figure— unmistakably, the Duke—seated squarely in the middle of the park, collided head on with hers. Memories of the experiences they'd shared recently rushed in to make this encounter a thousand times more excruciating than their almost identical convergence in Mobile and, therefore, a *déjà vu* of extraordinary power. Clarissa began to wonder if any of the events of the past months had actually happened.

The Duke's inability to respond to her evoked in her the most heartwrenching pain for him but also overwhelming personal devastation. Quite automatically, she grasped a crumpled piece of paper lying beside his hand on the bench and read its contents.

Carnival

concealed
 and naked
 les enfants
delivered again
   to the bondage
     of remembrance
  to provide
    and endure

disavowed
  symbols
 pensioned with pain
delivered again
   to the kingdom
     of good intentions
  and slavery
     to tradition

wounded
  by generations
 imbedded
and delivered
  again and again
    til misery
  explodes their masks
     of tolerance

FRENCH QUARTER FOLLIES

an absence
    of ills
      is a state of wellbeing
happiness hovers
        let the carnival begin!

gauzy disguises
      whisper the language
    of hope
to the really born
        and spirits soar
           delivered again
    to a prankish
        benevolence

laissez les bon temps roulez!

figures merge
    as marchers strut
  delivered again
to a meandering crowd
      spirits
        in search of meaning
    charms
        in search of deliverance

is life
    but circular
    like
the Kingcake?

Throw me somethin' Mister!

Clarissa's body responded. Automatically, with no fore-thought whatsoever, she ran away. Was this a cruel joke? Had the Duke been abused? Had he regressed again in order to protect himself? Was he rejecting her? In effect, yes! The poem suggested to her that he'd given up hope. Life no longer had meaning. As she ran toward the coffee shop to find her employer, these thoughts began triggering an emotional avalanche. Crashing disbelief in everything she'd ever seen, heard, felt, thought, touched, or tasted consumed her. What she thought was love felt like emptiness. She kept running—past the coffee shop, beyond the French Quarter, through the Faubourg Marigny to Elysian Fields Avenue. She needed more help than any one person could give. A short time later, her social worker from Chartres Mental Health Center helped her into the psych ward at Charity, whereupon, reaching her old room, she fell asleep instantly.

The ward psychiatrist, Fred, couldn't believe his eyes either. Only he could have identified the origin of the crumpled poem Clarissa carried with her to the ward. He himself had penned it and, in fact, had trashed it. Clarissa's intake interview with Fred lasted only minutes because of her acute distress and because she was well known to Fred. Even otherwise, had he tried to carry out complete reevaluation of her status, she might not have shared with him anything more than a description of the circumstances that brought her in, if that. The details were too painful. As it was, she only reported that she came upon an unresponsive figure in a period costume in Jackson Square on her way to work. In addition to the shocking nature of this experience and its subsequent emotional effects, Clarissa did mention that the unsettling nature of the poem added immeasurably to her distress.

For all Fred knew initially, this could have been a dead body she encountered. The later description of the figure in Jackson Square, however, the reappearance of another one of his poems, and the association between the two puzzled Fred enormously.

From an artist's perspective, Fred knew the figure well. From a clinician's perspective, he knew that the Duke and Dean were one and the same, and that Dean, an eloped involuntary patient, could have been forced to return to the ward some months ago. Because the police failed to locate him within twenty-four hours of his elopement, however, they'd all moved on to more pressing matters, and because the Duke seemed to be functioning well enough in the French Quarter, Fred chose to ignore what he knew. While keeping a trained eye on the Duke's behavior almost daily, Fred had the strong impression of significant improvement to the point that he seemed out of danger, but the recent immobility reported by Clarissa clearly represented a massive regression. This inability to care for himself, plus the potential for harm to the Duke, warranted intervention on Fred's part. Absolutely! He called the police, gave them a description, asked them to locate the Duke in Jackson Square and bring him to the hospital on an Order of Protective Custody.

Fred assured the police there would be no resistance on the part of the patient. The police didn't anticipate any problem with mistaken identity given the description provided them, nor would they be surprised about the patient's attire, Fred figured. This was, after all, the French Quarter, and these were veteran officers.

From a distance, earlier this morning, Maury's eye caught Clarissa just as she ran from the park. About that time, the heat of the morning had begun irritating The Ticketmaster as he lay tucked away behind the bushes in the corner of the park nearest Jax Brewery, camera in hand. Still very much invested in his charges as living characters, The Ticketmaster felt sorely disappointed in the reception so far accorded his herculean undertaking. He couldn't believe that Quarterites—or tourists, for that matter—could be so indifferent to history, but especially his fellow French Quarterites. What a revolting development!

The Ticketmaster's interpretations of the exchange or lack of it between Clarissa and the Duke coincided with hers, incidentally. He wondered, too, why the Duke didn't respond. Any congruence between his and Maury's beliefs about the Duke remained untested up to this point.

As time ticked by this cloudy morning, The Ticketmaster began to reflect on the wisdom of his recent actions, not to mention the legality. What is The Ticketmaster's problem? It started with depression in his mid-twenties, apparently. Five years ago, just before his thirtieth birthday, he got himself in *big* trouble for writing bogus invoices for furniture orders where he worked as an interior designer on commission. As if this weren't enough to get a grown man's attention, he later indulged in gambling to the point of going bankrupt, losing his side business and most of his personal property, including his Jaguar and townhouse. Lithium helped considerably, but arrived a bit late from a financial perspective. On occasion, however—and this was one of them—The Ticketmaster felt sure that he had no need for medication. Can the "historical" events of this day after Bastille Day then be attributed to a Lithium deficit? Yes, maybe, but even so, if history is any predictor, rather than being not guilty by reason of lunacy, the clever Ticketmaster will look for a way to be simply not guilty.

If the Duke is a sitting duck for Maury's strategic plan, then The Ticketmaster is a stool pigeon. Premeditation on the basis of paranoia accounts for the first of these two forecasts—foul as they are as metaphors—and hypomanic synapses account for the second.

Maury had to make his move. No amount of deliberation would deter him, so why deliberate? Maury's surprise strategy *must* work the first time. It had to, because a second chance would be highly unlikely. Walking slowly up to the bench where the Duke sat, still motionless, Maury did pause to deliberate, contradicting his previous resolve—but only briefly.

His faint utterance could have been lip-read, "the time is now," his mumblings resembling those of The Ticketmaster during his moment of truth.

Again he hesitated. Let's review this one more time, he thought. Maury learned a long time ago to double-check his thinking. What he didn't learn was to check it against a standard other than his own. Once again, he reviewed the timing and circumstances of both the Bead Lady's disappearance and the Duke's arrival. Once again, he astounded himself with his monumental discovery.

Maury positioned himself at less than an arms length directly in front of the immobile figure. With the finesse of an olympic fencer and driven by the need to know so characteristic of mad scientists, he thrust his right hand squarely into the Duke's crotch.

"There it is! *Voila!* The answer is here, right here in the anatomy," he said to himself, groping again to make doubly sure. "Right. Here it is!"

Not only not well endowed, as folklore would have predicted, the Duke clearly lacked the genital anatomy congruent with his external appearance.

"Aha! The Duke *is* the Bead Lady in disguise," Maury proclaimed, forgetting to be quiet lest he draw attention to himself.

The now alert Ticketmaster heard only the "aha." Because these wax figures were not anatomically correct, Maury, our hero, succeeded in proving nothing at all, no pun intended.

So surprised was Maury at the flash from The Ticketmaster's camera, that he never noticed the absence of any response, even reflexive movement on the Duke's part. For Maury, planning ahead took so much concentration he had little energy left to think things through—that is, beyond the mission at hand, so to speak. In this case, he hadn't even thought about how the Duke might respond. Nor did he have time to think of it now. By the time Maury could say "Bead Lady" and back out of the Duke's personal space, The Ticketmaster had caught the attention of a mounted policeman on Decatur and reported Maury's theft of the waxed figures from his museum on Iberville. Maury was caught red-faced and empty-handed! Off they went, two on foot, one on horseback. Back to the police station, ho!

It was late morning by the time all the administrative paperwork was completed and the Duke was escorted in a wheelchair to the psych ward. He was seated in the day room while the psychiatric staff carried out their admissions procedures. The other patients were distracted by TV cartoons, so Clarissa's view of the goings-on around the Duke remained unblocked. She stayed in her room, feeling on the one hand grateful for the Duke's safety, but on the other, terrified for her own welfare without being able to relate to him.

It took the staff about thirty minutes to reach a conclusion about the Duke's condition. And, this followed two unrevealing mental status examinations and a neurologic examination with very unusual findings. The neurologic examination involved pin pricks, finally, with progressively deeper and deeper punctures, but no reactions—and no blood! One of the more astute medical students noticed very fine wax slivers around the puncture marks.

Attesting to her increasing psychological strength and native intelligence, Clarissa figured out the diagnosis even before the staff verified their collective findings and agreed

142

they'd been duped. Talk about empty-handed and embarrassed! Fred, the ward psychiatrist, was so thoroughly angered he began sputtering and almost lost it. "Incredible! What a bunch of rocket scientists we are," he shouted in a shrill voice that almost sounded like the Bead Lady's.

Fred managed at the last minute to gain control and to maintain his professional decorum, however. This, at least, gave everyone something to rejoice about because they always feared what might be behind Fred's facade. Meanwhile, using the keys the medical student lost while in her room during her previous hospitalization, Clarissa quietly let herself out of the hospital ward and joined the anatomically correct and very much alive Duke on Ursulines for lunch.

FRENCH QUARTER FOLLIES

REPRIEVE

Sophia brought Maury a candy bar from Fred's trash but no poems. Maury told Sophia the whole nine yards about how he'd been framed. He had to clarify to Sophia that the photograph he described remained unframed—he hoped—and that he was using a figure of speech about himself. "Falsely accused," he explained, trying harder. Her tendency to take things literally got in the way of conversation, whether meaningful, like this one, or not. Maury went on to report another event almost equally disturbing to him. His jailmates complained so bitterly about his hygiene that he had to be scrubbed down before a sense of equilibrium could be restored in the lock-up. Sophia understood his feelings about that pretty well, but in the back of her mind the words "framed" and "falsely" kept on reverberating. This is the kind of thing that made communication tough sledding for Sophia, not to mention relationships. Words got stuck. They piled up. The more words, the more confused she'd become.

Jackson Square looked like it does every December after the annual Christmas Carol Sing-a-long when candlewax covers everything. Sophia said it was closed to visitors. Maury wasn't impressed. They couldn't possibly blame that on him. He never attended the sing-a-longs. Maury's confusion stood on its own merit. Sophia hadn't caused it, although her style might have jostled his neurons a bit. Words didn't pile up in Maury's case so much as his own observations didn't all make it into the hard drive for processing. He would listen to accounts of different events or circumstances, and they would remain distinct like a series of small, discrete snapshots instead of pieces to be factored into the bigger picture. He would also miss some of the pieces. Although he picked up on the time sequence related to the Bead Lady's disappearance and the Duke's appearance, for example, he missed the significant differences in age, demeanors and states of mind, focusing only on gender as the decisive factor. His versions of what is going on in these snapshots are generally based on previous experiences. His overriding suspicions accounted for his moments of brilliance, too, but also for the background of fragmentation so characteristic of his mental activity. His ability to scan the environment seems limited to only one focus at a time and his resources are easily overloaded by the intensity of his vigilance. On the other hand, Maury deserved some credit in this particular case. Maybe he knew some things others didn't. Maybe he has more confidence in the possibilities of what can transpire in the French Quarter.

Maury stashed the candy bar, leaned against the bars, and sighed. His moment of truth brought no conscious satisfaction whatsoever. Uncharacteristically, he admitted this to Sophia. By now, he might not have been barhopping but he would be holding court on his corner celebrating his colossal discovery and his daring adventure. He knew for sure that nobody sober or otherwise would be willing to risk taking a situation like that in hand the way he did. At a deeper level, Maury began to feel reassured as he talked about it. At least his suspicions were validated. The Duke is a Duchess according to the critical piece of evidence— or lack of it—on which he focused, not knowing his prey was a wax figure, let alone anatomically incorrect.

In terms of consequences, which he hadn't considered in advance, Maury could now say he'd met the enemy—The Ticketmaster. The worst that could happen to him had already happened. Of course, it was heavy duty confinement, but it could have been another kind of restriction like black magic. Voodoo could have jeopardized his health or his life. Maury couldn't help thinking that his present circumstances related back to the Bead Lady through The Ticketmaster just like he used to think she affected him through mimes and Doberman "pinchers." Well, he'd been in jail before, no big deal! It could be worse. It could be worse.

The collusion between the Bead Lady disguised as the Duke and The Ticketmaster became a new thread in Maury's tapestry of problems, not to mention the revelation that the Bead Lady is truly a chameleon. In the past, her layers of black always betrayed her whereabouts. These new developments would require considerable thought, but at the moment Maury's attention focused on another dilemma—*his* whereabouts. Sophia stood on the other side of the bars, still sorting through words. They talked again. Bail wasn't an option, but wait! He had an alibi! Why hadn't he thought of that before? Until just a short time before he was caught red-handed—or more correctly, empty handed and red-faced—Maury was one of a band of gypsies whose merrymaking began in the early evening and ended rather abruptly sometime before sunrise. Then came the chores—catching up with the mule, cleaning up the broken carriage pieces, and washing up to decontaminate the injuries. He was alone less than an hour. How could he possibly have relocated the entire cast of Wax Museum characters to Jackson Square Park and reassembled them in that short amount of time?

At Maury's hearing, all the gypsies but Vincent, the rapper, showed up. Sophia rounded them up. Already feeling lucky to be exonerated from paying for his share of the damaged street sign, Vincent was afraid that he'd be required to chip in for damages to the carriage, so he reneged. Of course, the issue here related to the wax figures, not the carriage, but Sophia would have had trouble explaining what she, herself, didn't completely understand. She didn't try. Everyone swore on a stack of Bibles that Maury traveled all night with them and that he couldn't possibly be implicated in the theft and defacing public property charges. Their credentials weren't very impressive, especially when one of the witnesses claimed to be Michael Jackson. There also stood Sophia the bag lady, Ginger the prostitute, and Jake the custodian, all familiar, but surely not famous.

When Sophia smiled at the referee, his first impression—that she'd just finished a poppyseed bagel—quickly yielded to the real cause of the black spots on her teeth. Tooth decay represented one of the few common characteristics of this little band of gypsies, except for Vincent, thanks to floride.

The court referee decided in Maury's favor, finally. Albeit too late to celebrate in a style befitting, at least, Maury's estimation of the occasion, they all congregated on Maury's street corner hangout to drink rum and sing. Maury played the violin majestically while fiddling with the solutions to his newest problems. Strange as it may seem, this motley crew had bonded together.

The waxen groups had bonded in a different way for a different reason, not fear of the outside world or a wish for a common cause or any particular emotional need. The heat created a certain cohesion, an undeniable adherence to adjacent objects! Early that same afternoon, the police returned the partially melted, misshapen wax figures to their rightful residence on Iberville. The manager did not react kindly to the situation and demanded that The Ticketmaster, who'd called in sick, report to his station irrespective of his health status. In fact, the manager was beside himself with outrage by the time The Ticketmaster arrived. All the evidence—or, once again, lack of it—for this shocking escapade pointed to The Ticketmaster. Who else but he and the manager had a key? No signs of a break-in could be found. Yes, insurance would cover the costs of restoration. What about lost business in the meantime, however, and the deductible? Whether or not The Ticketmaster knew anything about this catastrophe became a secondary issue when the manager finally calmed down long enough to realize his employee's condition, which worsened—if that was possible—at the thought of no pay while the museum was closed for repairs.

The Ticketmaster's call in sick proved to be bonafide, after all, but both The Ticketmaster and the manager had physical illness in mind. The Ticketmaster was higher than a kite. Ideas flew past faster than lightning. He might even have mentioned Ben Franklin at this moment! Sentences became salads of gibberish. A shot of Haldol at Charity helped a lot. The Ticketmaster became the third admission from the French Quarter this very day, although one had already eloped and the second required no attention whatsoever. The Duke still sat, or shall we say sat—very still—in the day room. Discharge for this kind of patient represented an unprecedented challenge. The only patient to recognize the Duke, The Ticketmaster responded to the waxen figure quite positively. Others were wary to say the least. So were staff. Spooky, they thought. Scary, so lifelike yet so lifeless.

The Duke's daunting influence on the ward was palpable for reasons quite obvious to all concerned, and all, except The Ticketmaster, were *very* concerned. His presence for The Ticketmaster proved to be incredibly effective, more meaningful than any known form of therapy for his or any condition severe enough to require clinical attention. This life-size toy soldier became his constant companion, and The Ticketmaster's rate of recovery miraculously exceeded that of any patient ever treated for mania or, for that matter, any disorder on the ward, bar none, regardless of severity. And what a relief for the staff that they didn't have to solve the problem of disposition regarding the Duke. Discharge plans for a wax figure can be challenging as they discovered, especially in the absence of a known guardian. Was this case worthy of publication? Fred, the ward psychiatrist, decided to report the case at the weekly ward conference and again later at departmental grand rounds.

Clarissa found the Duke's anatomically correct and physiologically fully functioning counterpart in real life to be exceedingly therapeutic, too. With the help of her companion she recovered very quickly from her acute distress. The Duke showed unusual concern. Having been confronted with the possibility of losing him helped Clarissa reach out even more. It didn't feel risky. The Duke's growing awareness of his importance to her helped his healing immensely. He began talking with her about some new emotions with which he was feeling some uneasiness. This, too, drew them closer. Clarissa's employer noticed that they were holding hands as they walked toward the river in the evening.

At grand rounds, Fred reviewed the literature on the historical and contemporary treatments of bipolar disorder, manic phase, and then enlarged his discussion to include lesser known treatment approaches, sometimes called adjunctive therapies. These included pet therapy, plant therapy, and some other activity oriented approaches like music therapy, play therapy for children, and psychodrama. No references in the literature could be found on life size doll therapy. Fred presented a synopsis of a paper he collaborated on, titled, "The Benign Exploitation of Human Emotions: Adult Women and the Marketing of Cabbage Patch Kids." Some long time ago, with a colleague, Fred had presented this paper at an annual meeting of the International Psychohistorical Association in New York City. He fondly remembered the intrigue of the audience, whose questions extended the presentation beyond its scheduled time by almost an hour. "This study of the interaction between adult women and Cabbage Patch dolls provided a window into the ways in which many people cope with emptiness and loneliness." Fred concluded, with a demeanor deserving of acknowledgment for his scholarship, untiring attention, and artful approach to this subject (see insightful footnote* below). He also summarized the psychiatric history of his patient, Alger, whose two-day hospitalization turned out to be the shortest in hospital history for a full blown manic episode.

Although he was born in New York City, Alger's parents had immigrated from West Africa as young adults. Having no brothers or sisters, he had more attention than otherwise would have been available, but some of it proved destructive. The absence of an extended family deprived Alger of the kind of safe haven kids need when parents are distracted or abusive. Both conditions applied here. Alger's mother and father worked hard to make ends meet and the father's explosive temper caused Alger untold difficulties. Although infrequent, visits with aunts, uncles, cousins, and grandparents in West Africa helped some with his overall identity, but the stormy, unpredictable household he grew up in, and his own genetic predisposition, left him with a tendency toward unstable relationships, his own moods being both the cause and effect of discord. When he was sixteen, his father died of a heart attack, and at seventeen, he was orphaned. He endured the suicide of his chronically depressed mother with no show of emotion. Neither professional or much other help was available to him at this point in his life. Fortunately, his parents' estate paid for his education in full and then some. Although he floun-

dered and switched majors frequently, Alger succeeded at graduating with a degree in Art History. Partly related to his final choice of majors
and its usefulness in the job market, a very chop-
py work history followed his college years. Perhaps his original interest in theater also helps
explain his attraction to the Wax Museum. Considering his deterioration since about age twenty-seven, the match might be a good
one—steady employment, less stimulation than
theater, an historic genre, and the availability of
people to interact with but in a structured setting.
His manager, too, couldn't help but be astounded at Alger's attachment to the wax figure of the
Duke and the effect of the relationship on his
rapid stabilization. Perhaps partly as a result of
staff efforts to incorporate the Wax Museum
manager into Alger's treatment, and partly out of
his sensitivity to Alger's bond with the Duke,
Alger was allowed to keep his position. Alger's
gratitude for this second chance expressed itself
in renewed dedication to his work.

Alger's astonishing recovery was credited to the presence of
the Duke. Fred briefly reviewed the very minimal use of medication which was limited to one rather low dose of Haldol and
Lithium, a drug which requires a considerable period of time to
take full effect, certainly longer than two days. The audience
reacted visibly and audibly to the two day turnaround of signs
and symptoms. Fred's final discussion centered on developmental and current dynamic implications of full-size, life-like mannequins in the treatment of psychiatric disorders using Kohut's
theoretical construct of twinning as a basis for his presentation.

Except for the museum, activities in the French Quarter had
become business as usual. Everything slowed in the summer.
Back into his music and other routines now for several days,
Maury could not forget about his recent exploits, nor did he
recover fully from his feelings about being robbed of his moment

of glory. Now consistently vigilant for the Bead Lady, the chameleon voodoo Queen cross-dressing in a Duke's outfit, Maury became more preoccupied. He spent his time collecting mental snapshots of everything "under"—the underground, undersides, underworld, and underwear. His little support group provided some solace, though each had their own fixations and foibles to address.

The French Quarter was quiet in July, Bastille Day being only a small blip in the annual calendar of events. Several days after his release from jail, Maury walked down Iberville whistling 'La Marseillaise' on his way to find Sophia whom he hadn't seen recently. No doubt he'd find her making her rounds. Maury felt queasy coming up to the Wax Museum. He began wishing he'd chosen Bienville or St. Louis Streets, but instead of switching he moved only as far away as the opposite side of Iberville Street and kept walking. The dusk and the distance caused him to squint, but when looking over his shoulder as he frequently did he could have sworn he saw The Ticketmaster carrying the Bead Lady—cross dressed as the Duke—into the Wax Museum on Iberville. Sweat poured into his smelly overcoat. "Isn't this where I came in?" he muttered.

FRENCH QUARTER FOLLIES

EN GARDE!

Heads bobbed busily on Maury's corner at St. Peter and Royal. His little band of gypsies huddled to discuss the latest news. Vincent, the rapper, had to split with his friends to be there. He enjoyed hearing the news of the culture he lived in, and no one in the French Quarter would have information more current or more colorful than this enterprising group. They'd been meeting fairly regularly lately, about the same time each evening after dark. Their antennae tapped a limitless range of resources from tarot cards to the *CityBusiness* news, trash bags, the flea market, hallucinations, historical markers, graffiti, the *Times-Picayune*, astrology, delusions, science, gossip, weather reports, porn mags and Windsor Court menus. Topics often shifted more quickly than heads could bob or hands could gesture.

Sophia always brought an earful from the carriage drivers. Their contacts turned up tidbits about who's in town, movies underway and where filmings were located, incoming shows, political meetings, and the like. She picked up a lot. Sorting it out was another problem. Jake's contributions came from the art world—the latest prints, paintings, and scuttlebutt about the movie and theater people, who has AIDS, who's been arrested and why.

Maury's unique contribution centered on music and musical events, but his domain also included thinly disguised reports of happenings in the underworld. Tonight, however, his attention rested on *all* recent events in the French Quarter. His suspiciousness required that he scan for information. Ginger shared pillow talk—Mafia news, political strategies, and business deals. Michael Jackson seemed to be outside the loop—too many internal distractions—but he didn't refrain from sharing them frequently. His latest was a belief that he was chosen to sing the Star Spangled Banner at the first Saint's game of the season. Vincent brought intelligence from the Market area, particularly about drugs, their quality and comparative costs. He could recite a veritable catalog of street pharmaceuticals.

Current events included The Ticketmaster's recent stint at Charity. Maury listened closely. Everybody in this little corps except Jake and Vincent had been there at least once. Sophia held the record. No one but Maury seemed to see this event as newsworthy. An unusual looking nun dressed in a natural linen habit hadn't been seen frequently on the streets of the lower French Quarter recently. Current events did not include the Duke. No one but Maury could remember when they last saw him. Actually, and unbeknownst to the intelligentsia, a resident of the Central Business District who needed a house sitter had arranged with Clarissa and the Duke to housesit at her home for two weeks. Clarissa's employer highly recommended them, hoping their relationship would benefit as well.

"Here's the deal." Maury interrupted the hubbub. "We need to talk about the Bead Lady."

He proceeded to share with the abruptly hushed audience his grave concerns about the Bead Lady's undercover presence in the French Quarter. Everyone in the group shared a significant degree of concern about this subject. At the deepest level, interest in the supernatural bound them together. They were whispering. Without repeating his recent experiences in Jackson Square Park, Maury nominated the Wax Museum on Iberville as the den of iniquity most deserving of investigation. The vote was unanimous even before he revealed his latest discovery. When the group heard about the diabolical duo recently seen entering the museum together, they descended a few more rungs on the ladder of civilization. Mob mentality replaced their usual marginal imbalance.

Bastille Day had come and gone but this little *corps* of Quarterites still embraced the spirit of rebellion. Deriving strength from each other and their pumped up leader, their resolve quickened as they discussed ideas. Storming the Wax Museum would require considerable planning. It couldn't be just one of those spur of the moment things, Maury cautioned the crusaders. A survey showed that not one of the group had prior experience in this kind of activity. Rehearsals were in order.

ANGELS AND PANCAKES

Michael Jackson impersonated The Ticketmaster as the others filed past, paying their fees and picking up brochures about the displays mounted inside as well as other French Quarter activities. They looked studious. They stayed focused. Disguises assured their anonymity. Everything's working. They're inside. What next? Find the Bead Lady! What about other customers? What about closing time? Is there an alarm system? Nobody thought about police surveillance. *"Jesus!" How do we remove the Bead Lady from the museum? What about a net? Is there a way to remove her venom once and for all? Drugs, maybe.*

While these partners in crime role-played their strategies, most of the residents in the French Quarter were asleep. Fred, the psychiatrist at Charity who lived on Dauphine not far from the museum, was an exception, having decided to once more review the puzzling cases he'd encountered this year. He'd consulted the literature frequently on exotic disorders and unexplained circumstances. Fred's preoccupations involved a depressed young woman admitted twice who had in her possession poems he'd personally written and thrown away, a paranoid street musician who eloped during a showering of Mardi Gras beads onto the nurse's station floor, a catatonic young man who disappeared mysteriously and sometime later showed up in the French Quarter in historical Mardi Gras attire, and a manic museum Ticketmaster whose mannequin-assisted recovery astounded the experts. Is this the therapy of the future? That distraction kept coming up. For some patients, adding mannequins to managed care will really cut treatment costs. On the other hand, mannequins sometimes stir up conflicts and create candidates for treatment, as evidenced by circumstances in which Clarissa and Maury were involved.

For the life of him, Fred could not make any sense of these situations. To make matters worse, all of these bizarre cases followed the simultaneous disappearance of the Bead Lady from the French Quarter and Fred's mynah bird, Emily, from his cage in Fred's living room. This memory never dimmed. The crowning blow to his clinical ego came as the result of the admission of a mannequin to the ward which identically matched the recent description of the formerly catatonic young man from Omaha. In his sleep deprived state, Fred began to wonder if everyone has a double somewhere in wax form. Then he wondered if he, himself, might be suffering from something like a delusion of doubles. Capgras' Syndrome flashed into his groping mind immediately. As a lowly medical student, he'd even diagnosed such a case once—a nebbish of a man insisting that the woman responsible for bringing him to the clinic so brusquely must be a look-a-like imposter posing as his wife. Had Fred's clinical prowess, his formerly recognized sixth sense for solving sticky problems, begun to wane?

Maury's little brigade completed their plans that same night. By this time the next night, their mission would be accomplished. Each had a distinct role and everything was synchronized, although watches were scarce commodities among them. Sophia took care of that deficiency in a jiffy from her stash of trinkets. Although they feared the full moon as much as any psychiatric emergency room staff, they agreed that they couldn't postpone their mission any longer. Besides, the light might be beneficial. One thing they hadn't thought about was the weather, but considering that any success for this crew would likely be accidental in nature, it was difficult to tell if the gaps in their collective thinking would work for or against them.

The appointed hour arrived. This nervous but determined little salvation army gathered early at an "undisclosed destination" in order to avoid attention. Unfortunately, Michael Jackson's hallucinations at the time it was announced caused the destination to be undisclosed to him as well, so Jake had to retrieve him from their habitual meeting place, Maury's corner. Now they were late. Should they take a cab? No, their paraphernalia would hardly fit even in the trunk, and besides the driver would notice something's fishy. If there were a seventh, it would have been natural to expect background music from Snow White and the Seven Dwarfs as this band of vagabonds echoed "Off to Work We Go" and began trudging across the French Quarter. Maury in particular felt irritation at their late start. The museum would close in forty minutes. They chose the late time to avoid the likelihood of other patrons.

Their *esprit de corps* waned a little by the time they reached Iberville Street. This turned out to be the hottest day of the year, a scorcher! The layers of clothing required to conceal their tools caused quite a lot of discomfort. Maury suffered most in that god-awful overcoat of his and any passing pedestrian would have suffered from the odor. Also unbearably hot, Maury's wig kept slipping from perspiration. As was his custom in times of crisis, he cross-dressed to avoid recognition. This time he wore Ginger's blonde wig to avoid being recognized in his usual cross-dress outfit. All of this was, of course, based on the highly questionable assumption that anybody cared. Ginger wore a black wig this evening, another one of Sophia's discoveries, and a black cape "borrowed" from a theater party she'd attended several years back. She resembled a vampire, with the exception of her teeth ,which were stained, stubby, and crooked. Inadvertently, Sophia's disguise, in large part, resulted from the absence of her usual odor. This afternoon she slipped and fell into the mule watering trough at the stable and came out half clean. Sophia was one unhappy camper for awhile. Because her outfit for this evening's gala came fresh from somebody's trash, Sophia's presentation this evening was almost as unrecognizable as her usual self as it was inappropriate. She wore a baggy polka dot clown outfit and a floppy velveteen hat. The outfit concealed the ropes she carried and the hat hid her rope-like hair equally well.

Jake looked like a locomotive engineer in coveralls, floppy work cap, denim shirt and hiking boots. His coveralls had pockets big enough to conceal flashlights and hammers, in case they had to break locks. Vincent looked like he always looked—bright pink hair standing straight up on the top, head shaved around the sides, gold earring, black clothing on very white skin, an olive tee-shirt, hightop black shoes, and a tattoo in black on his left arm that resembled a centuries-old wrought iron design. He claimed it was copied from the earliest example of Spanish iron work in the French Quarter. For some reason, the group trusted him to carry the money they'd gathered to pay their admission. The rest had their hands full. Michael Jackson trailed the pack as they rounded the last corner before reaching their destination. He wore ordinary clothing. He had no need to make a statement to the establishment through his appearance nor did he want to disguise his identity. It was so unmistakable it would have been futile, he thought. He wore sunglasses—to protect his eyes, he said.

Through the entrance to the museum lobby and up to the ticket desk they sauntered, having changed their gait from a dysrhythmic march to a southern stroll just outside on Iberville. Everyone tried to look amiable and studious as they browsed the counter and brochure rack for items of interest. Vincent fumbled forever to find the money entrusted to him. Yes, he had been sorely tempted. It would have bought beaucoup joints, but he came up with the funds. *Six tickets, please!*

Throughout this foreplay, Alger, The Ticketmaster of Jackson Square fame, did not recognize either Maury or Sophia and he hadn't ever seen even the undisguised versions of the other troupers. He worked diligently these days and protected the establishment to the very best of his ability. Since his encounter with the International Society for the Study and Enactment of Anachronism, Alger's propensity for social interaction resumed at its previously low level. He had few outside contacts. He talked with Sophia on her rounds on occasion, thus his earlier invitation to join this very group on the carriage ride. His life centered around the museum and his waxen friends, especially the *Duc d' Orleans*. Alger's remarkable recovery and new work ethic pleased his manager immensely.

The Ticketmaster mentioned that the museum would be closing in thirty minutes and wondered if they'd like to reconsider. "No," said Ginger, the designated speaker for the group, "we're leaving town in the morning. We'll hurry through," she added, wondering how her adlibbing would be received by the group.

So far, so good. The group's odd manner of dress and the bulkiness of their configurations did not go unnoticed, nor did the pungent odor which quickly permeated the lobby escape discernment. Alger thought the latter far exceeded the usual variations in body odors, regardless of nationality.

The odor soon followed the entourage as it moved into the bowels of the dimly lit, black-walled museum proper, its soft dramatic lighting focused on a whole series of lifelike scenes depicting the history of the region, but New Orleans in particular. As a result of a keen sense of the obvious, the few patrons lingering this late in the evening accelerated their pace. The same aroma which followed this little entourage as they passed through the lobby now preceded them into the purified atmosphere of the museum proper. This is just one example of where lack of awareness worked in their favor. Their chances of similar successes were countered-balanced by their elaborate strategies, all of which were undocumented and most of which were misremembered, not to mention unsound to begin with.

Upon entering the museum proper, the little band of faux troubadours felt satisfied that they'd successfully passed the test of their disguises, the first entry on their mental list of obstacles to overcome. A jumble of words and emotions arose from their group mass as they moved forward. They were awestruck by the drama which unfolded before their eyes. Jake noted that their plans hadn't allowed for emotional reactions and that they would have to move on. Maury's leadership skills had fallen victim to the heat and his foot soldiers were compensating. His presence, at least, lent a semblance of organization to their efforts. They had to move quickly now. Ginger urged them on.

A nun in a natural linen habit caught Maury's eye as they moved forward. But halfway down the first row of scenes, their search ended. There in the soft lighting of an 18th century drawing room stood the *Duc d' Orleans*. The emotions that slowed them down at this point were extremely intense. Everyone knew that they had just entered the domain of the infamous and powerful Bead Lady who had obviously adopted a new persona and who obviously resided in this very drawing room.

"Quickly, quickly," Vincent piped up. "Let's get on with it." They were all scared.

"All clear," whispered Jake as he returned from reconnaissance to determine the presence of other patrons.

While Jake was gone, Sophia whipped out of her billowy bag an amazingly close but smudgy and somewhat threadbare reproduction of the Duke's costume. No one in the French Quarter could compete with Sophia for resourcefulness. As if their lives depended on it, they all huddled around Michael Jackson in the drawing room and dressed him to match the Bead Lady's disguise. He didn't resist.

DR. PAUL RODENHAUSER

As chance would have it, the moment the lights began blinking to indicate closing time coincided with the most critical moment in their plan of plans. But, they decided not to worry when Jake pulled out his big flashlight. *It didn't work!* They panicked. Ginger hightailed it around to the exit into the lobby in order to attract The Ticketmaster's attention. In her haste, however, she tripped over a power cable. There they all stood in pitch darkness. One flashlight, the very small one, finally worked. Ginger's script required that in a few minutes she'd bring The Ticketmaster through the main entrance into the museum proper under the guise of needing to ask one final question. The little troupe of makeover artists would leave through the exit, simultaneously, of course.

After capturing The Ticketmaster's attention, Ginger proceeded slowly toward the entrance where Vincent listened behind the heavy door for their approaching footsteps. So far, so good. But everyone was running low on adrenaline. "Here they come," Vince barked in a whisper. Out went the little flashlight.

Mass confusion consumed the troupers as they clinched their final blow to the most destructive force ever known to the French Quarter. In the darkness, they had a fifty-fifty chance of getting it right at this point. With the dexterity of drawing a sword from its sheath, Maury whipped out a huge fishing net from under his soggy overcoat. No ordinary net, this one meant business and so did Maury. Using his last ounce of strength, he blindly flung the net over one of the two *Ducs d' Orleans*. Were it distinguishable, the *Duc's* skin color would have helped considerably in this, the most valiant battle ever staged against the underworld. As Ginger and The Ticketmaster entered the museum from the lobby, the scalawags were on their way out the exit to the lobby. Last to leave the museum proper, Jake accidentally kicked the power cable. The lights came on to find Ginger and Alger standing squarely in front of a perfectly posed *Duc d' Orleans* whose skin seemed remarkably dark. Alger checked the lighting system.

FRENCH QUARTER FOLLIES

NOT SO GERMAN

Confusion continued among the brigadiers as they fled into the moonlit night down Iberville and across Dauphine with their Bead Lady in a bag. Had they snared the right Duke? When they finally could agree on what was a safe enough distance from the museum to slow down, they stopped, exhausted from the emotional tension and the weight of their prisoner, not to mention the intense heat. *Thank God!* The figure inside the net did not resemble their comrade, Michael Jackson. They were home free. So taxed were these warriors by their mission to capture the leader of the underground, that they totally neglected to consider in advance what they would do with their prisoner. By this time Ginger had caught up with them, so they enjoyed the benefit of full membership in order to maximize their collective resources in solving this monumental problem.

They thought of the psych emergency room at Charity. Surely the Bead Lady would qualify as crazy enough, but would she benefit from treatment? What would change after she got discharged? They'd still be haunted by this wretched witch. Deciding to take matters in their own hands as was the custom in the days of old, they took the immobile figure to what was once the village plaza, now Jackson Square, and they placed the deplorable voodoo queen on display there—under guard, of course. She was not going to leave their sight again. So, enclosed in a massive fishing net, tethered to a stationary bench in Jackson Square, the transvestite Bead Lady became a community exhibit, a symbol of evil.

Whether or not the Bead Lady would understand the punitive nature of this public display had not been considered. This situation was to be the case, of course, only until this little group of nearly delirious masterminds could come up with the next move, logical or otherwise. They agreed they would take turns in shifts guarding her from the cover of nearby bushes, the same place Alger hid that fateful photogenic day. Maury remembered the price all too well.

Actually, Maury and his troupe had outstripped their ability to be creative. It seems that exhaustion had lowered them yet another rung on the ladder of civilization. They were simply repeating a vignette from the recent past that had been deeply imprinted in their memories, either by experience, as in Maury's case, or by repeated descriptions. In his previous state of mind, The Ticketmaster would have been delighted to know he made an impression. The case of the captured Bead Lady rested through the hot night.

When Clarissa passed Jackson Square the next morning enroute to work from the CBD, she startled at the sight of the netted Duke in the park. She could only guess that some pranksters were still playing games with the same mannequin she'd encountered recently. She knew her Duke slept soundly at home. Until her curiosity about her experience with the wax dummy earlier that day was satiated, however, she had to discuss the situation several times with her employer and her Duke. Both agreed it must have been a discarded replica from the Wax Museum.

Clarissa got along very well with her employer, an extremely skilled baker, well known in the community as a generous, warm-hearted, gentleman named Jean. His breads and pastries were in great demand, and his fantastic French King Cakes with almond filling were unequaled anywhere in the city of New Orleans. Previously, his shop on Ursulines Street belonged to a German immigrant who'd maintained the establishment as a bakery for thirty-some years. This being Jean's thirteenth year of owning and operating his bakery, he was surprised at still being confused with the previous owner, whose temperament and philosophy of life contrasted sharply with Jean's. Whereas the previous owner revered perfection, Jean cherished living for the moment. The previous owner worked around the clock. Jean worked half-days. The previous owner abstained from alcohol. Jean loved wine. The previous owner never took time off. Jean vacationed as often as possible. The previous owner was constricted and stingy. Jean was demonstrative and generous. The previous owner had an authoritarian manner. Jean was *laissez faire* through and through. This is not to say Jean was not dramatic and temperamental at times, but mostly as an expression of passion rather than authority. Clarissa considered herself exceedingly lucky to have responded to the ad for this position. Jean and his wife, Marya, represented the good parents she so desperately needed. They obviously cared about her very much.

Originally from Strasbourg in northeastern France, Jean learned the art of baking in his home town as a youngster. His aunt and uncle, his father's sister, provided for him what he and his wife embodied for Clarissa. They'd operated a bakery all of their lives, so Jean grew up knowing everything about baking. Wanderlust took him to Paris where he succeeded as a pastry chef in one of the best restaurants and then on to Martinique where he met his Creole wife, Marya. As a couple, they found that the French Quarter offered them the best of all possible worlds, and environment new to both of them, yet one in which they both felt comfortable. They appreciated the economically progressive, democratic social structure, as well as the city's unique culture, rooted, as it was, in French customs.

From the moment they met the Duke, Jean and Marya were touched by his need to belong. His feelings of emptiness became so painfully obvious during their drive back from Mobile. Because they had no children of their own and because they had ample space, they had offered the Duke their small guest quarters as a temporary apartment. The Duke's disposition flourished in response to their care and Clarissa's obvious interest. Jean and Marya felt the chemistry between the Duke and Clarissa held the key to a wonderful future for them. They were obviously good for each other.

By the time Jean reached Jackson Square to investigate Clarissa's concerns about the mannequin, the sun was almost overhead. The exhausted gypsies, each of whom had agreed to guard the Bead Lady in shifts of two hours, had all crashed in exhaustion. Sophia shook the others as soon as she awoke. The members of this motley crew rubbed their eyes in disbelief as they examined the remains of their prisoner. Jean watched in amusement from the gate. The empty uniform of a 18th century French lieutenant lay on the pavement, draped over a mellifluous puddle of very warm wax.

DR. PAUL RODENHAUSER

PERDIDO

The Duke and Clarissa were living together without recognizing it. With matchmaking in mind, Jean and Marya had taken the initiative in recommending them as housesitters to a friend who lived on Perdido Street. Both readily agreed, being inclined as they were to be helpful. When Clarissa worked, the Duke stayed close by the house and when she returned, he occasionally strolled to the fringe of the Quarter where he picked up a few dollars by posing for photographs. They stayed home together in the evenings. Although they had visited each other's apartments over the past four months or so, they had not sleep together, in fact, both had significant unease about sexual feelings, let alone sexual feelings in the context of a close relationship. Over the time they had spent together, however, they'd both moved to about the same place with regard to discomfort. They were both about the same distance from achieving sexual intimacy.

In the evenings they talked about their daily experiences, about their beliefs, and about themselves. Dean, the Duke, had finished college after a five-year struggle to put himself through. His grades suffered because of the hours he had to work to pay for room and board and tuition and books. Hardly was there enough for food and clothing, let alone entertainment. This year, since his arrival in the French Quarter, he'd entertained himself by reading fiction and biographies. This interest not only provided an education in language, literature, and history, it also gave Dean a sense of affirmation. He could identify with many of the characters in novels and incorporate their personages, their values, their beliefs, and relationships, into his enlarging repertoire of thoughts and feelings. Dean experienced a kind of restoration, if not reconstruction, over the past year. People have to experience wholesome dependency before being able to be truly independent. That's common knowledge. Indeed, Dean's regression took him back almost three centuries. Now that's a bit unusual, but wasn't he fortunate to have that opportunity? No telling how far backwards some people have to travel before being able to exist in the present, comfortably.

Dean obviously had the advantage of resiliency despite the appalling severity of his distress and he had the luxury of a generous and unique support system. The whole French Quarter became his playpen and he grew up all over again. Captivating in appearance and mannerisms, he naturally attracted attention and there was no real requirement to perform. Although still painfully shy, Dean now had the ability to integrate his thoughts and his feelings. He lived in the present without retreating to an inner world and he demonstrated ability not only to relate to people but to discriminate between superficial and deeper levels of relations. Physical contact to a point became comfortable and Dean learned to both trust his feelings and predict the responses of his environment. To the extent that anyone can trust another, Dean found himself trusting Clarissa, a growing feeling that started in Mobile just after Mardi Gras.

Not everyone has the wealth or critical combination of inner and external resources available to Dean and Clarissa, the chemistry between the two of them being a major pillar in their support system. Maury and Sophia, for example, just go slip slidin' along in their parallel lives. Things get a little better, things get a little worse. That's how it's been for Maury. Hard as he's tried, he can't seem to control the underground. Hard as Sophia's tried, she can't keep her thoughts sorted out. Jake can't seem to get out from behind the broom and Ginger, from under the bed covers. Vince will need considerable help, it appears. And then, there's Michael Jackson.

Back at the museum, Michael Jackson held it together as long as he could. He relaxed throughout the night after his comrades departed in darkness. But had anyone thought about morning? In fact, the planning brigade, that committee of the minds in which he held full membership, hadn't given any more thought to his plight than they did to their plans for their prisoner. The others were, of course, outdoors, free as birds to do what they wanted even if there were currently mesmerized by the second disappearance of the Bead Lady.

Michael Jackson conceded that maybe he, himself, didn't have the capacity to know ahead of time that he might be stranded in this drawing room indefinitely but, he began to think, shouldn't somebody have figured this out? When would this shouldn't end? Impersonation is one thing, but this is ridiculous. He, by trade, did not impersonate wax dummies for God's sake! This experience didn't compare at all to the kind of things he'd become used to, like singing the Star Spangled Banner at sports events. There's not even an audience here. His thoughts spoke too soon. The clock struck ten and the first patrons were let into the museum. Noticing one of the kids in one family munch on a granola bar reminded Michael Jackson that not only did he not have breakfast, but the likelihood of any food in the future was nil. And what about taking a leak? *Hey, what's wrong with this picture, folks?*

"I'm tired of this shit," sounded funny coming from a wax mannequin, especially the *Duc d' Orleans* standing in a French drawing room, but that's what he said. And with that, Michael Jackson walked! Off the stage and out the entrance he stomped, stopping long enough to ask The Ticketmaster the directions to the restroom. Patrons were dumbfounded. Three-hundred years later, the *Duc d' Orleans* takes a potty break!

The Ticketmaster, Alger, lost it momentarily but quickly regained his composure. He ushered the patrons to the street and closed the museum while hoping against hope that his manager would not choose this time to drop by. He locked the door securely and waited for Michael Jackson to return from the restroom. They talked a very long time then they went out to have breakfast. Passersby greeted the Duke as they were accustomed to doing but the Duke seemed a little tense this morning, they thought, and tanner than usual. His French seemed a little flimsy, too.

To the same degree that Michael Jackson had been feeling abandoned, deprived, and neglected all morning since awakening, he now felt befriended, cared for, and well nourished. Michael Jackson informed Alger to the best of his ability about what happened and how he got to be impersonating the *Duc d' Orleans* since closing time last night. He didn't name names because he couldn't quite remember them, having considerable difficulty with recent memory because of inner interferences. Alger knew very well that there were no duplicates of the *Duc d' Orleans* in the warehouse, so his need for Michael Jackson became all consuming. No Duke, no job. He was certain of that. Having not had this much attention for as long as he could remember, Michael Jackson had no problem agreeing to a deal. He would impersonate the Duke from ten to five each day in return for a place to sleep, meals, and five dollars a day for cigarettes and stuff. The museum, which became a happier place instantly, reopened immediately.

On her way home from working the breakfast shift only, today, Clarissa caught a glimpse of the black *Duc d' Orleans* with Alger who, of course, she didn't know. She felt extremely confused, but hoped that by the time she reached Perdido Street, she'd have come up with some rational explanation. Fortunately, she found Dean at home. They spent the late morning and early afternoon having a leisurely brunch with a mini-bottle of Mumm sparkling wine. Clarissa's anxiety and sense of helplessness associated with the multiple Dukes and the effects of the wine stirred unusually strong feelings. Both Clarissa and Dean felt a little overwhelmed by these newest developments.

Like Dean, Clarissa had the benefit of inner strength, recent good fortune, and a support system to help her to this point. She'd come a long way, particularly in the past few months. Life no longer caused her to struggle with sharp-edged emotions churning inside like a Cuisinart without a control button. She no longer felt that everybody in the world received a letter instructing them to ignore her and her tendencies to think in self-destructive terms seemed to have dissipated. Clarissa trusted her feelings and to the extent that anyone can trust another, she trusted Dean.

Early that afternoon, it rained as an electrical storm passed overhead. Dean and Clarissa simultaneously felt sleepy so they slipped into bed, the same bed. The wetness, the wine, the darkness, and the magnetism of their soon naked bodies created such feelings of engulfment that their bodies were thrusting before they were aware of their union. His penetration was so deep and their desire so intense that the heat of their climax held them together. Their hearts melted—like wax—and joined into one.

DR. PAUL RODENHAUSER

ENSEMBLE

Perdido turned out to be a key of sorts, but not the Perdido Key folks in these parts think of when they want to get lost. That's not to say that Dean isn't a traveler. In a little over a year, he sojourned from Omaha to the French Quarter to Charity through Mardi Gras to the early 18th century to Mobile and back to the Quarter. Maury's version of the odyssey detours Dean through the Wax Museum on Iberville instead of Mobile. The payoff, this young man's miraculous metamorphosis, would astound both believers and skeptics of behavioral change. Dean's transfiguration took him from belly-up to belly-down in less than a year. This, the most dramatic aspect of his odyssey, reflected an agonizing internal process which began as a state of surrender, a freezing of emotions and a physical immobility as convincing as that of any waxen figure ever observed. Likewise, his persona was empty. At this point in the course of Dean's odyssey, he showed every evidence of thinking clearly, feeling and functioning well, actually even copulating—belly-down—his position confirming the finale, the culmination of his inner voyage. Dean no longer felt like wearing his uniform.

Michael Jackson wore his uniform everywhere and with pride. His impersonations of the *Duc d' Orleans* at the Wax Museum became so popular that the museum extended its business hours by five hours per day. "M.J.," as he is affectionately called backstage, learned to impersonate the Duke not only in appearance and mannerisms, but also in voice, including a very convincing accent. His monologue, now staged four times daily, explains to visitors from all over the world the interests, activities, and accomplishments of the Duke. The Duke delicately avoided referring to his reputation for being a bisexual athlete, his main claim to fame. Nor did he reveal that it was his son's success as the French Regent, not his, that determined the name, New Orleans. He did include in his monologue the history of the exploration of the region by Sieur d' Iberville and his brother, Sieur d' Bienville, who founded the city and served four terms as governor of Louisiana.

Admission fees at the museum increased several times as word of the Duke's lively, inventive performances spread far and wide. Now a living history museum, it's as if all the figures respond to the Duke's deep voice with sparkling animation. Imaginations dance with history every time he speaks. Many patrons have heard his narration so many times they could recite it themselves.

The terms of M.J.'s employment, including his salary, have changed considerably. M.J., who is fortunately able to isolate his hallucinations and delusions long enough to please his public with flawless impersonations, is the object of envy for many, but particularly the little band of gypsies so instrumental in his success. How naive they were that sweltering evening when they dressed M.J. in the Duke's costume right there in the drawing room. Another beneficiary, much to Maury's chagrin, The Ticketmaster, Alger, has become a very happy man. As the new manager of the museum, he now has his own assistant, not to mention a handsome salary. His assistant manages the routine aspects of the business, mainly the bookkeeping, the lobby, and the front desk. Although he oversees the entire establishment, Alger's interests are solely in the area of artistic effects, more specifically theatrical presentation and historical research. The impact of his imagination and ingenuity has transformed the Museum into a must see centerpiece of Louisiana and New Orleans history.

What's also wonderful for Alger and M.J., and vitally important to them both, is their friendship. Neither of them ever made it to the chum stage in their respective lives—until now. They are the best of friends. Each offers the other a certain talent and they both thrive on the success of this once dark, dreary museum. Its former corpse-like, mildewed figures are now as spiffy as any mannequins can be and they no longer give the appearance of prisoners saying, "help me!"

What are incomprehensible achievements in the eyes of his

fellow French Quarterites might be considered natural consequences by M.J. since, from his perspective, his success emerged
from a delusional system. Most delusions don't pan out in con-
sensual reality like M.J.'s did. Despite his perceived reasons for
his "arrival" on-stage, M.J. still felt a sense of belonging to the
little group at Maury's corner. Not only did M.J. drop by from
time to time, Maury and his other cronies came to the museum to
see M.J. as often as passes allowed. The bad blood between
Alger and Maury improved considerably when the possibility of
other museum speaking roles became a topic of conversation.

Maury's suspicions didn't change much. Whereas by all out-
ward signs, M.J.'s beliefs, bizarre as they be, were incorporated
and utilized in a constructive direction, Maury's beliefs didn't particularly enhance the quality of his music. He remained fixed on
the whereabouts of the Bead Lady and talked about it incessantly.
Mimes and Dobermans continued to pale in his thinking as time
went on. While Maury saw no signs of gains from his own recent
exploits, he couldn't help but notice M.J.'s remarkable success.
Whereas Sophia's mood quickened in response to M.J.'s good fortune—and she always beamed for days after her visits to the
museum—Maury's mood remained about as flat as that pealed-off
puddle of wax recently deposited in Jackson Square Park. He continued to keep his finger on the pulse of the Quarter, though.

No news had reached Maury from the neighborhood around
Ursulines Street lately. Jean and Marya continued to be busy with
their daily chores at the bakery as the regulars and tourists kept
coming back for more. Ironically, one of the things Clarissa had
grown curious about in recent times related to Jean's whereabouts. He worked half-time, yes. That fit with his philosophy of
life. Clarissa could understand that, but where did he go the other
half-time? He didn't seem to be at home. Upstairs, over the bakery, where the couple lived, Marya seemed to be busy, but alone,
most of the time. Once he finished working in the bakery, Clarissa hardly ever saw Jean around. Likewise, this man with two lives
worried about where Clarissa might be. She hadn't shown up for
work for two days, nor did she respond to phone messages.

The little band of veterans from the storming of the Wax
Museum continued to meet regularly on Maury's corner to catch

up on Quarter events. This little support group knew nothing of the baker's activities, but they were particularly concerned about not having seen Clarissa or the white Duke recently—an odd development, they thought. Maury especially had to know everybody's whereabouts and Sophia followed relationships closely.

"There's another strange development," Sophia mumbled, "come to think of it." She then proceeded to blurt out news of a budding relationship between Jake and Ginger.

Furthermore, the *corps* learned that Jake gave away his dog, Glendale, to Vince, the rapper, who now had a home for himself and the dog, thanks to his new job as custodian at the Wax Museum.

Maury's Quarterite counterpart for bewilderment about odd happenings, Fred, the Freudian, continued to ponder the recent events in his experience from every angle he could think of. For the first time in his life, his conclusions entertained the possibility that some things related to human behavior are no more explainable than the workings of the universe. An introverted, studious and dedicated physician, Fred had joined the staff at Charity and the ranks of French Quarter residents about five years before any of these bizarre events began, or at least entered his awareness. A native Southern Californian known to be as liberal as they come, Fred surely couldn't fathom reality as he currently perceived it.

Fred and Maury had similar missions, although they approached them in very different ways from the beginning—one immersed in the occult, and the other in, some would say, a cult, albeit shrouded in scientific methodology and grounded in neurology. Both fought similar battles, most of them clearly windmills in Maury's case, but not exclusively. An untrained observer can easily see that, but if not in Fred's profession, where are the observers who can explain these uncanny incidents? Fred worried about these unexplained happenings. He'd naively thought that psychiatry could provide all the answers. Who does know? he wondered. Who does one ask? The clowns in Jackson Square? The tarot card readers? The artists? The musicians? For some reason—Freud would probably know why—Fred forgot about the mimes!

Never underestimate the power of the mimes, Freddie, the

committee of the mimes. Clowns and artists will come and go but mimes are here forever. They know what's going on. They could explain it to you, Freddie, but the question is, will they? Mimes are mute.

Except for the mimes and, of course, Fred's thinking, the landscape of the Quarter did continue to change. The white Duke never reappeared. No one saw him anywhere anymore, not even Maury, not even on the fringes of the Quarter or on Perdido Street. Dean and Clarissa became *los perdidos*.

As bits and pieces of stories reached the nightly powwow on the corner of St. Peter and Royal, Maury began to wonder out loud if the white Duke gave up impersonation for "impassionation." The *corps du jour*, the little band of storm-trouping gypsies, would all laugh but for as many different reasons as there were members of the little clan. Although it would be difficult to know whether or not anybody really got it, Maury's humor did contain truth. Our subject might have chosen "insemination" instead of Maury's high falutin' term, but the dude who disappeared surely preferred undressing to make love over dressing to kill.

FRENCH QUARTER FOLLIES

LAGNIAPPE

In these parts, one can occasionally expect a little something extra as in a baker's dozen. At the little boulangerie on Ursulines, *les petits pains*—like these little stories—are always supplied in batches of thirteen. That way, if one is devoured on the way home, a full dozen remains. Had readers digested this lagniappe story first, it's hard to say how their hunger for the remaining dozen would have been affected. They may never have known our friends Dean the serial killer, a.k.a. the White Duke, or Clarissa ,the college drop-out, or Maury, the street musician, or Sophia, the bag lady, or Ginger, the prostitute, or Jake, the custodian, or Vince, the rapper, or Alger, The Ticketmaster, or M.J., the impersonator, a.k.a. the Black Duke. Fred the Freudian didn't offer much more than a blank screen so don't count him in. Charity provided our people with at least a refuge and it probably always will. Ah, mention of the baker and his wife, Jean and Marya, almost escaped our list of characters.

Some would say mimes shouldn't be included in our cast of memorables for reasons similar to the case of Fred the Freudian. Mimes are blank screens, too, but I will argue against exclusion on the basis of poetic license if not prescience.

Allow me to become transparent. I am Jean, the narrator of this sack of stories, the voice who spoke to Maury as he lay flat on the sidewalk, the village baker who produces pains de siegles by the basketfuls on Ursulines, the matchmaker, and the voiceless mime on the pedestal, the mime over matter, if you will. My wife and I followed Iberville and Bienville to New Orleans. My origins supernaturally go back, yes, to Strasbourg but seventeenth century Strasbourg. And, while, Marya's voodoo beliefs are no exception to those of the people of the Antilles in that era, her voodoo powers are exceptional, exquisitely so. We know all about travel through space and time, through centuries both forward and backward. We know all about appearances and disappearances, incarnations and possessions, Ducs and Duchesses, New Orleans, Montreal, Paris, the Antilles, and far beyond.

Maury, your intuition serves you well. Our colleague (Marya's and mine), the Bead Lady, lives on. Occasionally known as Sister Beatrice Letitia, she currently levitates on Ursulines wearing a natural linen habit. Look closely and you might recognize her as the legendary Parisienne, La Marquise Marietta DuPuy de la Poste, but that's yet another story! But, on the other hand, Maury, Dobermans don't have the power. Try Catahoulas. Vincent, beware. You are next. And Fred, you've been had! It's that simple.

No mental hospital can compete with the French Quarter, folks! As for the mynah bird, well, he either existed or he didn't. But, if he did, then he told this story.

---

* Footnote: Fred's tendency to digress, as evidenced in this presentation, always increased under stressful conditions. Recent events, in particular the brief hospitalizations of Clarissa, the Duke mannequin, and now this manic patient—stressful in their own right—reminded Fred of the yet unexplained, disarming events and circumstances during the admissions of Clarissa, Dean and Maury some months back.

THE LIFE OF CHRIST
IN THE 21st CENTURY
Edwin Christian Allman

THE LIFE OF CHRIST IN THE 21st CENTURY

"Coincidence is God's way of remaining anonymous."
—Goethe

In the year 2037, nearly four decades into the 21st century, a world government has been forged by the once-bitter Cold War rivals, the United States and Russia. Along with their allies in the 10-nation European Community, and supported by most of the major nations of the world, the two countries created a World Federation government that has eliminated hunger and most major armed conflicts. Religion and spirituality are largely incidental. In the new world order, advanced technology and information systems have made a kind of universal peace and prosperity possible. On a certain college campus in New Orleans, however, a professor of photography is inadvertently sowing seeds of doubt about the World Federation goverment's ultimate moral authority.

Dr. Richard Bannister agitatedly wiped away the beads of perspiration from his forehead as he looked expectantly at the bored faces in his classroom. Ruggedly handsome, with an unruly shock of sandy blond hair, Bannister could pass for a slightly disheveled model in a men's clothing advertisement. He was stylish in a rough way, but his clothes look as if they'd been ironed while still on his body.

Drumming the lectern impatiently, Bannister scanned the classroom, waiting for a response. He cleared his throat. "I see that the lack of air-conditioning hasn't helped heat up any of your brains," he said, rolling his eyes. Turning to a replica of the *"Shroud of Turin"* mounted on the wall behind his lectern, Bannister raised his voice. "Doesn't anyone have a comment about my theory on how this image could have been formed?"

A collective groan arose from the thirty or so students sitting behind him impatiently and uncomfortably in the heat.

Bannister pointed to a section of the blackboard on one side of the Shroud replica where he'd written:

> "PREMISE: There is no rational explanation for the image on the Shroud of Turin."
> "FACT: The World Federation Science Institute contends the image was somehow painted onto the cloth in the 13th century."
> "QUESTION: Why would an agnostic who is skeptical of 'miraculous' explanations for the cloth contend that one possible explanation for the image is a burst of radiation from the body it is alleged to have once covered?"

Bannister shifted around to face the class. again. As if on cue, a stiff, humid breeze from the open window caused the Shroud replica to flutter crazily in place.

Bannister raised his eyebrows in mock horror, nodded his head in the direction of the animated display, and focused his attention on the class again. "I do believe the Shroud is making a statement!" His lame attempt at humor fell flat.

One student, a lithe, beautiful young woman with long, dark hair, shifted in her seat near the middle of classroom. Her liquid brown eyes seemed to sparkle as she raised her hand tentatively. Immediately behind her, a skinny, emaciated young man with spiked orange hair and eyebrows pierced with several silver rings, chortled, "Here we go again—Margaret LaTour on the God trip!"

A prim, neatly dressed blonde to his right snorted, "Oh, shut up, Joey. If she wants to believe in ghosts, what's it to you?"

"Sure, Angela," Joey retorted, fingering a ring on his right eyebrow. "Let's play pin-the-tail-on-the-poltergeist. That's perfectly acceptable speculation in a photographic theory class!"

A few half-hearted chuckles erupted from the seats around them.

"Quiet," Bannister interjected, irritably. "Look, Miss LaTour... I'm perfectly willing to concede that you have a right to your religious beliefs, but they aren't relevant to this discussion. I mean..."

A dreamy smile played at the edge of Margaret's lips, "You mean, don't speculate about what is impossible to prove one way or the other?" She was silent for a moment, then, calmly cut off Bannister before he could respond. "I think what you mean, Professor, is that you are uncomfortable with any explanation that doesn't come neatly wrapped up in a package of scientific terms. You want facts, Professor. You don't want the truth."

Joey howled derisively, "It's God, I tell you. It's God himself, right there in that cloth!" The classroom was punctuated by a chorus of chuckles.

Bannister suddenly slammed his fist on the lectern. "Cut it out! Jeez, this is our second class on this subject and you people *still* don't get it!"

Angela piped up, "Get what, Professor Bannister? We've been listening to you drone on for the last hour about this shroud thing. You made such a big thing about being an agnostic, about how you don't believe its miraculous, and yada yada. You say you want facts, but you've spent all this time making fun of the World Federation Science Institute. They said it was a fraud, but you think they're crazy. It's not miraculous, but the Science Institute is hiding something. Which is it?"

Bannister sighed heavily. He looked wearily at Angela, and then turned his attention to Margaret. "Look, I'm not making fun of your religious beliefs..."

Then to Angela, "And I'm not saying the World Federation Science Institute is crazy, either. I'm simply telling you there's more to this than..."

Angela rolled her eyes, "There's always more to the story...but what's the point? The image was formed by a burst of radiation? Puh-leeeze!"

"Dammit, Angela!" Bannister exclaimed, his freckled face reddening. "That's NOT what I said! Now, for the last time—there, it's right there on the blackboard—I said that's one possible explanation! I've also said that, so far, there's been no other rational explanation for how that image got there."

Joey grunted, "Sounds pretty damn clear to me!"

". . .About as clear as your complexion, Joey. The speaker

was a beefy, crewcut, jock type sitting near the back of the class.

"Bite me, Dick-head," Joey retorted sarcastically. "I'm crushed, really," he added in a mock-wounded voice.

"All right, all right," Bannister cut in, laughing, despite himself. "We don't need any more love poems between the gutter punks and dickheads...er, excuse, Jason," he corrected himself, addressing the jock, as the classroom exploded into laughter.

"Now, if we can return to the subject...Angela, Margaret...As I was saying, what I've tried to do is point out there really has been no explanation except for the burst of radiation that we can't rule out. All the research teams, save for that bogus bunch of toadies at the World Federation..."

"There you go again!" Angela fumed. "You do think the Science Institute is crazy!"

"No, not crazy—I just think they have an agenda," Bannister raised his voice. "For some reason, they're ignoring the carbon dating that suggests that the cloth could, in fact, be over 2,000 years old. I'm simply saying that, in the absence of any proof to the contrary, their position is as suspect as the religious groups. I'm sorry, Margaret. Who simply accepts on faith that the cloth is miraculous?" Bannister looked at Margaret, shrugging his shoulders, then paused abruptly.

What is it about her face? She's...glowing!

Margaret looked up from a piece of paper on which she was doodling. She smiled at Bannister and he appeared shaken.

What is it about her eyes?

Bannister recovered, but his voice was quavering.

Angela interjected, "So we're back to the same old, same old, eh?" The cloth is a mystery. But just because it's mysterious doesn't mean it's miraculous; isn't that what you said? So what's the point? This discussion is going in circles!"

"Yes, I, ah..." Bannister reluctantly shifted his gaze from Margaret to Angela. "Yes, I agree —it doesn't mean it's miraculous, but I...ah...but I don't think it's necessarily not miraculous either...I..."

"Hey, Dr. Bannister, you okay?" It was Joey, looking on with concern.

Bannister finally recovered, "Oh, yes...It's just that, well, I

179

think it's ridiculous that the Science Institute seemed to go out of its way to prove that the cloth is a hoax. Well, I know they did no such thing. In fact, I think it's mighty strange that they're even commenting on this at all. I mean, whoever heard of the shroud as a matter of serious concern, I think that's what they called it, until these appearances, whatever they are?"

"Oh, yeah," Joey said excitedly. "We keep hearing on the news that this sphere of light is hovering over these villagers in Tibet and some strange man keeps popping up, performing miracles. If I was some Techno Master with the World Federation government, I'd be pretty upset, too. Ain't no place for miracles when we've got the God of Technology to save our asses!"

Bannister chuckled, "A very good point, Joey. I think those rings in your eyebrows might be a lightening rod for illumination!"

Margaret raised her hand. "Dr. Bannister?"

Bannister nodded in her direction.

"I was wondering," she began, her eyes strangely luminous. "You've said you don't think the image was necessary formed miraculously..."

"That's right..."

"But all you seem to be saying is that it can't be explained. That one of the only rational explanations is one that nobody, especially the World Federation, wants to accept. I'm just puzzled by one thing—why are you even bringing this up in a class on photographic theory?"

Bannister brightened, "Ah, good question. Why the *"Shroud of Turin"* in this class? Because, ladies and gentlemen, if the image was formed by a burst of radiation from that body, whoever's body that actually was—and it's a helluva point to ponder at this stage in history—it is history's first photograph, 1800 years before the officially recognized first photograph! It's a negative from a positive. THAT'S worth studying, don't you think? I say it's..."

A series of short, shrill beeps interrupted Bannister. "Ah," he said, somewhat disappointed. "The class-is-over-alarm. And the natives here are no doubt anxious to get to their next class. We'll pick up where we left off next time."

Before he could finish, most of the students were filing out. Bannister looked distractedly at his notes on the lectern, opened his briefcase and started to gather up his papers. Looking up, he was startled to sense someone in front of him.

Margaret, standing in front of the lectern, appeared not to notice Bannister. She was staring past him at the image of the shroud with incalculable serenity on her face.

"Margaret?"

Bannister's face registered a look of naked astonishment.

Her eyes! There's a light, I see it!

Slowly, Margaret turned to Bannister with a knowing smile.

Bannister stammered, laughing nervously. "If...I didn't know better, I'd think you half-expect that figure pinned to the wall to walk over and give you a hug!"

Margaret ignored Bannister's feeble attempt at humor. Instead, she returned her gaze to the image of the shroud. "Wouldn't it be wonderful if it's true, Dr. Bannister?"

"Er, wonderful? What?"

Continuing to stare at the image, she began to speak in a sing-song, almost child-like voice, "For more than two thousand years, you have either dismissed me or have done things in my name that are obscene..."

Bannister looked nervously behind him, if unsure of the source of the voice. "I really don't..."

Margaret continued, "Oh, yes. Some believe I have been here and will come again. Some believe I am yet to come. Some say I was never here at all, just a figment of tormented imaginations, yearning for salvation from a source other than themselves. Perhaps the time is near; perhaps it is time for the truth."

Bannister was clearly uncomfortable. He laughed nervously, and affected a stiff formality. "Uh, Miss LaTour, class is over. I don't know if it's, er, 'time,' as you say, but that stranger's appearances are sure making some very powerful people nervous."

Margaret continued, "I mean, the man— if it is a man, I mean, and not some sort of tabloid news creation—is making everybody crazy. The World Federation is calling him some sort of high-tech prankster. but why go through such lengths to discredit him, or it, or whatever? Maybe they just can't stand the thought of some-one—or something—out of their control."

Bannister shrugged, still discomfitted by Margaret's apparent, rapturous preoccupation with the Shroud image.

"Well, Margaret…I mean, Miss LaTour, I need to lock up the classroom, and uh…" He cleared his throat. "Uh, how about a cup of coffee?"

Suddenly alert to her surroundings, Margaret blushed, "Sure, why not?"

Bannister gathered the remaining papers into his briefcase, then snapped it shut. He nodded toward the door and followed Margaret out. As he left, he turned out the lights and closed and locked the door behind him.

In the darkened room, the replica emitted a blaze of sparks.

* * *

The night was still, eerily black—the only source of light from a fingernail-slice of moon, reflected on the calm surface of a small pool, situated in a slight depression of a craggy mountain peak.

Suddenly, a cold wind swirled violently to life, shaking the branches of a small tree at the pool's edge. If anyone had been within 100 yards, they might well have found themselves driven to their knees in pain first by the ear-splitting, machine-like hum which filled the air, then by the blinding light from the huge spinning sphere that suddenly hovered over the pool.

The menacing lightning sparks thrown off from the spinning sphere would certainly have mortified the average onlookers as the crackling energy burst like firecrackers on the surface of the pool.

Enveloped by the shower of sparks, the water began to boil. Just as suddenly as the spectacular light show had begun, all motion ceased and the sphere faded. Slowly, the shape of man emerged from the froth, shook himself vigorously, and walked to a nearby tree. As he approached, the tree glowed, and a dazzling cloak, undulating in a kaleidoscopic pattern of luminescent colors, appeared on one of its lower branches. The Stranger, his skin glowing and bronzed, radiating what appeared to be a light from the just-vanished sphere, slipped into the cloak, his eyes registering something akin to profound amusement as he turned from the pool. He looked briefly at the sky and turned to a path that led down the mountain.

EDWIN CHRISTIAN ALLMAN

*   *   *

As the first orange rays of the sun licked the edges of the nearby mountain peak, the village came alive with the sounds of the people beginning their day's work. A round-faced child, in sandals and a simple gray smock, ran in circles around a small woman carrying a basket. Other women, dressed simply in smocks, gathered at a well near a cluster of neat, modest huts, drawing the day's supply of water for cooking and pottery making. Several men gathered nearby, bartering clothing and foodstuffs from a series of makeshift stalls.

All of the villagers, with one exception, were relatively short, dressed simply in the village's traditional attire. Rhea Lan Chang was different. Unusually tall by her region's standards, she was dressed in the trademark silver jumpsuit worn by World Federation officers. A metallic triangle-in-circle insignia just below her left shoulder identified her as a World Federation Behavioral Officer, a hybrid judicial officer and counselor for the village of about 20,000 people.

She strode purposefully through the milling crowd, her bearing businesslike but nevertheless cordial as she briefly greeted passing villagers by name. As she walked, she appeared to be consulting with a hand-held computer, talking in staccato bursts. Passing several huts, she turned in the direction of the village's lone modern structure, a sleek, two-story glass and steel building with a gleaming sign that announced—in the native dialect, as well as English, German, and French—that it was a regional command station for the World Federation government.

Arriving at the building's entrance, she placed her hand against a dark panel.

A disembodied voice commanded, "Identity confirmed. Rhea Lan Chang. State your purpose."

"Chang. Scheduled meeting with Science Officer Jamaal Husington."

"Appointment confirmed," the voice replied.

A door opened noiselessly. As Chang entered, she nodded to a stern man with steely blue eyes and Aryan features, a silver-suited sentry with what appeared to be a small magnet in his right hand.

THE LIFE OF CHRIST IN THE 21st CENTURY

Damn goons, she thought to herself. As if these peaceful peo-ple are suddenly going to attack them with pitchforks! Idiots!

She smiled curtly to the officer and walked straight ahead to another door with the name "First Science Officer Husington - Tibetan Regional Command" stamped on rectangular piece of metal off to the side.

As if responding to her thoughts, the door opened. As she entered, she looked over the shoulder of a man with his back to a desk to a wall-sized video monitor, blurry with rapidly-changing images. Without a word, the man turned and stared intently at Chang. His broad, black face registered obvious worry. He nod-ded at Chang to take the chair in front of his desk. As he did, he pulled a metallic card from a terminal and waved it at Chang.

The son of an Ethiopian couple descended from the coun-try's royal family, Husington was an elegant looking man of per-haps 45. Evidence of his breeding and education adorned the walls: an undergraduate degree in economics from Oxford; advanced degrees in physics, artificial intelligence, and astrono-my from Harvard and Stanford; numerous commendations for humanitarian causes. His stature was further embellished by a plaque on the wall behind his desk that read, "Jamaal Husington: Honorary Inhabitant of Silver Station, the first city on the moon. Thank you for making it possible."

"You know what this is?" Husington asked abruptly.

Chang shook her head. "Your message said it was inter-esting."

Husington lets out a sharp sigh, "I do tend to understate. Please, forgive me. It's more than interesting. I assume you know this is about another appearance by that damned sphere and that…that, stranger, whoever the hell he is."

"Not really. I just heard some of the villagers babbling this morning. I didn't take it seriously."

Husington snorted. "Oh, it's serious, all right. Look at this!" He flipped the metallic card across the desk in Chang's direction. She scooped it up and looked intently at it for a moment. Slowly, she looked up, stunned.

"My God! He's…"

Husington cut in, "The previous two transmissions were isolated. The third one, two days ago, was at Lake Superior in the U.S. We've heard that a news crew actually got something on tape. The tape supposedly shows that he actually evaporated it and refilled it! But the World Federation military just happened—oh, yeah, just by chance!—Ha!—to have a couple of harrier ships nearby and the troops moved in and confiscated the tape. Now, just yesterday, we got reports of fifteen DIFFERENT sightings, all the same damn time!"

Chang's face registered profound shock. Before she could speak, Husington sprang up from his chair and threw his arms up the air.

"Oh, yes—all...at...the...same...time! I wonder how our illustrious Herr Koehn is going to explain this one?"

Chang visibly sagged in her chair. "He certainly might think this is the excuse he needs to call an election of the Federation Council. We all know he thinks he should have control of the Federation military, isn't that right?"

Husington nodded grimly. "After that light show we saw last night...even if none of the villagers were actually there to see the source of all that stuff that happened, we'd have a tough time convincing Koehn or anyone else that our sector didn't experience one of those sightings."

*   *   *

Outside, the small boy, who'd been running circles around his mother, suddenly stopped and looked toward the mountain. He was struck dumb by the sight of a dense fog rising from the base of the mountain. His eyes wide with wonder, he turned and ran after his mother, shouting excitedly and pointing behind him. "Keee! Keee!"

His mother turned, as if to quiet her son, then she, too, was rendered speechless. Suddenly, she shrieked Rhea Lan Chang's name in her native tongue and turned in the direction of the Federation building.

As she reached the entrance, she was greeted by the sentry who opened the door, weapon readied, at the sound of the commotion. He warned the excited woman away, simultaneously pressing a keypad on his belt.

Husington heard a familiar warning beep on his monitor and he arose and motioned for Chang to follow him. As he approached the door that led out of the building, he quickly signaled away the sentry, who was struggling with the hysterical woman.

Chang following closely behind, moved in to comfort the woman.

"Dammit, Chang!" Husington barked. "What the devil is she saying?"

"I...I don't know... But come quickly, there is something." Her voice trailed off as she hurried with the woman, who had broken away and was running toward the moving cloud at the base of the mountain." Husington and the sentry, dumbfounded, chased after the fleeing women.

Moments later, the village woman, Chang, Husington and the sentry arrived at a spot a hundred yards away from the Federation Building, joining a throng of villagers who were screaming and pointing toward the fog, now swirling with brilliant hues of blue, gold, and silver. Suddenly, an unbearably loud hum filled the air, followed by the appearance of a huge, lighted, spinning sphere hovering just a few hundreds yards above the base of the fog. The villagers, frightened, covered their ears and grimaced in pain.

*   *   *

The Stranger walked slowly toward a desolate stretch of the mountain, a look of profound sadness on his face. The few huts that dotted this side of the mountain were falling apart, perched precariously on dry stakes. As he drew nearer, he saw perhaps a dozen listless, emaciated women and children, clustered along the barren, hard ground. There were no green plants anywhere. A small girl rose from the group and took a few unsteady steps in The Stranger's direction. Despite the bleakness of her surroundings, she somehow managed to smile.

With a broad grin, The Stranger broke into a slow gallop, pausing briefly to scoop up the little girl into his arms. With the girl cradled in his arms, he walked toward an old woman, her eyes blinded by cataracts, kneeling near one of the huts. Gently putting the little girl down beside the woman, the Stranger knelt next to the woman and took her face into his hands.

"You knew I would come for you," he said softly.

"Yes, Master. We have always known. It is written!"

The Stranger smiled, his eyes glowing with the light of the sphere. "You've known me in your hearts through the ages. Now, see with these eyes how your faith has rewarded you."

With that, The Stranger placed his hands on the old woman's eyes. Laughing, he removed his hands and the woman's eyes turned a blazing blue. She looked up through her tear-blurred eyes and beheld The Stranger's handsome, bearded face, framed with long, flowing auburn hair. She reached up to touch his face, then reached out to feel the cloth of his dazzling cloak, alive with the magnificent, flowing colors of the rainbow.

She looked again to his face, and nodded knowingly as he appeared to change before her eyes: first from a handsome red-haired man he was transformed into a Buddhist monk, then into a young black woman, then an old white man clothed in a black robe. Before her eyes, he became a young Chinese girl, an old woman, a young man with a black skull cap, and then…the same Stranger she first beheld when her sight was restored.

"Yes," she said simply. "You are all that we are, all that we have ever been."

Standing, The Stranger looked out at the desolation and murmured, "It is time, precious child. Time to remake the world into my father's image. Time to banish the fear and the great darkness. Time to wonder."

With that, he arose and spun around twice, his magnificent cape swirling around him. With a shout, he stopped suddenly, raised his arms in triumph and walked again toward the path that led down the mountain. Turning to the faces behind him, he exclaimed, "It is time! Be alive!" With that, he raised his hands again. As he did, the barren land suddenly sprung to life. The leafless trees sprouted lush green leaves, the huts repaired themselves, and the villagers simply stood up, robust and healthy.

THE LIFE OF CHRIST IN THE 21st CENTURY

*   *   *

Still dumbfounded by the fog, which seemed to swirl in place, Husington and Chang managed to quiet the villagers' fears somewhat. The hum had subsided and the sphere was gone. But, as they debated whether or not to approach the fog, Husington and Chang were driven to the ground along with the villagers as the hum returned, its sonic resonance louder than before.

At the peak of the light and sound, The Stranger emerged from the fog, astride an impossibly white, extraordinarily large stallion. As man and horse approached, a shower of sparks trailed them, tracing their movements like the after-burn of a rocket.

From the Federation Building, a half-dozen heavily armed sentries emerged and hurried to join Husington, Chang, and the villagers. Husington waved at them to lower their weapons.

"Get back, damn you! Get back!"

As The Stranger drew closer, he appeared to be transform- ing. Chang noticed with astonishment that he appeared to be changing into every known ethnic and class type imaginable. First, he was a Scottish nobleman, then an African princess, an adolescent Eskimo, a Rabbi, a Spanish priest, a woman in busi- ness suit.

Husington saw the same thing, except, The Stranger looked like …Husington when he looks at himself in the mirror. Then The Stranger looked like…Chang! No, he looked like Husing- ton's mother …was it his father?

Inexplicably, the villagers lost all fear. En masse, they ran to greet The Stranger, smiling and shouting excitedly. The expres- sions of the still-dazed Chang and Husington indicated that something or someone was approaching…what?

They seem to know who he is! He's speaking to them as if he had just left on an errand yesterday and has come back to tell them about his trip!

The Stranger dismounted, smiling, having returned to his first incarnation. He knelt and opened his arms, as if in welcome. Chang fainted. Husington, distracted from The Stranger, reacted to her immediately. "Officer Chang!" To a sentry, he barked, "Get her some water! Hurry!"

The Stranger broke free from the crowd and walked the few steps to Husington, kneeling beside Chang.

"Not to worry, Dr. Jamaal Husington, World Federation Science Officer."

Husington nearly fainted himself. "How the hell ...??"

The Stranger merely smiled. Rising, he clapped his hands together, opened his cloak, and chuckled as a flock of doves flew out. One alighted on Chang's chest, flapped its wings, and flew away. Chang awakened with a start.

The villagers, obviously delighted, cheered and applauded. The Stranger bowed deeply. As he straightened, he stepped in front of the sentry who was returning with the glass of water for Chang.

"I'll take that," The Stranger said, raising his hand. As he did, the glass floated out of the sentry's hand, hovered for a moment in mid-air and then settled into The Stranger's outstretched palm. Ignoring the shock on the faces around him, The Stranger examined the glass, looked at the still-prone Chang and chuckled, lifting the glass to his own lips, "Since you appear to be okay, I'm sure you don't mind. I've been on the road for awhile and I'm parched."

Turning to Husington, muttering under his breath, The Stranger snapped his fingers, which seemed to be the cue for the glass of water to vanish in mid-air, and replied, "Yes, you're quite right, Dr. Husington. It's a heck of a way to introduce myself. But, how do I say this politely? What's that term? Expletive deleted, right? Well, I'm not the 'expletive deleted' you think I am!"

With that, The Stranger slapped his knee, hugely amused with himself.

Rhea Lan Chang, still dizzy, rose unsteadily to her feet toward the sound of The Stranger's voice. For the first time, she saw The Stranger's face clearly. Clearly, she thought to herself, he's human... or, not human? Something about his eyes..."

Mirrored windows that stretch forever into space. Galaxies of a million suns, infinite wisdom, a time before time.

Chang tried to speak, but The Stranger shook his head. Addressing her directly, and then the crowd, he spoke in a voice that was at once a whisper and a shout, "I have a message for Herr

Koehn. I believe he is the head of the World Federation military, is that not right?"

Not waiting for an answer, he continued, "Here's the message: 'Gotcha!' Which is a way of saying, 'Three nines, no surprise. Turned upside down, no disguise'."

With those cryptic words, The Stranger smiled, bowed deeply, and motioned for Chang to stand beside him. Without a word, as if in a trance, she complied.

Husington watched, gape-mouthed, as Chang began to speak in the voice of The Stranger.

"He is the way and the truth and the light," she began, "He is life's beginning and life's end. He is called by many names, but His message is the same as it has always been. His gift is love. He is to proclaim the kingdom of that gift that is already within each of us. Do not despair. Rejoice in the truth of what you can become."

Rhea Lan Chang, emerging from her trance, looked dazedly around her. Husington and the villagers were staring at her, perplexed. She looked to the spot beside her where the Stranger had been, but he was gone, as if he'd never been there.

*　　*　　*

"The flight was terrible, thank you very much," the slightly overweight man said, irritation and fatigue obvious in his voice.

"Look, Franz," Jamaal Husington began as the two men walked rapidly across the square that led to the skyscraper whose gleaming insignia identified it as the World Science Federation Institute. "I know bringing you here to New York from Florida isn't your idea of a vacation, but that professor in New Orleans isn't going away. Something's happening, and it seems to be linked to his lectures at Tulane."

"Yes, yes, I know, Jamaal." Franz Brightbill wiped a lock of his silver hair off his reddened forehead. Despite the crisp fall air, he was sweating profusely from the exertion of keeping up with his companion's pace. The elder man had once been Husington's physics professor at Stanford, but he obiously deferred to his young friend now.

Husington, despite his stature as the Federation's leading science officer, remained deferential to the man he still considered his mentor. Approaching the building, Husington hastened to open the door for Brightbill, who nodded mockingly. "Oh, get over it, Jamaal—I'm not in my grave yet," but his grim face lightened in appreciation of the gesture.

The two took an elevator which soon opened to a long, forbidding hallway leading to a door a few yards away. Their identification verified, they entered a huge room, crammed with computers, oversized video monitors as well as a staff of white-coated professionals and the familiar uniformed sentries.

Ignoring everyone, Husington and Brightbill walked directly to a video monitor. Husington touched a keypad on a nearby desk and the monitor sprang to life.

The two men looked at each other with quiet understanding.

"It's bigger than we thought," Husington said.

"Bigger, but not so insane," Brightbill mused, nodding his head, his face registering a gentle challenge.

Husington rolled his eyes, "Oh, come on, Franz! I know you've got this thing for God and resurrection and all that but surely you don't…"

Brightbill interrupted angrily, "Why is it so difficult to believe, Jamaal? Something like these sightings have been predicted for thousands of years, well before the birth of Christ. This isn't exactly according to script in the Good Book, as it were, but you'll have to admit we can't explain who he is. And even the World Federation Army and all of Koehn's scientific gadgets haven't been able to get hold of him. High-tech prankster? Give me a break!"

Husington looked wounded, musing, "How can you stop something that appears and disappears at will?"

Brightbill snorted, "Something to cheer about, no? I am sure our great military leader must be breaking heads all over the place! Ha! Let him be furious!"

"Well, as long as he doesn't get furious with me. He wanted us to meet because he needs answers. He thinks you might know something; why don't I know…"

"No, my young friend," Brightbill admonished, "he just

wants me here because it will look like he's being generous and open-minded to have a scientist who also happens to be a religious nut—like me—saying crazy stuff. He thinks it will be a useful distraction while he hides the fact that either he doesn't know what's the hell's going on, or that he knows PRECISELY what's going on and doesn't want anyone to know he knows."

"Dammit, Franz! What's that supposed to mean? Quit talking in riddles!" Husington waved his arms in disgust.

"Oh, calm down, Jamaal. Koehn's given us a few days before we have to deliver our next report. As for what I meant, who cares? If all of this is what I believe and pray is right, Herr Koehn isn't much longer for THIS world.!"

"Jesus, Franz! Is this some kind of messianic trip for you?"

Brightbill chuckled, "Be careful what you ask for; you just might get it!"

Husington, ignoring Brightbill's taunt, turned his attention to the monitor again. A nondescript, humorless man with a nametag that identified him only as "Situation Leader - Henderson" arose from a nearby desk and greeted Drs. Husington and Brightbill crisply. He handed Husington a print-out and waited expressionlessly.

Husington studied the print-out, his agitation visibly growing. "Holy mother! Franz! Look at this!" Turning to Henderson, Husington asked, "What do you make of this?"

"I don't know, sir. This report just came in about forty-five minutes ago. I can tell you that Commander Koehn saw it within a few minutes of the transmission. He wasn't, er…happy, sir!"

Franz Brightbill began chuckling quietly, then laughed out loud, startling Husington and the Situation Leader. Several curious faces looked up from their stations.

"Amazing!" Brightbill cackled gleefully. "Simply amazing! First sighting of the sphere ten days ago, over Acapulco. Then the report of the sphere, this time, along with this…man…this stranger. He evaporates Lake Superior, refills it, and vanishes. Third sighting, simultaneously in fifteen different locations around the world. Each one accompanied by the same man, who gave the same damn speech! And last night! Hahahaha!"

Husington was unable to control his anger. "It's not funny,

Franz. This is dangerous…"

"Dangerous?" Brightbill matched Husington's anger with more of his own. "All these sightings, simultaneously around the world? Dangerous to whom? He shows up last night in THIRTY locations simultaneously. At airports! None of the aircraft could take off! Their instruments had all shut down! At terminal wards in hospitals. Dying patients get up and walk out! Cured! You saw the man yourself! Didn't you tell me he turned a burned out village into an oasis, overnight? Instantaneously, I think you said…"

Husington sagged noticeably. Curtly, he turned to the Situation Leader. "That will be all, officer." Turning to Brightbill, he motioned to a door off the main room. "Franz, may I have a word with you in private?"

Following Brightbill to the small office, Husington slammed the door behind them. Fuming, he stared fixedly at the older man.

"Look, Franz, I couldn't say it out there, but you know damn well I didn't mean dangerous the way it sounded."

"Yes, we know Koehn is going to use these, er…incidents to browbeat the Federation into making him Supreme Commander—or whatever ridiculously grand sounding title it is they give these days—of the World Government. So what?"

"So WHAT, as you damn well know, is that Koehn is going to use this and the tension in Asia to really take control. This Stranger is just an excuse, and you know it!"

Brightbill nodded eagerly, "Yes, I certainly do. But what's the problem? Let him! Let him wrap his bloody hands around the World Federation. If this strange man is who he says he is, there's not a damn thing we can do about it, is there?"

Husington, unable to control his exasperation, cried out, "Christ! And what if he isn't? What then? Are you willing to let Commander Koehn take over, just for the sake of proving your stupid theory?"

"Okay, Jamaal, here's my rational side speaking. How about this? If you didn't know any better—and you do—wouldn't you be inclined to think Koehn is staging these incidents himself for precisely the reasons we've been yelling about?"

Husington raised his hands in submission, "You're impossible."

Brightbill nodded in agreement. "From the impossible, the possible becomes interesting. Let's have a drink—on you, of course."

*　　*　　*

In the kitchen of his apartment in the French Quarter, Bannister stirred a pot of beans, looking out the French doors near the stove as a blue jay taunted an irritated cat. Hearing the phone ring, he turned the flame low and trotted to the next room.

Answering the phone, he was at first delighted, then concerned. It was Margaret LaTour. "Professor Bannister? I don't have time to explain, just listen. I've given it some thought, and I think I've decided to drop your class."

"But why?" Bannister asked almost pleading.

"I said I don't have time to explain now, but you'll understand soon."

Perplexed, Bannister sighed, "Okay, I'll take your word for it. But I'm sorry you find it necessary to leave the group."

Inordinately depressed for a reason he couldn't fathom, Bannister walked back to the kitchen after hanging up the phone and turned off the stove. Impulsively, he grabbed his light parka from the kitchen table, and headed out of the apartment—where to, he didn't know.

A couple of blocks away, around the corner from his apartment on Chartes Street, at St. Philip, he ducked into a small bar called Molly's. The music on the jukebox was an old Meters standard, an upbeat slice of New Orleans' funk that had several patrons dancing and laughing.

Heading to the bar, Bannister sat and ordered a beer, suddenly realizing that he was depressed because he already missed Margaret. As if reality were his to create, Bannister looked to the seat next to him, shocked to find the bar stool that was empty just a few minutes ago was definitely now very much occupied—with one very real Margaret LaTour.

"Why if it isn't my old professor," Margaret said, eyes twinkling.

What is it about those eyes?

Struggling to maintain his composure, Bannister retorted, "I knew you'd say that!"

"What? That you're my professor?"

"No, that I'm your OLD professor."

"Well, old man, care to kick up your heels with your darlin' little girl?"

Bannister was flummoxed. *Didn't she just drop his class with more than a hint that she may have thought he wanted more than just coffee that day after class?*

"Well, this may come as a surprise to you, but I'm not that old and I don't like being rejected. Besides, I'm a lousy dancer."

Margaret's face lit up with a mysterious, knowing smile. "You shouldn't feel that way!"

"Feel what way? Old, rejected or that I'm a lousy dancer?"

"No, none of it. I dropped your class because, well, now that I'm not your student any more, it's a little more okay to tell you that I like you."

Thoroughly charmed, Bannister finally relaxed, "In that case, shall we? Margaret led Bannister to a spot on the floor by the juke box, pulled him close to her, and embraced him tightly, burrowing her face into his shoulder."

After a few minutes, Bannister pulled back slightly and lifted her face to his. "I must say, Miss LaTour, you sure do know how to confuse a man."

"I'm not trying to confuse you—just the opposite. I do know something about you...about us, I mean. That's the other thing—the shroud, I mean. I had a dream the other night. The Stranger, the man connected with all those sightings. I mean, I've never seen him, but I know it was him. And you're going to meet him, a lot sooner than later."

Bannister frowned, "I think I'm getting a headache. Let me see; you dropped the class about the shroud because you think maybe you're attracted to me, so you find me within minutes of dropping the class to tell me that I'm going to meet the man in the shroud. I mean, I liked the simple explanation better."

Margaret smiled, "Okay then—I won't tell you that your life is going change when you meet him. I won't tell you that you have something very important to do and that The Stranger is going to destroy an evil man. But…" she puts a finger to Bannister's lips, "But I will tell you one thing—if you don't take me home with you right now and make love to me, I will never, ever speak to you again."

*   *   *

Bannister stood in the doorway between his bedroom and his living room, fascinated by the swirl of lights playing on the front door. He looked briefly back to the bed and watched as Margaret opened her eyes, sat up, and pointed to something behind him.

He turned and watched as his front door dissolved into what looked like a video monitor. On the screen, he saw a man dressed as a clown who flashed a series of cue cards that read, in rapid succession:

MESSIAHS FOR SALE OR RENT!

YOU'RE IT!

TAKE MY PICTURE, SELL YOUR SOUL

KINGDOM COMES IN MANY MODELS - BUY NOW!

Then Bannister's vision evolved into an image of the man writhing on a cross, his head bowed in agony, or was it pleasure?

The man on the cross looked up at Bannister with a smile and winked. As he did, he wrenched his right arm away from the cross and stretched his hand up and out of the screen. When he brought his hand back into view, he was clutching a silver-leafed sheet of notebook paper, which he then extended out of the screen near Bannister's face, imploring him to read it.

At that point, Bannister awoke with a start, pleased to see Margaret bending over him.

"Hello, you handsome old professor!"

Bannister rubbed his eyes, a sheepish grin on his face, as he pulled her down into an long embrace.

Slowly, Margaret wrestled her way out of Bannister's arms, got up and headed for the bathroom door across the room.

Monumentally pleased with himself, Bannister got up, looked at the clock on the nightstand, and reached for the phone.

"Nothing's in the fridge," he said half to himself. Louder, he said, "Pizza time!"

Finishing his order, he put down the phone just as Margaret emerged from the bathroom.

"As it happens," she said, pushing Bannister onto the bed, "I do like shrimp and black olive."

"Now, how did you manage to hear…oh, never mind. Okay, it's confession time. Who the hell are you?"

Margaret smiled, "Your little Cajun princess, cher."

"Yeah," Bannister mused, more curious than pleased. " You seem to have been struck out of thin air and plunked down into my life like a little piece of angel's gold."

"Why, professor, you do have a way with words!" Margaret rolled her eyes.

"But they're just words, Margaret—you're real…but why? How did you find me so soon after we got off the phone…"

Margaret put a finger to Bannister's lips, shushing him. "You dreamed about the shroud last night, didn't you, Richard?"

Bannister shrugged, averting her gaze, now more luminous than ever.

"You did, didn't you," she goaded, shifting her weight on the bed as she leaned close to his face. "Let me tell you about your dream. You said in class that the image was a negative, but in the dream it converted to positive."

Bannister's face registered surprise, but he said nothing.

Margaret's face began to take on an eerie glow; her eyes dreamy, unfocused. "And in your dream, he came to you—he was laughing about something. But he wouldn't tell you what it was. He said something you didn't catch and then he disappeared. But before he did, he pointed to your front door and made you understand that whatever it is you are supposed to do will start for you very soon."

Before Richard could react, there was a soft knock at the front door.

"Probably the pizza I ordered while you were in the bathroom." Bannister stood up, pulled on a pair of shorts and padded into the living room. Opening the door, he gasped audibly.

The man at the door was certainly dressed as a pizza delivery driver, but Bannister realized with a start that there was something all-too-familiar about the man's face. It was the same man Bannister had seen on the cross in his dream: the same man, unbeknownst to him, who appeared to the Tibetan villagers and to hundreds of other people. The same luminous eyes, the same mocking expression that seemed to communicate indomitable joy and unspeakable sadness.

Bannister was transfixed, nearly speechless. He exclaimed, "You!"

The Stranger appeared perplexed. "Of course, you did order this, right?"

Bewildered, Bannister simply stared. Recovering, he held out $20 to pay for the pizza, but The Stranger waved him off. Instead, he handed Bannister the pizza along with a note. Bannister read it, then looked up at The Stranger with an angry start.

"Look, I don't know who the hell you think you are, or what the joke is...but...I...DON'T know you! And I'm not going ANY-WHERE with you!"

Margaret, drawn to the room by Bannister's tone and volume, entered, "Richard, what's going..." She stopped dead in her tracks, openly astonished at the sight of The Stranger, and fainted.

Richard turned in the direction of Margaret's voice and rushed to her side. He looked back to the door just as The Stranger turned to leave.

"Hey," he yelled after him. "Where are you going?"

Bannister rushed to the door and out into the hallway, shocked to discover that The Stranger had vanished, as if he'd never been there.

He was even more violently surprised when he returned to Margaret's side. As he glanced at her crumpled body, he was shocked to discover that her hands begun to bleed profusely. He gently scooped her up and took her to his bed. He grabbed the phone, dialed, and shouted into the receiver. "Emergency! Please hurry! No, I can't hold! She's dying, damn you!"

*　　*　　*

The Stranger walked slowly along the oak-lined street that leads to the New Orleans Museum of Art, pausing at a sign near the entrance that reads, "The Human Race in Darkness and

Light." He smiled as he read a caption touting their wax recreations of beloved and notorious historical figures, —from Martin Luther King, Jr., Joan of Arc, and Elvis Presley to Adolph Hitler and Attila the Hun.

He looked up calmly as the sphere loomed over the museum, briefly flickered, then faded.

He walked up the steps and into the museum. As he did, the darkened main gallery began to lighten, the illumination seemingly emanating from The Stranger himself. Slowly, he scanned the room, then walked slowly among the life-like figures, finally stopping at a recreation of Marilyn Monroe, a look of profound sadness and pity on his luminous face. He stared fixedly at the waxen face of Monroe, her expression frozen in a sad smile.

The Stranger stepped back slightly, and passed a glowing hand over her platinum-haired head. Laughing, he looked down to a spot beside the figure and smiled as a rainbow of sparks leaped from the floor. As the sparks dissipated, he nodded his head as a beautiful brown-haired girl of perhaps three years of age rose from the floor, as apparently alive as The Stranger. She looks up at The Stranger and smiled, the light in her eyes as brilliant as his own.

The Stranger knelt and hugged her. Standing, he took her hand and led her among the remaining wax figures, repeating the hand gesture at each one, and recreating toddler versions of King, Hitler, Elvis, and perhaps two dozen others, just as he had with Monroe.

Outside, a passing group of college students, out for a night's picnic in the park, became startled by the light and the sound of the sphere, and the play of shadow and light that seemed to be coming from inside the museum.

Inside, The Stranger and the children laughed and danced to the light and the pulsating hum of the sphere. As the light and musical syncopation of the sphere reached a crescendo, the children formed a circle around The Stranger, pausing briefly to wave to the curious college students who made their way into the main gallery. Then The Stranger raised his arms and he and the children vanished before their startled onlookers' eyes.

THE LIFE OF CHRIST IN THE 21st CENTURY

*   *   *

World Federation Military Command Center, Berlin

Christian Koehn, a formidable-looking Aryan with close-cropped blond hair and steely blue eyes, impatiently drummed the huge glass and steel table that served as his data command station.

He stood abruptly as an equally herculean-looking man entered the room. Dwarfed by Koehn's oak-like, 6'7" frame, the silver-suited officer visibly grimaced as he stopped in front of Koehn's command station and craned his neck to see the World Federation Commander's face. He saluted crisply.

"First Security Officer Josef Kurtz, sir!"

Koehn's lips formed a hard grin. ""I know who you are, Kurtz. Report."

Kurtz winced. "Sir, it is not unexpected, I…"

Koehn eyes hardened. "Not unexpected, no. Idiot! I already know WHAT the report says. I was not asking about that bumbling Husington's report—I want YOURS!"

Kurtz gulped, but remain expressionless. Koehn brightened momentarily, but maintained a subtle menacing edge in his voice.

"No, my trusted friend, you did exactly as you were told. So what is your take on this?"

"I think it's clear that Husington and Brightbill have no idea…" Kurtz began.

Koehn's face darkened, his rage reddening his face. "Brightbill? Why is he involved in this investigation? When I authorized you to assemble this team, I did not give permission to make a saboteur part of it!"

"But, sir, you also gave explicit instructions that Husington could bring in whomever he needed. There were no restrictions."

"Well, as of now, there are," Koehn said. "I want him taken off this case by the end of the week. Go on…"

"Husington and Brightbill have come up with nothing of use to us. All the sensing devices in orbit are functioning properly. We have enough credible eyewitnesses to believe the sightings are authentic. We've virtually eliminated any possibility that the telecom net was sabotaged. By all accounts, sir, whoever is causing these disruptions either possesses technology far in advance of our own, or…"

Koehn snorted, "Or what? He is the Messiah. Ha! But enough of this. Let's assume this…this…thing, is out of our control for now. If so, let us see how we shall work this to our advantage." Koehn turned to a huge video monitor behind his station. "Let me show you something."

Koehn sat at his desk and rapidly keyed in a series of codes. As he did, a series of faces flashed on the monitor.

"This Messiah Magician may be out of our reach for now, but these individuals…they are not."

Kurtz registered the faces. In rapid succession, the faces of the 11 members of the World Federation government's ruling council popped up on the screen: the president of the council, Santo Diaz from Brazil; Seeyan Latu, Africa; Marcus Leeper of the United States; Sarah Whiten, the European 10, Annabella Pogue, Canada and the others.

As each face appeared, Koehn maintained a running commentary. "Diaz is ours, so are Mandela, Quoriz, Pogue. I'm not sure that we can count on the council members from Free Asia, Australia or India, but I am confident there will be no problem with Switzerland, Mexico, Russia, or the at-large representative when the matter comes to a vote."

"Er, what matter, exactly, sir?"

Koehn appeared to ignore the question, and instead keyed in another code. As he did, Kurtz' face registered a vague note of alarm.

"So, we, or rather, *I* know, Officer Kurtz, we have at least seven votes. But, of course, we know we need nine votes to confirm a new president, do we not?"

"Sir, I…"

Koehn slammed his fist on the data station's steel countertop. His eyes were like glassy blue ice. His voice was strangely quiet it seemed to Kurtz' ears. "Listen to me! When I made you First Officer, it was with the understanding that your loyalty is to me, not the Federation council, was it not?"

Kurtz swallowed, nodded, then stiffened. "That is correct sir. And you have never had reason to question my loyalty."

Koehn's brief smile was quickly buried under a mask of cold resolve. "And let us make sure that remains the case. I want those other two votes secured, Kurtz. And I want them secured well before I call for a leadership vote two weeks from now. Get your reprogramming team together and get it done, understood?"

Kurtz saluted. "It will be done, Commander Koehn." He turned to leave, but stopped in his tracks as Koehn calls out a final admonition.

"Oh, and Kurtz…"

Kurtz turned.

"I don't want to hear any more reports of your conscience getting the best of you, is that clear?"

Kurtz saluted again. "No, sir. Not this time." *At least not in the way you might imagine, Herr Commander,* he muttered under his breath.

*   *   *

Bannister bent worriedly over Margaret who had been comatose in her hospital bed since he checked her into Touro Medical Center after her collapse at his apartment two days earlier. He looked up as a nurse entered the room and gently but briskly motioned him to one side. As she checked Margaret's vital signs, she looked up, mildly irritated. "I'll only be a few minutes, Mr. Bannister. Would you mind waiting outside?"

Bannister nodded, grumbled inaudibly, and made his way to the door. With a forlorn backward glances, he exited the room into the deathly quiet hall. Walking toward the nurse's station, he recognized the tall, balding man in doctor's whites who'd treated Margaret the night she was admitted to the emergency room.

Turning, the man greeted the approaching Bannister. "Ah, I was just about to come looking for you."

"Uh, Dr. LeBron?"

The man chuckled, "Still having trouble with our local pronunciations, I see? It's LeBlanc. French, you know."

Bannister smiled sheepishly, despite his fatigue and worry.

"Unfortunately, my Yankee brains followed me South when I left Rochester to come here last year. Sorry."

"You'll be fine once you've got another Jazz Fest under your belt. Once you can sing it, talking comes easy." LeBlanc smiled, then consulted his clipboard. "Let's see—you're Richard Bannister, the young man who came in with Miss LaTour…"

"Yes, that's right," Bannister sighed, the weariness returning. "Well, I was just wondering—I mean, she's been in a coma for two days, and…"

LeBlanc looked up, frowning. "No, I'm afraid you don't quite understand. It's not exactly a coma, in the classic sense of the word. She is in a state of deep shock, true—the loss of blood alone could have killed her. But a coma's not exactly the right word…"

Bannister, puzzled, blurted out, "Then, just what exactly is it?"

"I'm not sure I can tell you, exactly. It's as if something is preventing…no, wait a minute," LeBlanc paused. "Let me show you this chart." He unfolded a large piece of paper on which there appeared to be a series of inky jagged lines.

Bannister shrugged. "And…?"

"This is a map, if you will. It's a map of her consciousness, so to speak, obtained from the amplified EEG. The digital readout seems to indicate that she's actually vacillating between a state of deep REM sleep and a light first-stage waking sleep. There doesn't appear to be any medical reason for her to be unconscious. It's almost as if…"

Bannister's eyes widened. "Almost as if she doesn't want to wake up…" He finished LeBlanc's sentence.

LeBlanc, clearly surprised, nodded.

At that moment, the nurse who'd shooed Bannister away, exited Margaret's room and approached the two men. Addressing LeBlanc, she said, "Her signs are still stable. She's healthy as a horse."

LeBlanc turned to Bannister, an expression of concern on his face. "Mr. Bannister, they tell me you haven't slept in two days. Why don't you go home and get some rest. There's nothing you can do tonight. I assure you, she's in no danger now."

Bannister nodded wearily, helplessly, and turned toward the hall leading to the main exit. As he emerged into the cool night air, he distractedly pulled a pack of cigarettes out of his pocket.

As he did, a slip of paper fluttered to the ground. He bent to pick it up and, straightening, he recognized it as the note the pizza delivery man had given him earlier. On the note is the cryptic message, "Quit stalling. Call now!" followed by a phone number.

Agitated, Bannister spied a nearby pay phone and rushed to it. He dialed the number and nearly dropped the phone in shock when a voice answered before the first ring.

"What took you so long, Dr. Bannister?" The voice was teasing, mocking, but strangely musical and soothing at the same time.

Nevertheless, Bannister was furious, "Listen, you son of a bitch! I don't know you, do you hear me! Get out of my fucking head!" Nearly hysterical from the stress and lack of sleep, Bannister suddenly sobered as he noticed the looks of alarm by a passing elderly couple.

Quietly, urgently he whispered, "Get out of my head, do you hear me!"

"Come now," the voice replied, this time gentle, compassionate. "You know better than that. Come on, Dr. Bannister. Have a beer, relax..."

Bannister's rage was suddenly, inexplicably gone "Okay," he said, the fatigue creeping back into his voice. "Where?"

*   *   *

Bannister rubbed the two-day stubble on his face as he walked up the stairs of the Balcony Bar on Magazine Street, a few blocks from the hospital. It was a Monday night and only a few young locals were there. All eyes were on the wall-sized monitor broadcasting the football game between the New Orleans Saints and the San Francisco 49ers. No one appeared to notice or care as Bannister's tired, ruffled form settled gratefully into one of the wooden, high-backed bar stools.

A pretty young woman behind the bar walked over and smiled vacantly, "The mixed drinks are downstairs, but we got Bud, Bud Light, and Local Poison on tap."

Bannister attempted a sardonic smile, "All three,—set me up and knock me down, darlin'."

The bartender affected exasperation, then, seeing Bannister was serious, shrugged and grabbed three mugs, methodically filling one after the other. Before Bannister could reach for his wallet, he felt a strong hand on his shoulder. He turned and gasped. He stared, dumbfounded, at the face of a man dressed in the style of Amish farmers. But the man, to Bannister's eyes, looked eerily familiar.

"You! Who are you THIS time? Matthew the Amish farmer?"

The man, powerfully built and dressed in traditional black broad cloth, simply smiled, his eyes luminous, almost taunting. Bannister looked worriedly around him. The bartender, the video monitor, the other patrons at the bar, appeared to be floating away into a dense, glowing fog.

Bannister felt his chest tighten. He stammered, "You...you're the guy who delivered the note with that pizza! Why don't you get a life, asshole!"

Matthew's smile disappeared, replaced with a stern, warning glance. "No, Dr. Bannister, I think it is time that you got *a* life."

Bannister's fear was rapidly replaced by a sense of outrage. "What do they pay you for this? Are we on some sort of reality television or what?"

""What do they pay me? The same thing they pay you, Dr. Bannister...blood, sweat, tears...hope, glory, faith...whatever rewards are appropriate for playing games with the shroud."

Bannister's irritation crested into genuine anger, "You spout all this stuff as if I'm supposed to know who you are and what's going on. What are you, some high-tech spy for the Federation?"

Matthew chuckled. "The World Federation doesn't need spies, Professor Bannister. Your life is an open book! The question is, what do YOU really want? You pretend to be an agnostic when what you really want to believe is that the cloth is miraculous. Over there, look..."

Matthew motioned to the barstool next to Bannister. Bannister was astonished to see his portfolio case, the one he used to cart around his shroud replica and research papers.

"You bastard!" Bannister screamed. "You all but kidnap me from the hospital and steal my lecture notes...!"

Suddenly Bannister stopped, as if he was finally aware of the absurdity of the scene he was acting out. He raised his arms in exasperation.

Matthew smiled, approvingly. "Now, see? It's not so bad, is it? You saw him in your dream, did you not? Margaret told you about the dream, did she not? You love her so much, you pretended to humor her. Even though your dream told you she spoke the truth."

Bannister turned and laid his head on the bar. "Damn you…damn you…damn you."

Matthew patted Bannister gently on the shoulder. "You are not alone, Dr. Bannister. If you will come with me, I think I might be able to answer some of your questions. Won't you come?"

Bannister, looked up at Matthew and nodded wearily. He grabbed his portfolio case, stood and allowed Matthew to guide him out the door. As he exited, he was vaguely aware that he was no longer in New Orleans. As his feet sank into a foot of wet snow, he realized he was somewhere else entirely.

Lancaster! Amish country.

Matthew gently guided Bannister across a narrow road to a waiting horse-drawn buggy. He helped Bannister into the buggy seat and joined him, taking the reins.

Matthew nodded to Bannister, then turned his attention to the horse. "It is not far, is it, Nellie," he said, snapping the reins.

As they rode, Bannister felt the tension of the past few days melt away. He breathed in the cold, crisp air, aware that despite his light parka the freezing temperature had not chilled him at all. He scanned the pristine countryside and fell into a long, trance-like silence.

Turning at last to Matthew, Bannister began, haltingly. "I …don't know what to think, Matthew. My dream told me something about you, but it wasn't you, exactly - and it doesn't make any sense, being here. A man, grinning, in pain, on a freakin' cross! I don't know why, but I seem to remember that Margaret knew this. What am I doing here? Where are we going?"

"Where and why and how are irrelevant for now," Matthew replied cryptically. "Just remember that it is you who chose this path. You also may choose to bear the burden of what this path represents. Or not…"

"And, what have I chosen?"

Instead of answering, Matthew handed the reins to a startled Bannister. "Shut up and drive!"

Bannister gamely tried to keep the spirited horse on the snow-covered road, but nearly lost control of it when he glimpsed a shadowy form ahead on his right. As they drew nearer, the form became clearer. Bannister yelped in surprise.

It was The Stranger, leaping down from the cross, blood dripping from his hands, marking the snow as he waved.

"Shit!" Bannister yelled, as the image disappeared. "You didn't see that?" he asks. "That was YOU! On the cross! In a different outfit!"

Matthew chuckled. "Me? Or was it you—your future?"

Bannister looked at Matthew challengingly but remained silent, feeling discombobulated. As the buggy passed by a small, quaint white clapboard house, Bannister suddenly imagined that he saw the inhabitants.

A beautiful, young, blonde woman, her hair braided and her face glowing, served steaming bowls of soup to her hardy, bearded husband and their twin, tow-headed daughters—miniature versions of the woman. Bannister suddenly saw himself at the table, waiting for the woman to serve him as well. He is not surprised when father, mother, and children turn to him and smile. As they do, Bannister looked up, as if on cue at the open sky, just as a huge, glowing, spinning sphere dissolves into the whiteness of the clouds.

Shaking his head, Bannister emerged from his trance and, as if he'd been driving the contraption all his life, expertly pulled to a halt in front of tiny wood-frame church, topped by a dazzling, golden steeple that seemed to stretch for miles into the sky.

Matthew hopped spryly onto the ground. "Time to meet our fellow travelers, Dr. Bannister. Are you prepared for your destiny? Never mind—your destiny is certainly prepared for you!" With that, Matthew motioned for Bannister to follow him up the three steps to the church entrance.

Entering, Bannister saw a miniature of the vast steeple on top of the church at the altar near the back, bathed in a bluish-silver light that he realized could only have come from the barely-perceived spinning sphere that he'd noticed earlier.

Bannister was disoriented by the miniature steeple and the light of the sphere although this was not nearly as disorienting as the people gathered in the church. People, Bannister realized without knowing quite why, were apparently there to see him. There were maybe fifty of them, equal numbers of men and women, all of whom could be clones of the blue-eyed, Dutch blonde family he saw in his trance.

Or maybe, Bannister thought to himself with a sense of rapturous bewilderment, *Matthew's children?*

Matthew, ignoring Bannister, walked to the back of the church and addressed the group. As he spoke, the people turned to face Bannister, still standing, hesitant, at the entrance. He scanned the room, almost desperately looking for an ordinary face. But each one was uniformly beautiful, pleasant, otherworldly—each with the same pair of luminous, knowing, glowing eyes. Bannister realized he should be wary and fretful, but he was instead calmed by the distinct lack of animosity in their faces, the sweetly innocent curiosity they seemed to have about him.

Matthew spoke more forcefully now. "…so, he has come, to prepare the way for our Army of Children. We feel his joy, his pain. We share his adventure. We teach, and we learn his path…"

*   *   *

Margaret wakes from a long, deep sleep, dimly aware of a strange, ethereal swell of electronic strings and pulsating chimes, syncopated, soaring keynotes fluttering over breezy, disembodied voices. She rises from her bed and walks hesitantly to a large picture window opened to a black, starless night. In the distance, the sphere looms over a glowing field, bursting with iridescent roses, the surrounding air thick with doves in flight. The waves of flowers seem to part, making way for the Stranger, astride a magnificent white stallion, trotting slowly toward her. A few yards away, the horse stops and the Stranger dismounts, leaping into the air and spinning like a top, his every movement throwing off a kaleidoscope of silver-blue sparks. He whirls and moves closer to Margaret, stops and raises his arms in exultation. As he does, a shriveled tree erupts from the ground, shimmers, then sprouts vivid green leaves. The Stranger moves closer, whirls, and again raises his arms as a scrawny miniature elephant leaps off the palms of his cupped hands. His cloak billowing and emitting a profusion of sparks, the Stranger stands still, his eyes locked into Margaret's. She claws at the air in front of her as the Stranger smiles, whirls, and fades into a blur of light. His face emerges from the whirlpool of light as a Tibetan villager. He whirls again and he is an African prince. Again, and he is Margaret, and Bannister, and her long-dead mother and father, and...

Margaret cries, "Who are you? Why are you?"

The Stranger, in the midst of yet another madcap whirl, stops, as if he's been rudely interrupted. He fades from view, instantaneously replaced by the image of a cross, dripping blood. The image fades into a red-hued Satanic figure, licking its lips with an obscene serpentine tongue that abruptly lashes out to within inches of Margaret's face. The Stranger reappears, dispatches the evil visage with one swipe of a daisy-covered lance, and turns to Margaret, smiling, beckoning her to step through the window. As she does, she realizes she is naked, waist-deep in cool, mountaintop pool. Feeling a hand on her shoulder, she turns to face the Stranger. They embrace and sink into the water as the sphere looms over head.

Margaret moaned as her eyes jerked open. Bannister, who had been asleep in a chair by her bed, was startled awake by her cries. He stood and bent over her. "Welcome back, darling. Do you remember anything?"

Instead of answering, Margaret's face hardens. "Turn it on! Now!" she exclaimed pointing to the video monitor on the wall. Dumbfounded, Bannister complied. The screen came to life. A talking head appeared over the commentator's shoulder as he talked. A montage of fantastic images flashed.

"...and World Federation officials said they were at a loss to explain the latest incidents connected with the appearance of the sphere. FEM director Emmett Finley said his agency is investigating reports on a new series of explosions at Mt. Vesuvius. He says that eyewitness accounts of a reversal of the lava flow have not been confirmed, but unofficial sources vehemently contend that event did in fact happen. Other reports of a man who seemingly stood in the lava flow and was heard to 'command' the lava to retreat, appear to be the result of mass hysteria, according to at least one Federation behavioral officer on the scene. In other news. . ."

Bannister turned the volume down. Margaret looked at him knowingly. "I saw him again last night, Richard. You did, too, didn't you? And for you, it wasn't a dream this time."

Bannister sighed. "I honestly don't know."

*　　*　　*

World Federation Council Summit, Zurich, three days later.

Christian Koehn sat forbiddingly erect as he half-listened to a speech by the Federation Secretary which he already knew would confirm his election to replace Santo Diaz. Kurtz interrupted Koehn's reverie with a light tap on his shoulder and handed him a note. Koehn smiled and returned his attention to the speaker.

"...so it is confirmed, by a vote of 9 to 1, with Free Asia abstaining, that Christian Koehn is the new President of the World Federation Council." With that, the assembly—11 Council members and 100 policy advisers—erupted in applause.

Koehn rose to his feet and made his way to the podium as he was introduced by the speaker, Canada's Annabella Pogue.

"Madame Secretary," Koehn began, "I do not wish to address the Council in full at this time. However, I have just received a report that assures that we will soon have this prankster and his 'miracles' under control. Until then, I thank you for your support."

*　　*　　*

The fighting at the Turkish-Iraqi border was horrific and brutal, the air thick with smoke and punctuated by the deafening screams of the wounded and dying and the steady report of gunfire and explosions. Kurdish rebels and Iraqi shock troops who were engaged in hand-to-hand combat on the streets, severed limbs with bayonets, shards of glass, blocks of concrete, and anything handy. One soldier, running to chase down a fleeing enemy tried to raise his arm and he screamed in horror as it was ripped from the shoulder by random mortar fire. It dropped heavily to the ground, spattering the ground and his fatigues with sticky red liquid.

Into the insanity, a lone figure walked calmly and serenely. Bullets, grenades, and rocket fire, and passing swipes of machetes and bayonets glanced off or passed through him with no apparent effect. As he walked, the sphere loomed overhead, filling the sky with a blinding light and an ear-splitting hum, instantaneously immobilizing the soldiers on the ground. As the sphere vanished, startled soldiers groggily regarded the passing Stranger with growing awe. Recovering his battle spirit, one enraged soldier rushed The Stranger with a bayonet. Turning, The Stranger raised his hands and laughed out loud at the shocked expression on the soldier's face as he suddenly released his weapon, which fell to the ground, now a writhing snake. The Stranger whirled and pointed to a shattered building nearby, smiling approvingly as the astonished soldiers watched broken walls and crushed foundations transformed into flowering bushes and pools ringed with cobblestones. Bombed out bunkers were transformed into playgrounds, teeming with laughing children. The sphere returned and The Stranger vanished.

*   *   *

Bannister stormed away from the main Tulane campus building, muttering angrily to himself.

"Hey, Dr. Bannister! Wait up!" It was Angela, one of his students. He turned briefly to the sound of her voice and continued walking toward St. Charles Avenue. Angela rushed to catch up, her blonde hair streaming behind her as she quickened her pace.

"Hey, what's up, Dr. Bannister?" she asked breathlessly, as she caught up to him and fell into stride.

Bannister strode up to the neutral ground that ran down the center of St. Charles Avenue. Quickly stepping back, narrowly avoiding a passing streetcar, and irritated, he turned to Angela.

"What's up? What the fuck is up?" Bannister yelled.

Angela's eyes widened at Bannister's outburst. "Whoa! Watch thy mouth," she exclaimed, laughing. "So, what IS up? You look like you want to kill your best friend!"

"I'm sorry," Bannister said, calming down somewhat. "It's just that my dean just informed me that the Federation Science Institute has been putting pressure on Tulane to cancel my classes on the Shroud."

"What? They can't do that!"

"Well, they did just that, which is why I'm going over there," he replied, pointing to a grassy area near a lagoon as he walked across St. Charles into Audubon Park. "Yep—if I can't take my class to class, as it were, I'll take my class with me. Spread the word—tomorrow's class is gonna be outside, in the Park."

Angela chuckled. "As good as done, Herr Doctor!"

*   *   *

The day was unseasonably warm for early December as Bannister set up an easel and the Shroud documents at Audubon Park. Most of the students in Bannister's class had shown up and were gathered around him in a circle.

As Bannister spoke, he was pleased to see that Margaret rejoined the class. He smiled at her and continued.

"I thought he'd be a little more into the class out in the open, but I guess I was wrong, eh, Jason?" Bannister nodded in the direction of the scowling jock.

"But I think he has a point though," Bannister continued. "Jason said earlier that the whole world is going crazy over these Stranger sightings and I'm playing Mr. Mystical by continuing these lectures. But I don't think anyone's proven that the Shroud is even remotely connected to these, er, events..."

Bannister paused abruptly, his eyes registering shock. Suddenly, the sphere appeared over the nearby lagoon, the wind rose and an ear-splitting hum filled the air. The students all covered their ears, grimacing in pain. As the sphere vanished, a dense fog lifted from the lagoon and The Stranger, resplendent in a brilliant multicolored robe, his auburn hair falling loosely to his waist, rose from the water.

Jason was the first to recover. Picking up a nearby tree branch, he leaped to his feet and rushed toward the approaching Stranger. "You sick bastard! You're dead!"

The Stranger smiled and sidestepped Jason's first swing, laughing gleefully. The student's face twisted in horror as the tree branch turned into a very live and prickly porcupine in his hands. He dropped the animal and watched, along with his amazed classmates, as it bounced once and rematerialized as a dove that flew lazily into the air.

The Stranger walked over to Jason, and passed a glowing hand over the cowering student's head. "Jason, my man, I think you need to grow up." Instantly, Jason transformed into a five-year-old boy. "And now, you've got the opportunity!"

The Stranger turned and faced the students. "Well, well — what have we here? I know I haven't introduced myself properly, but I trust I've managed to entertain you. In fact, please allow me to play a little Q&A with you. Anyone? No? Well, how about a riddle…"

The Stranger sighed dramatically. "In the old days, this particular form of riddle was called a 'knock-knock' joke, I do believe. Okay, here goes—Knock-knock!"

Silence.

"Come now, children," he said, mock disappointment heavy in his voice. "You can do better than that! Knock-knock!"

Angela, laughing now, piped up. "Who's there?"

"Savior."

"Savior who?"

The Stranger grinned goofily. "Why, Save yer money for a rainy day!"

He slapped his knee and laughed uproariously, immensely please at his corny pun. Despite themselves, the group, including Richard and Margaret laughed with him.

"Good," The Stranger said. "Now, let's try this one: Why is it you always find what you're looking for in the very last place you look?"

Silence.

"Because," The Stranger laughed, "when you FIND it, you STOP looking - and that was the LAST place you looked!"

Bannister feigned irritation. "Jeez, as much trouble as you've caused, you should tell a few jokes to break the ice. But who the hell ARE you?"

The Stranger, as if seeing Bannister for the first time, smiled-mischievously. "Tsk-tsk, Dr. Bannister. You don't remember that wonderful shrimp and black olive pizza I delivered to your door last week? Did you somehow forget nearly driving that horse and buggy off the road? Nearly killed me, you did—and I was already pretty bleedin' banged up as it was!"

Bannister was struck dumb, a glimmer of understanding slowly creeping into his wide eyes.

The Stranger twirled his cape and bowed. "Who am I?" he asked, taking a step toward Bannister.

"I am a clown." His face transformed into a postcard perfect circus clown.

"I am the earth." The Stranger's face swelled into a spinning globe.

"I am the sun, the moon, the air. I am the sky. I am mystery and love and light," he whispered musically, his form shimmering with a bluish-silver light, mirroring the elements in a way that seemed to be pure suggestion, without concrete substance.

"I am within you and without you. The beginning, and the end, and the beginning once more."

The Stranger turned serious. "I believe it's time to accept questions from the floor, er...I mean, the ground. Angela?"

Angela jumps. "How? Oh, jeez—what AM I thinking!" She giggled. "Of course you'd know, Morph Man! Okay, how do we know you're not some sort of high-tech prankster. I mean fifty years ago, some old magician named David Copperfield made the Statue of Liberty vanish in thin air. With the technology now, ANYONE can do tricks like that."

"Ah, yes! And so they can," The Stranger said. "But you see, we all have the ability to believe what we choose. But some beliefs are valid, some are not. And belief in a Supreme Being, which I am sure some of you think I'm pretending to be, is— and always has been—a matter of faith. It was never intended that there be any material proof of something that is other than material…"

He paused, chuckling, then added, "Which is certainly not to say, 'immaterial!' I can assure you that faith itself is not immaterial. It's the very fabric of life, as is love. Without one, the other is impossible. I'm simply a messenger. What people choose to believe—and more importantly, what they choose to believe IN—is entirely up to them. Some of us here now will see that in the coming days, including - and perhaps especially - your Dr. Bannister."

With that, the Stranger began to glow. As he disappeared, two Federation harrier anti-gravity hovercraft roared up to the spot where the Stranger had just been. Josef Kurtz leaped out of the first craft, followed by two dozen heavily armed troopers. Startled by the sudden turn of events, the crowd scattered. Bannister grabbed Margaret's arm and turned to flee, but Kurtz leveled his stun weapon and fired, hitting Bannister in the legs. Immobilized, Bannister urged the panic-stricken Margaret to run, but she refused. In the last minute before Kurtz could reach her, the Stranger reappeared and pulled Margaret behind a nearby oak tree. Kurtz rushed around the tree only to discover a wisp of illuminated fog swirling up into the branches and finally melting into the sphere which itself soon vanished. Enraged, Kurtz returned to Bannister and jerked him to his feet.

"Where is he," he screamed into Bannister's contorted face. Bannister pointed to the tree. With a shout, Kurtz knocked Bannister unconscious with the butt of his weapon.

*　　*　　*

Margaret sees the Stranger approaching, astride his white stallion, its eyes ablaze with the light of the sphere. The Stranger dismounts, smiling, his arms open in invitation. When they kiss, Margaret feels faint, then awakes with a violent shudder.

The Stranger leaned over her and Margaret realized she was back in her own apartment. Impulsively, she reached up to touch the Stranger's face, jerking it away with a pained shout. She looked at her seared flesh and moaned. The Stranger passed a glowing hand over Margaret's and she watched in amazement as the ugly red welt miraculously disappeared. The pain was gone.

The Stranger straightened and walked to the window. "I suppose you're wondering what you have to do with all this?" he quizzed distractedly, almost as if he was addressing the trees outside the window.

"I suppose I should…"

He continued to stare out the window. "Let me put it this way: you don't seem to realize that you are just as capable as I. You can perform these miracles that everyone seems to think I perform. You are ready, I hope, to accept the possibility of miracles. But I believe you're wondering if I mean 'miracles' in the sense of those, er…tricks. I did in the park. As Angela said, anyone can do tricks. The real miracle is love and the capacity to believe and imagine and create a world that is ruled ONLY by love. THAT is the miracle. And everyone already has that gift. Too bad so few choose to claim it."

The Stranger waved away Margaret's question, his face plastered with a maddeningly goofy grin. "Hey, cher," he said, affecting her Cajun accent, "are ya hungry? Let's you and me take a walk, yeah. I wanna show you a few things about illusions."

The Stranger took her hand and together they left her apartment on Royal Street. Three blocks from the apartment on Royal, the two of them walked hand in hand into the heart of Jackson Square, laughing and skipping alongside the iron fence that ringed the park in front of the imposing St. Louis Cathedral.

As they moved through the crowd, an angelic elderly lady leaped out of her wheelchair and danced a jig, much to the amazement of the woman pushing her. Two young teenaged tap dancers in ragged bluejeans and T-shirts suddenly found themselves bedecked in tuxedos. The dapper duo tapped over to a spot where a dreadlocked guitarist just found himself riffing on a gleaming new Stratocaster, his battered acoustic box instantly a thing of the past. Four young black men reintensified their acrobatics near the cathedral as the Stranger and Margaret bounced by, inventing celestial Zydeco dance steps as they went. Everywhere tourists in Bermuda shorts and thong bikinis dropped their shopping packages and joined the mushrooming, New Orleans style second line dance sprouting in the Stranger's wake. High above, the sphere blinked on and off in a visual symphony of light.

*   *   *

Kurtz and his specially trained team of Federation behavioral officers were frustrated as they looked at the bruised and bleeding figure of Richard Bannister, splayed out on a tiny, hard cot across the room. A silver-suited officer addressed Kurtz.

"Permission to speak freely, sir."

Kurtz nodded impatiently.

"In my opinion, he knows nothing, sir. I would have a great deal of trouble continuing the interrogation beyond this point."

Kurtz nodded solemnly. "I'm inclined to agree. Even under the stress of the synaptic reordering instruments, he is clearly as ignorant as we are about the origins and intent of the man and the sphere."

Kurtz sighed, clearly troubled. Briefly, a look of pity crossed his face. He touched a square on a panel connected to his belt and Koehn's image materialized on a monitor mounted on the wall.

"Yes?"

"Sir, I understand your frustration, but we have tried all of the available techniques. He cannot take much more punishment. My honest opinion, sir?"

Koehn stared, his face hard.

Kurtz continued, "He knows nothing. His lectures on the shroud were purely academic. We have it on good authority that Bannister is an agnostic."

"Very well—but I reserve the right to question him again myself." Koehn, not waiting for a reply, touched a key on his pad, and vanquished Kurtz' image to the electronic ether.

Koehn was tired, worried, his face betraying uncharacteristic doubt. He touched a keypad and turned in his chair to the monitors behind him. "Dammit!" he screamed to the empty room. Momentarily in shock, his mood quickly turned violently angry as the full frame picture of The Stranger stared back at him, grinning madly. Koehn frantically pushed every button on his keypad. Each time, the images flickered, disappeared, and popped back instantly with the face of the Stranger.

"We meet again, anti-Christian Koehn! Whatsa matter, big boy—technology got your metaphysical tongue?"

*   *   *

Bannister stirred, opening his one good eye. He briefly touched the other, swollen shut. Before he could take stock of his injuries, the sphere, no larger than a baseball this time, materialized, replaced almost instantly by the figure of The Stranger, hovering over him, suspended in the air beside the cot.

Bannister recoiled in fright. The Stranger landed softly on the floor beside Bannister. As his feet touched the ground, Bannister realized the pain was gone. Unaccountably, at least to himself, Bannister laughed, surprised he could move his facial muscles without wincing. He leaped up from his cot. The Stranger playfully jumped back, raised his arms, disappeared momentarily, then reappeared sitting on a plush, purple velvet couch that floated several feet above the floor. A silver crown of thorns was perched at a rakish angle above his grinning face.

"Last time I saw YOU, you layin' down on de job like a wino on a three-day binge. Now you're practically a new man, Dr. Bannister. In fact, I think you ARE a brand new man!", he teased.

The Stranger touched his crown, smirking. Bannister's eyes betrayed pure confusion. "Like it? Last time, it was a real pain in the noggin. I kinda like the new version better, don't you?" At that The Stranger laughed, nearly losing his balance before catching himself in mid-fall.

Suddenly angry, Bannister shouted, "After all this shit you've put me through, go ahead and fall, you smug bastard!"

The Stranger turned serious. "Oh, come off it, Professor. It was YOU who decided to conduct those Shroud classes. Then you took your act to the park when the school told you to stop. But, naah, the self-righteous Dr. Bannister decided to do as he darned well pleased, despite the risks. If you think you're going to pin your predicament on me, you're sadly mistaken. You made your choice. I didn't have to come here and heal those wounds, you know."

Bannister looked up angrily, "And you don't have to stay, either, you arrogant asshole!"

The Stranger shook his head sadly, then brightened. "Knock-knock! Who's there? Savior! Savior who? Save your self-pity fer your mother, wimp!"

Bannister's shoulders sagged. "I honestly don't know what you mean."

The Stranger looked mortified. "Oh, but I think you DO! Remember a flashback you had not too long ago, about playing doctor with little Mary when you were a child?"

Bannister nodded, no longer surprised at the Stranger's prescience.

The Stranger continued, "Well, your mother blistered your little fanny for that, didn't she? You were raised believing that touching little girls was nasty, naughty, sinful business. But when you were older, guess what? Suddenly, it was okay, even healthy to touch grown-up girls, especially if they happened to be your wife. Two similar acts, two very different belief systems. Which one was valid?"

Bannister, perplexed, remained silent.

"You're here," The Stranger said, "because Christian Koehn seems to think you're the key to get to me. Well, I'm here to demonstrate to YOU that the Shroud may have some basis in reality—your reality, if nothing else. Like it or not, Richard, the Shroud really is miraculous. Your theory about the burst of radiation? Yep—that's EXACTLY what happened. A MIRACLE! Trouble is, it's still not proof of a Supreme Being, is it? But the Federation—or at least Herr Koehn—fear that it just might be the kind of proof that upsets this society's worship of technology and, therefore of THEM—the ruling elite. But everything anyone knows about this, ultimately is wrong. The point is, all the proof in the world won't change anyone's belief or lack of belief in a Supreme Being. Seeing is not necessarily a basis for belief. And that's as it should be, Richard. Because if something so obviously miraculous, so obviously beyond the need for proof, isn't enough to make people at least consider that it came with the miracle the first time, well, Richard, I'm afraid miracles aren't all they're cracked up to be."

"Don't feel so bad, Richard. Humanity didn't get it the first few times around, either. The miracles were designed only to show people their own potential for their own innate possibilities, their own miracle-making and their own sense of magic, faith, and most of all, love. Koehn and the Federation would have you believe that 'magic' and belief in miracles is inherently dangerous or stupid or both. But dangerous to whom? After all, if people can create their own miracles—create their own magic and love—what do they need the Federation for? But most people are too lazy to try it for themselves and, naturally, the Federation likes it just the way things are. My father's kingdom—our father's kingdom—is already here…"

The Stranger pointed to Bannister's head. "…and here." He touched Richard's chest next to his heart.

The Stranger began to glow. As his body faded, his voice lingered for a moment longer. "Don't let them kill your capacity to create a miracle in your own life, Richard. It's there. All you have to do is claim it."

* * *

Bannister, despite the implied threats, had yet to meet Koehn in person. Instead, Koehn decided to speak to the professor via a two-way monitor.

"I don't have to ask whether or not you understand the charges. I'm sure your training at MIT is proof enough of your intelligence."

Bannister looked back at Koehn evenly, his voice measured and calm. "It really doesn't matter whether I understand the charges, now does it? Your goons have already told you I don't have the foggiest notion of who or what the stranger is. Isn't that enough for you?"

Koehn rolled his eyes in disgust. "Oh, but don't you? Seems you two were quite friendly when he was in your cell. I wonder if you'd care to explain that?"

"Only if YOU would care to explain why you and your stupid goons couldn't seal off the cell and trap him," Bannister smirked, obviously pleased by Koehn's annoyance.

EDWIN CHRISTIAN ALLMAN

*　　*　　*

Franz Brightbill stood beside a woman in a wheelchair, facing the window of her hospital room, her eyes blank, devoid of any awareness of her surroundings. Brightbill spoke softly, well aware that this pretty and young but much older than her years woman couldn't hear him.

Almost to himself, Brightbill whispered, "I promise you he will not go unpunished! I remember you as a young girl, so sweet, so trusting. My God, what he did to you! Twenty years! Twenty…years!!"

Brightbill clenched his fists, then relaxed as he bent down to kiss his sister, then shuffled sadly out of the room.

In the darkened room, a pinpoint of light danced like a beacon of shame on a single teardrop that rolled slowly down the woman's cheek.

*　　*　　*

Bannister was increasingly alert, his wounds all but healed from the trauma of his interrogation. He sat at a large table, listening as a mid-fiftyish, gray-haired gentleman with a mockingly kind face consulted a sheaf of papers on the table between them.

Camille Bergeron, the attorney assigned to defend Bannister, looked up at Bannister with a tight smile. "Let's see. You're the first, last, and probably only case that will be tried in Los Angeles Coliseum. Looks like you've got the charges to match, too! Accessory after the fact for interfering with Federation broadcast signals. Secular sorcery—oh, that's a new one! Oh, yes, misappropriation of Federation university funds. Yessir, when you piss people off, you make sure you soak their pants but good!"

"And they got me just the right legal guy, too. I piss people off, and you lick it off their boots," Bannister shot back.

Momentarily taken aback, Bergeron recovered, "Oh, I do all right, I guess. A couple hundred thousand Fedmarks for three hours work. Not bad for a bootlicker, wouldn't you say?"

Bergeron motioned for the security officers to lead Bannister to the waiting car which will take the accused Professor and the security team to the makeshift courtroom on the floor of the coliseum.

As the procession rolled slowly into the coliseum, Bannister noted with astonishment that the stadium was packed. More than 100,000 people had filled the stadium and tens of thousands more were outside in the parking lots, watching the proceedings from temporary video monitors set up for the occasion. Earlier, a news net commentator said that the trial would be carried live and was expected to draw an audience of up to 6 billion worldwide — more than half the people on the planet.

Yeah, Bannister - it's a helluva time to be an agnostic!

As Bannister's vehicle reached the court staging area, he stole a glimpse at Koehn, who was staring at nothing apparently, his eyes eerily vacant.

Koehn surveyed the scene from his perch atop the platform on which the "courtroom" had been fabricated. From his vantage point, he could see the makeshift jury box and he had a panoramic view of the assembled crowd as well. He was smugly self-satisfied, alert to his surroundings, but he remembers:

Koehn is speaking to an unseen Persona, someone for whom he feels great reverence. "For as long as I can remember, from my days at school, I knew I would face my destiny in an arena as grand as this," he says.

"You were my understudy," the unseen replies. "Soon you will be my master. Your glory will spite the defiled holy ones. You will rule all that is above and below."

Koehn's face is radiant with intense, mad joy. He instinctively touches a scar on his scalp and is transported—a dream within a dream. He is on top of his naked teacher, her face twisted in fear and revulsion. "You dirty Jewish bitch! You filthy, vile bloodsucker! You will worship my hatred for you!"

The unseen intones, "They accused you..."

Koehn is transported to a courtroom, the judge pronounces him innocent.

The unseen interjects, "They murdered you..."

Koehn is transported yet again, feeling his skull crush under the weight of the chain the mob used to avenge their neighbor...

EDWIN CHRISTIAN ALLMAN

The unseen's voice rises triumphantly, "After three days, you arose from the dead. You openly admitted defiling the teacher, yet you were exonerated. It is time for the world to see your true power. Let their blood flow in rapture and their love turn to fear, forever."

Koehn was suddenly alert. The monitors sprang to life as the judge settled into his seat in front of Koehn and two fellow observers from the Federation Council. Koehn looked pointedly at Bannister, who returned the gaze with a mixture of fear and anger.

Bannister looked around expectantly at the crowd, relieved to see that Margaret and Matthew were sitting just a few rows above him. He turned his attention to the judge who was reading the charges.

"Representatives of the Federation, members of the prosecution and the defense, ladies and gentlemen. You have no doubt heard of the charges today against Richard Bannister, former professor of photography at Tulane University. For the record, let it be noted that Dr. Bannister has been charged with a number of crimes, the most serious of which concern treason against the World Federation government. All of the charges are the direct result of Dr. Bannister's alleged association and complicity with a prankster who has been disrupting World Federation business over the past few weeks. The government will prove that he, in his role as a professor, intentionally disseminated scientifically discredited information that has severely disrupted the Federation's ability to govern. Because these pranks continue, and because Dr. Bannister has refused to renounce his heresies, both the Asian and African factions have submitted articles of secession from the Federation. They claim that if the Federation cannot control the misdeeds of one man, they can hardly expect to ask their people to continue their allegiance to a one-world government. In view of the seriousness of these charges, and Dr. Bannister's part in the consequences, it is the court's right and duty to allow Mr. Bannister's accusers, the World Federation government, to present a more detailed rationale for bringing Dr. Bannister to trial. We will hear from the Federation's Council president, Christian Koehn. Council President Koehn?"

Koehn rose to speak. "Thank you, your honor. It is our contention, and the record bears this out, that the Federation stands for truth and justice. But of greater importance, to the quality of life for the world's citizens, the Federation stands for world order—order which has resulted in peace and prosperity unparalleled in human history. Yet two men—Dr. Bannister, and his unidentified cohort—have conspired to create a mockery of our society. They would have you believe that magic and sorcery are somehow preferable to established codes of order. But ignorance, whether in the name of freedom or justice, has long been the scourge of mankind. The Crusades licensed religious fanatics to murder thousands of innocents in the name of an unseen God. So it was with the Middle Eastern, Asian, African, and Bosnian crises in the latter 20th century and the African and Indian schism at the beginning of this one. Dr. Bannister seeks to continue this brutal legacy by helping further the disruptions of a man who performs so-called miracles on this society. A miracle -maker by the way, who has triggered civil disobedience and threatens possible regional wars that will severely disrupt—maybe even destroy—the quality of life we have come to enjoy over the past thirty years.

Bannister could contain himself no longer. He jumped to his feet, but was quickly restrained. As he was forced to his seat he yelled, "But Koehn already knows the answer! His own behavioral officer says I don't know what's going on!"

Exasperated, Bannister looked again in the direction of Margaret and Matthew, startled to discover that they were surrounded by the luminous faces of the people he met on his journey to Amish Country.

The Army of Children!

No sooner than the shock of recognition registered with Bannister, there was a roar from the crowd, immediately drowned out by an monstrous, overwhelming hum. The sphere, blinding in intensity, magnified the stadium lights a thousandfold as it hovered just a few hundred yards above the hushed stadium.

For a moment, the huge stadium monitors went blank, then blinked on again. The Stranger's grinning face appeared.

"Greetings!" his voice boomed from the speakers. "And

may I add that it's a FINE night for a crucifixion—or is that FIC-TION?"

The Stranger's face faded from view, replaced by what looked like a toy doll, writhing on a cross of something resembling like pink plastic.

Bannister jumped as he felt a hand on his shoulder. He turned to regard the gently smiling stranger, resplendent in his robe. Winking, he pulled back the robe to reveal a white T-shirt emblazoned with the words, DYSLEXIC ATHEISTS DON'T BELIEVE IN DOG.

"Sorry I'm late," The Stranger said to Bannister, then to the crowd, "but I had to replace the batteries in the sphere. Six hundred million 'D' cells aren't exactly cheap, y'know?"

The crowd had fallen deathly silent. The figure of The Stranger stood before the judge's platform, regarding Koehn and the rest of the officials with a look of amusement.

He fixed his gaze on Koehn. The video monitors seemed to show The Stranger looking in all directions at once - crazily, impossibly, each monitor showed a different face. Each monitor showed a figure wearing The Stranger's oddly luminescent outfit. One was a young black woman, another a small white boy, and yet another revealed the face of an ancient Chinese man.

Koehn, far from appearing to be outraged or even shocked, looked supremely satisfied. He looked at the judge and nodded. The judge nodded in return and lowered his head to his microphone.

Addressing Bannister, the judge said, "Dr. Bannister, it appears that you have complied with our request. The charges are hereby dismissed without comment."

As the astonished crowd murmured, an even more perplexed Bannister simply stared back at the judge. A security guard walked to Bannister's table and motioned him to a chair beside Margaret and Matthew. Sitting beside Margaret, he regarded her with a look of puzzlement. Smiling, Margaret reached for his hand and squeezed it softly.

On the platform below, the judge continued, addressing The Stranger. "I see you have decided to join us! I must say, this is a rather anticlimatic end to a most infuriating few weeks. I…"

Koehn interrupted, "May I, your honor?"

Flustered, the judge merely shrugged. With a curt nod, Koehn stood up, walked to the judge's podium and lifted the microphone. He regarded The Stranger with malevolent contempt. But to the obvious shock of the officials on the stand with him, he addressed The Stranger as he would an old adversary.

Koehn affected a tone of casual indifference. "My, my, here is the Holy Prankster, come to taunt us again with his useless message of love and stupidity! Dressed, as always, in his bargain basement rags of many colors!"

The Stranger smiled and bowed deeply.

"Yes, indeed," Koehn continued, his voice rising, "you come again! A man clever enough to elude our investigators, yet stupid enough to think his appearance here will have any lasting effect on the Federation's authority. Surely you know, this changes nothing!"

The Stranger smiled sadly, nodding. He raised his arm in a gesture of mock surrender, whirled to regard the crowd, whirled again, then stopped, facing Koehn once again. But oddly enough, the monitors seemed to show that he was looking directly at each one of the cameras ringing the floor.

Finally, he spoke. "Just as we agreed, so very long ago, Herr Koehn!"

In the stands, Bannister's face registered shock. He turned to Matthew with a quizzical look. Matthew shook his head slowly. Gravely, he placed his finger to his lips and returned his gaze to the floor.

"So," Koehn thundered back at The Stranger, a profound note of sarcasm in his deep voice, "to what do we owe the monumental inconsequence of your visit?"

The Stranger, chuckling, pulled a small metallic disk out of his cloak and waved it dramatically. "Oh, just some inconsequential information that was handed to me just a few minutes ago by your trusted number one officer, Josef Kurtz, courtesy of one very helpful Dr. Franz Brightbill. I believe you are acquainted with his sister?"

Koehn's face reddened vividly. The Stranger cut him off as he opened his mouth to respond.

"Let's just say, then," The Stranger said, "that I have a hit record that's gonna go to the top of the charts all over the world, Herr Koehn. But enough of pleasantries. You want to know why I am here, I believe. Your strategy has worked, I admit. You knew I would not allow Dr. Bannister to suffer much longer. However, wouldn't you also admit your strategy has backfired? I mean, I am living proof that the Federation's power—your power—hasn't been enough to eliminate the seeds of doubt I've planted everywhere else. Now, here I am, right in your little playpen, and still you are powerless!"

Koehn, recovering, yawned dramatically, simultaneously motioning to a group of security officers a few yards behind them. Weapons drawn, they advanced on The Stranger. But before they reached him, the Stranger wheeled and opened his cloak. From his chest, a rapid stream of what appeared to be marshmallow cream erupted, instantly immobilizing the guards.

The Stranger turned again to face Koehn. "Stuck-up little soldiers, aren't they? Didn't even bother to say hello. But, back to your little problem, Herr Koehn. This will take only a few minutes and then you can go back to your games. If you can!"

Koehn made a movement as if to charge The Stranger himself, but also found himself immobile. Enraged, he screamed, "Enough of your tricks! It is not your time and you know it!"

The Stranger appeared hurt, "Oh, you wound me, sir! You're right, it is not my time! But it *is* time for the world to wake up to who you really are, stripped of your medals and your promises of peace and prosperity…"

The Stranger smiled in the direction of Matthew, Margaret, Bannister and the Army of Children were now making their way, single file, down the stands illuminated by the light of the sphere, silently spinning just 100 yards above the floor.

"You brought Dr. Bannister here to make an example of him. The Shroud, the sphere, my appearance here—they are all symbols of rebellion against the world government of yours. A world government that purports to offer security and order and a souffle' in every pot, as it were."

"Yet for all your power, you cannot control what you call the pranks of a single man. You dismiss me as a prankster, yet you claim I am a threat to world order. I am not a threat to anything or anyone. It is what I symbolize that scares you so—the power of love, the power of faith in human self-determination."

"In my time here, you have seen deserts turned to verdant gardens. The dying have seized the gift of life. A volcano's lava flow has been reversed and made harmless. Entire armies have laid down their guns."

"More than two thousand years ago, one loaf of bread and a single fish became a meal for five thousand people, or so the legend goes. But that and miracles more wonderful than that were not enough to change even one doubter's beliefs. Those who would will it, openly challenged the message. These are not miracles, they said! He—whoever he was—did not really want you to believe that the Kingdom of Heaven is within you! NO!"

The Stranger seemed to grown larger, more luminous as he spoke. His eyes appeared literally, to be on fire.

"NO! They told you that He willed you to follow Him and, in his absence, a bunch of officials in priest's robes or government uniforms or technocrats lab coats. YOU! YOU cannot find such wisdom for yourselves! NO, they tell you, follow us! WE know the truth!"

The Stranger paused, shook his head sadly, then continued, "Now, millenniums later, the Federation says, 'You cannot think for yourselves! We will do it for you! Only THEN will there be peace and prosperity.' If there be only one truth, then by goodness it should come from one church, or a State or—in your case, Herr Koehn—one man strong enough to enforce it!

"I have come to bear witness to a much more intriguing and productive possibility: that power comes from love, and faith comes from love and that love itself resides exclusively within and among each of us. We cannot measure it but we surely must learn the boundaries of the Kingdom. And we surely must learn that it is within us, not 'out there' somewhere, codified into a bunch of laws and rules that serve only those who make them!"

As The Stranger spoke, the sphere slowly began to intensify in brilliance, spinning faster and faster. Then it started throwing out a profusion of sparks that stretched into a beam which struck the faces of the Army of Children as they encircled The Stranger.

The Stranger looked rapturous, as he raised his arms, the coliseum seemed to whirl in the vastness of space. "It is a miracle, this life of ours. Each one of you can create your own universe . No, perhaps I should say each one of you IS your own universe. You are the masters of a rich and infinite domain that is uniquely your own, yet is intimately and eternally connected to each other's universe."

As the Army of Children drew in a tighter circle around the Stranger, the sphere descended to a point just a few feet above their heads. The coliseum was suddenly plunged into a cacophony of sound and light, reverberating with an unbearable hum. Just as suddenly, the monitors went blank and a cold, stiff wind arose, nearly knocking Koehn off his feet.

The Stranger's voice was barely audible above the noise now, but he could be heard clearly. "I have come today to take with me those of you who would transcend this madness in this limited place. Those of you who remain, wise or not, may or may not resume your search for the great *I Am*. Many of you will be told that my appearance here was a trick. But I could not allow Dr. Bannister to suffer any longer on my account. Nor will I sacrifice myself for a cause for people who will use my message to enslave others."

The Stranger looked fixedly at Koehn, all trace of amusement gone from his eyes. He motioned to a spot just behind Koehn who turned with a gasp to see the stern faces of Husington, Brightbill, and Kurtz.

The Stranger shouted over the now-deafening roar of the sphere, "Herr Koehn, you indeed have a date with destiny, but not the one your 'Other' foretold. Watch the monitors, Herr Koehn!"

Koehn instinctively looked up at the monitors and the Stranger's voice was lost in the ear-splitting noise. As Koehn looked, The Stranger and the crowd around him seemed to dissolve into the unbearable light of the sphere.

"Watch the monitors, Herr Koehn!" came the disembodied voice of the Stranger.

Koehn turned to face Brightbill, who calmly walked toward

him, holding a metallic disk. He handed to disk to Kurtz, who placed it into a nearby recording device fed into the monitors. On the screen, the tortured face of Brightbill's sister loomed like an avenging dragon. "I accuse you, Herr Koehn! I accuse!"

Brightbill motioned to Kurtz, who in turn nodded to nearby security guards. Koehn looked up challengingly and commanded, "Stay where you are, officer!" Ignoring him, the officers advanced on Koehn, seized him roughly and whisked him to a waiting vehicle which took him away.

In the stunned silence that followed, a deep, melodic, disembodied voice, much different from the Stranger's lighthearted tenor, rose in the vacuum.

"There is one who comes after who is greater. Will you look within in time to find what has been there all along? Will love conquer your fear?"

*　　*　　*

Dr. Richard Bannister stood at the lectern in his classroom once again. He slowly rolled up the Shroud replica and placed it, along with his research papers, into his portfolio case. He looked wearily, helplessly at Margaret, who followed him out the door. As he turned out the light and closed the door, Bannister heard a loud voice from a door down the hall.

He and Margaret entered the door marked "Faculty Lounge" barely acknowledging the curious stares and whispers of some of his colleagues. Instead, they train their attention on a monitor built into the wall.

A news commentator was standing in front of the World Federation government headquarters in New York, talking at a rapid, breathless pace:

"...and from reports from the World Federation Science Institute, all records of the sightings of the sphere have apparently been confiscated for further study by a Council faction headed by Canada's Annabella Pogue. Experts say that it will be a few days before a final analysis can be made..."

"In related news," the commentator's voice-over continued over images of an ashen-faced Koehn, shaking his head, mouthing the words, 'No comment.'" The World Federation Science Consultant, Dr. Franz Brightbill urged the Federation Council to reopen the long-sealed tapes documenting Koehn's trial for rape while he was in college. A highly placed source with the Federation Justice Department, who asked not to be named, has meanwhile confirmed that the alleged rape victim, who is Jewish, is, in fact, Dr. Brightbill's sister, institutionalized nearly twenty years ago after Koehn's exoneration."

Bannister and Margaret looked at each other with a mixture of disgust and amusement.

"Meanwhile," the commentator continued, "A CNN/Microsoft poll shows that a combined forty-eight percent of the worldwide viewing audience believes the Stranger's appearance was a hoax perpetrated by rival Federation factions. Thirty-three percent of those polled believe that the appearance was part of a promotional video for Steven Spielberg III's new docudrama entitled *"The Christian Koehn Story."*

Bannister motioned to Margaret, who followed him out of the faculty lounge, down the hall. They emerge from the building arm-in-arm, striding briskly. Bannister stopped at a trash receptacle and, grinning at Margaret, lifted the lid, threw it noisily to the sidewalk, and tossed in his portfolio case. He winked at Margaret, then grabbed her arm as they walked toward the Avenue, sparks flying from underneath their feet.

A filthy, decrepit wino emerged from the nearby hedges, awakened from the fog of his hangover by the noise Bannister made when he tossed the lid onto the pavement. Groggily, he made his way to the trash receptacle, looking for a discarded treasure; something to sell or use, or…

Peering in, he then jumped back as a profusion of bluish-silver sparks leaped out. Regaining his courage after the sparks dissipated, the wino again peered in and bent down to reach for something. As he pulled it out, he was fascinated by the rich, luminous colors and the soft fabric of the cloak, he tentatively tried it on.

A passerby, a harried, bearded professor, noticing the wino, quickened his pace past the bedraggled, aging man he'd seen every day for the past three months. But then he stopped dead in his tracks when the wino turned to face him.

Instead of a filthy, ancient-looking bum, the passersby saw a young, joyful, vibrantly healthy man, his eyes glowing with the light of the sphere.

—THE END—

CHARLES J. HEBERT

An attorney practicing in New Orleans, Charles J. Hebert graduated with a law degree from Tulane University. The grandson of a respected South Louisiana judge, Hebert was one of 10 children who grew up in the small Cajun Louisiana town of Jennings. There, his sense of place, and his reverence for eccentic and colorful characters that populate this region, were nurtured. *The Signing* is his second novel, following last year's critically-acclaimed, *Swimming to Atlantis*. He lives with his second wife and two children on the north shore of Lake Ponchatrain, near New Orleans. He is currently working on several other projects for publication and film, and his short story, *Chinchuba Pond*, will be published by Pontalba Press in early 1999.

EDWIN CHRISTIAN ALLMAN

A media and marketing consultant, Edwin Christian Allman is a former music critic for a daily newspaper and network television affiliate. Allman has broad experience in journalism, advertising, corporate communications and political consulting and speech writing in New Orleans and Atlanta. *The Life of Christ in the 21st Century* is based on his Renegade Films screenplay by the same name. Currently, he is completing work on what he calls an "alien biography" entitled, *White Noise Memories*. Two other screenplays, *Mr. Tambourian Man* and *The Black Heat*, are also in the works. An amateur actor, he has appeared in numerous community and improvisational theater productions, including his own one-act black comedy, *The Great River Road Kill Recipe Conspiracy*.

DR. PAUL RODENHAUSER

Dr. Paul Rodenhauser, who attributes his creative successes to the transcendental influence of his parrot, Laffite, is a professor of psychiatry, Director of Medical Student Education in psychiatry and Assistant Dean for Academic and Counseling Services at Tulane University School of Medicine. A graduate of the Thomas Jefferson School of Medice, Dr. Rodenhauser's literary inclinations began to take flight when he moved to New Orleans. His poems have appeared in The Pharos and the Journal of Poetry Therapy. His poem, "Interviews with a Homeless Man" was included in the 1998 collection of New Orleans poetry called *From a Bend in the River*. Also in 1998, his one-act play, Mr. Lafayette's Rocking Chair, was produced at the New Orleans Contemporary Arts Center.

234